# BITTERROOT: A NOVEL

"Deceptively easy to read, this book strikes at the heart of loss, and the alchemy of change. Suzy Vitello is a gifted writer with a deep understanding of people and places. *Bitterroot* is an exceptional novel by a great talent."

— Rene Denfeld, bestselling author of *The Child Finder* and *Sleeping Giant*

. . . .

"A deep and unforgiving look into many difficult and timely issues, ranging from same sex marriage and reproductive rights to grief and bigotry. Vitello depicts nuanced human relationships with grace, dignity, and beautiful turns of phrase. The plot will rope you right in with a cadence that's accessible and engaging throughout. Don't be surprised if the book keeps you up late into the night. This is one you won't want to miss!"

—Jacqueline Friedland, *USA Today* bestselling author of *He Gets That From Me*

. . . .

"In Vitello's novel, a young widow grapples with an attack on her family. Hazel finds herself at the center of a trial that unleashes a flood of racism and resentment against her family that has been building for generations. Vitello's crystalline prose elegantly captures the numbing grief that grips Hazel for much of the novel ... memorable characters nimbly embody the larger cultural forces at war in contemporary America ... A gripping and emotionally intelligent tale of resentment and loss."

—Kirkus Reviews

"*Bitterroot* is an intricate novel—a tapestry of family dynamics, generational trauma, and the pursuit of social justice in a small town. The prose is captivating and immersive, and the story pulsates thanks to its rich, small-town atmosphere."

—*Foreword Reviews*

• • • •

"Among the reasons we readers love a novel are two that seem impossibly at odds: a compelling plot that keeps you up way too late flipping pages as fast as possible, and dazzling writing with such beautiful phrasing you are inspired to slow your reading down to savor each sentence. Paradoxically, *Bitterroot* by Suzy Vitello possesses both hallmarks of excellence.

Bitterroot's believable characters pop off the page and its profound themes will inspire many provocative discussions, long after the last page is turned. I love this book."

—**Debby Dodds, author of *Amish Guys Don't Call***

• • • •   •

"As a plot person, I could not put this book down. Talk about one surprise/revelation/ unexpected turn after another. Never mind that the sex scenes were deliciously inventive. I loved the unlikely hero, Hazel, a benign name, but she draws dead and maimed bodies for a living, as the only forensic artist in the Silver Valley. 'When our father died ... yellowed with cirrhosis ... I chose watercolor.' Through a rollercoaster-from-hell life, and against all odds, she rises to the challenges of a family full of faults. One of the last lines: 'May we bloom where we're planted.' That's Hazel."

—**Jan Baross, author of award-winning, *Bye-Bye Bakersfield***

# BITTERROOT

*A Novel*

## SUZY VITELLO

Sibylline
PRESS

AN IMPRINT OF ALL THINGS BOOK

Sibylline Press
Copyright © 2024 by Suzy Vitello.
All Rights Reserved.

Published in the United States by Sibylline Press,
an imprint of All Things Book LLC, California.
Sibylline Press is dedicated to publishing the
brilliant work of women authors ages 50 and older.
www.sibyllinepress.com

Distributed to the trade by Publishers Group West.
Paperback ISBN: 9781960573964
eBook ISBN: 9781960573100
Library of Congress Control Number: 2023947585

Book and Cover Design: Alicia Feltman

# BITTERROOT

*A Novel*

## SUZY VITELLO

For all my sisters.

# PART ONE

# ONE

THE KNUCKLE RAP AT THE DOOR WAS ALL BUSINESS.

Betsy Jones, the real estate agent, was my first guess. She'd been after me to clean out my parents' house for years, and now that I'd finally ordered the Dumpster, she was a regular visitor. She wouldn't let up about the time-sensitivity. Hiking interest rates, the trend toward post-COVID buyer's remorse for zoom town dwellers. Daily, she'd text me:

> Folks are heading back to the big cities. You want to capitalize on your inheritance? Tick-tock.

But even with Betsy's no-nonsense demeanor, it was too heavy a knock for her. This was a man's knock. Kento, I thought. But why would he knock? Maybe because he knew Corinda was here—a last minute decision. She needed the money, and we needed the help.

"Coming," I yelled as the knock gave way to the annoying chimes of the '70s doorbell of our childhoods.

The door was mid-July sticky. It'd been raining all morning, but hot. Humidity made things swell, and as I wrenched it open, cursing in my head—the OCD-plagued Betsy would make us fix it before the open house—I felt Corinda's warm breath on my neck. Why did she always hover?

The state trooper on the cracked cement stoop was already removing his hat. Behind me Corinda yelled, "What happened? Is it Kento?"

My brother was due in any minute from Seattle.

"No!" she yelled, before the cop could answer.

"Ma'am?" said the trooper.

As for me, my brain hadn't caught up to my eyes yet. I absorbed the whole of him like a quicksand dream that stretched yawningly forward. I worked my way from his bald head to his muddy shoes in slow motion.

I said, "Can I help you?"

His gaze leapt over me, mistakenly addressing Corinda with a steady, somber tone. "Mrs. Mackenzie?"

"No," Corinda replied, her hand settling on my shoulder. "She's Mrs. Mackenzie."

In Grief Group, during the formal meeting, the focus is on coping. On moving *through* it. But after the meetings, in the parking lot, all of us vaping, sipping the remains of cold, ground-littered coffee, we always returned to the *What ifs*. The, *If onlys*.

It's human nature, right? Rewinding to a time before. Fantasizing an alternative outcome because we'd poured that extra cup of coffee. Or perhaps, in rewriting history, we *had* bugged our loved ones about their skipped mammogram. Or we'd chosen to live on the other side of Steeplejack, away from the veins of lead. Better tires. New helmet. Right instead of left. Or, in my case, insisting our mother get checked out after complaining of shoulder and back pain. And our father? Well, no regrets there.

"I'm sorry," said the trooper. "It was quick. Instant."

I felt blood drain my face. My vision turned black and starry; invisible cotton filled my ears, blocking sound. Corinda kept me from falling to the floor, her meaty arms hooking my pits. Maybe it was a mistake? How did the cop know to come here?

I wiggled away from Corinda's clutch. Both of my hands on the stoop's railing as the trooper recited the details, per his training. I caught stray, muffled words: "pronounced at the scene," "traumatic," "coroner," "next of kin." Oh, my God.

The suddenness of accidental death blasts in before your heart can absorb it. Shock, they call it in Grief Group. The banality of tasks lining up in the brain, a crutch to leap a person over the chasm of trauma. Ethan's parents in Spokane, sitting in their recliners, towels behind their heads to keep the upholstery grease-free. I had to call them, didn't I? Would they be watching *Jeopardy!* right about now? I pictured exactly that: Skipper and Mac, sipping gin and tonics and trying to guess the questions to the answers. My hand lurched up and swam in air, then back to the railing, as if I was conjuring magical powers, rewinding the clock to ten minutes before. Restoring the blissful unknowingness.

Behind the trooper, Kento's Jetta crunched up the gravel drive. Corinda thundered past me, down the steps of the stoop.

The trooper offered one more condolence before departing. He'd specified where I should go, what I should do. Next steps for the spouse of the suddenly deceased. Something about preparing myself to see the body in its calamitous state. I was to bring a support person. Corinda's hunched figure obscured my view of Kento, still in the driver's seat of his car. She was no support person. I shouldn't bring her to the cold basement room of drawers, said my internal voice. A voice that was joined by my mother's words reverberating against my skull, *Keep that girl away from our Kento. She nothing but trouble.*

In the end, they both accompanied me to the morgue. I was too shell-shocked for a squabble, and Kento, my passive twin brother who'd never warmed to my husband, seemed comforted by Corinda's presence. She was a buffer. Willing to take on the messy task of calling Mr. and Mrs. Mackenzie, absorbing the blow, as long as she could sit shotgun next to my brother while I curled up in the back of his sedan, leaking keening noises. Her incessant chatter about nothing landed as white noise accompanying the breath caught between my diaphragm and throat.

# TWO

MY HUSBAND WAS DEAD.

Ethan and I had been married just a fraction of the time we'd known one another. We'd been high school sweethearts. Him: debate team and co-captain of the soccer team. Me: voted most likely to get a tattoo on my 18th birthday. Which I did, of course—not the smartest box to check in the Northern Idaho town where we were raised.

We broke up when we left for college, as most high school sweethearts do. Me to an East Coast art school, him to U-Dub, and then Lewis and Clark for law. But after a solid taste of big cities, we found our way back to Steeplejack, got married, and bought a trailer house on five acres surrounded by Douglas firs between Coeur d'Alene and Steeplejack, spitting distance from a bike path that spans the Silver Valley. In our Bitterroot foothills trailer, we magnetized an ever-evolving sketch of our dream home to the refrigerator, right beside our word puzzle scores—an ongoing bid for the Scrabble throne.

We weren't in a hurry to build our dream home. We were going to take our time. Do all the things young marrieds do. Travel, establish careers, contribute the maximum to our IRA each year. We'd start our family as soon as we knocked off that school debt and had secured a favorable construction loan. We thought we had all the time in the world.

Steeplejack is that quaint silver mining town you pass through on your way from Seattle to Missoula. A ribbon of a highway winding through the South Fork of the Coeur d'Alene River, and if you're road-weary, it's where you might pull off the 90 for some of Helen Michael's huckleberry pie.

Especially after *Sunset Magazine* did that feature. Or maybe, being sucked in by the promise of quaint yet comfortable, you'd bunk down at the Connors' bed and breakfast because you heard about their freak chickens that lay double-yolk eggs—the tastiest north of Utah—and you want to sample them for yourself. You might pop into Lottie's Notions and buy a silk-screened hoodie with the Steeplejack logo: a mountain whose peak is in the shape of an anchor—which was how that mountain was before the miners blew it up and dug out all the silver. If you do peruse Lottie's, maybe you'll buy one of my creations. I understand they still have a few in back—but you'd have to ask specifically for them. And be warned: Hazel Mackenzie is a name that might start a fight if the wrong person hears it.

I married into Mackenzie, happily giving up the surname Zapf. In a world where convention looks to the alphabet for rank, a *Z* name in a small town always means last. Kento, my twin brother, when he married his husband, there was no question of him keeping Zapf—or combining his birth and married names with a hyphen, for that matter. For him, the beneficiary of our Japanese mother's only satisfied request, taking on his husband's name, Saito, was a no-brainer. Had our mother been alive, she would have secretly smiled that the child she named for her own father would have found love with a partner descending from the Fujiwara clan, while at the same time, pretending that Kento would someday marry a woman and produce a child.

When we were kids, Kento and I invented a game we called *I don't*. A sort of nuptialized version of "Would you rather," wherein a person offers two shitty scenarios, and the other person has to choose between them. In *I don't*, Kento and I took turns inventing hideous partners for one another. In hindsight, I'm sure Kento used this game to test the waters. It soon became clear that the partners he dreamt up for me included romantically intriguing elements. He spared no exacting detail. Sure, there may have been a limb missing, or an extra thumb, but the way he described my would-be husband's thick eyebrows, his sonorous voice—yes, my brother did use the word *sonorous*—it was obvious where his preferences lay.

Ethan Mackenzie, however, was not Kento's type.

In fact, they were bitter rivals on the soccer pitch. The year Steeplejack High made the Idaho quarterfinals, they were both starters. Co-captains. Kento, his ordered personality, his acumen for project management, was a classic defender. Ethan, outgoing, charismatic, was the goal-scoring forward. In that quarterfinal game, they were pitted against a favored team from Boise. The Boise team scored first, and in the second half, with four minutes remaining, Ethan equalized. The match looked certain to go to penalties when, with ten seconds left, Kento missed his mark, and Boise scored the winner.

It was the last time my brother touched a soccer ball.

Ethan, my perfect Ethan, had a flaw, and that flaw was holding a grudge. Even at our wedding reception, as Kento rambled through a circuitous, half-hearted toast, Ethan interrupted with a flippant, "I know you tend to be an over-thinker, but don't take too much time, dude. Keep it simple, like you should have done against Boise."

Kento stammered. His facial muscles fighting dejection, he managed a hasty smile and sat quietly down. My heart cracked.

And here he was, driving me to the morgue. If he harbored feelings of retribution, I didn't see them. They were reasonably polite to each other, those three years of our marriage. Thanksgiving, Christmas. But they tended to avoid conversation. Always choosing to sit on opposite sides of the table. Anemic fist bumps confined to parting ways. What was Ethan thinking if his spirit was still circling the sentient world? I felt his presence, as I had my mother's for weeks after her death. With every swerve and potholed bump, my body heaved. My throat emitted foreign squeaks all on its own. Corinda reached a hand behind her and patted my head, like you would a hurt dog on the way to the vet.

I had jumbled feelings about Corinda Blair, nee Luce, the girl with whom my gay brother lost his virginity in tenth grade. Corinda must have known, deep down, but she was still hopelessly in love with Kento. Years ago, one holiday season she took me aside at our parents' house. She was blunt. And drunk.

"Why won't he fuck me anymore, Haze? I mean, he used to. Is it that I put on weight? Is it because my ass is too big now?"

I reassured her, it had nothing to do with her or her ass. I said Kento was a complicated man. I gently suggested she move on, and she broke down in tears—the prelude, I'm guessing, to marrying a man old enough to be her father.

My mother, politely dying of ovarian cancer in the next room, overheard. Her words to me later, *She nothing but trouble*, continued to haunt me.

Corinda, currently estranged from her husband who'd been widowed and left with five kids to raise, was like that abused dog who keeps breaking free of its rope and finding its way to a willing guardian, before inevitably returning to its abuser. And here she was, patting *my* head this time. I scooted against the window, squishing myself out of her reach.

An old-school notebook peeked out from the passenger seat pocket. One of those black-and-white composition books left over from university. I grabbed it. Somewhere in my frozen brain came the lucid idea to take notes. With my parents, I'd had years leading up to their expirations. Advanced directives. Wills. Everything spelled out. But when it came to our own demise, Ethan and I had only ventured down Grim Reaper Road once, and it had been during a parlor game with Kento and Tom. Two couples pitted against each other in a "how well do you know your partner" series of questions. Ethan and I, we lost. But one of the questions was *bury or burn?* At least I knew, thanks to the game, that my husband wished to be cremated and spread in the hills above our property.

I clutched the notebook as we drove toward the morgue. My fingers turned white with the clench, and I focused on the antique ring on my left hand. It had belonged to Ethan's paternal grandmother, who'd inherited it from her husband's own mother—a woman who'd been badly burned in the fire of 1910 here in Steeplejack. The silver had come from a mine in the Bitterroot Divide, and I'd neglected to keep it polished. The tarnished ring glared back at me, an indictment of my negligence.

When we arrived at the place where my husband's dead body had been deposited, I froze. Kento turned off the car, wrenched around and faced me.

"I'm so sorry, Haze," he said, his eyes glassy with paralyzed tears. "Do you need a minute?"

"I need to polish this," I said, thrusting my left hand under his chin. "Can we go get some polish?"

Corinda sputtered. "Dude, what the hell? Who cares about—"

But my brother shushed her. Turned back around and started up the Jetta, peeled out of the morgue's pitted gravel parking lot, and off we drove to Steeplejack Feed and Seed for some silver polish.

Our mother's wedding ring had also been an heirloom. Our father, when he proposed, had promised a diamond "down the road"—a promise that, like so many others he'd barfed out, never materialized. When her mother—our grandmother—died, our mother inherited a ring that had survived immigration, internment, and thieves. Our mother wore it proudly, claiming that its power came from three generations of survival. When she became sick, and treatments exceeded what insurance would cover, she was forced to sell it. Or, rather, our father snatched it after chemo drained our mother of any padding, and after the ring slipped off her finger, onto the floor.

By then, the cancer had chipped away at Mom's brain—a reality that gave me comfort. She didn't fully register her husband's deceit. She never knew that he'd pocketed, then drunk, the measly thousand dollars the ring fetched. As for the medical bills, he'd simply declared bankruptcy, after placing the house in Kento's name.

At the Feed and Seed, Kento located the polish and a chamois. In the store's restroom, I untarnished Ethan's grandmother's ring. An hour later, we were following the coroner's assistant past the idle mobile morgue adjoining the ugly brick building of death. The mobile holding trailer had been pressed into service during the COVID spikes a few years back, and there it sat, waiting for the next interstate pileup or pandemic. I squashed the notebook against my chest, and the coroner's assistant led us through the door of the regular morgue and down the stairs to what she referred to as *the vault*.

Once down there, she turned to me. "Mrs. Mackenzie, I'm so sorry for your loss. I have to let you know though, your husband did sustain some fairly serious injuries to his face and head."

I tried breathing in around the phlegm that was building in my chest. Goosebumps speckled my bare arms. It was cold in the vault, and I hadn't thought to bring a jacket. I gripped the notebook harder.

For some insane reason, Corinda let loose with a whistle. The sort of whistle that's almost unconscious in response to an overwhelming situation. Kento cleared his throat in attempt to nullify her inappropriate utterance. Our footsteps and voices echoed off ceramic walls. LED lights flickered. We stopped in front of the subway-tiled wall. Eight framed doors were cut into the wall, two rows of four, stamped with letters, alphabetically, A-H. Attractive oil-rubbed bronze hinges and handles marked the doors, and if you didn't know bodies lay on the other side of them, you might wonder if the morgue interior designer had consulted Pinterest in search of a warm tone for the hardware.

In contrast, my ring shone north-star bright, the room's high lumens bouncing off the newly polished silver.

The coroner's assistant placed her hand on my shoulder. Asked if I was ready. Asked if I was sure I wanted to see my husband's body with my loved ones present. Asked if I wanted to remain standing. There was a metal chair folded in the corner of the room. If it would be more comforting to sit, there was that option.

I nodded yes to all the questions, but I wanted to stay on my feet. The thought of sitting on a cold metal chair viewing the body of my broken husband made my stomach lurch. I reached a hand toward Kento, still clutching the notebook in my other one.

The coroner's assistant was a young woman. Early thirties at most. Her oily skin gave off a greenish sheen, as one might expect from a person whose job was ushering the newly bereaved through the halls of death. Her eyes were squinty behind heavily framed glasses perched on a button of a nose. Her lips, stick-figure thin, and smeared with brown gloss. She wore her hair in a high bun, which gave her already stern look a boost toward unapproachable. Her name was Catherine. Or Cathleen. Or maybe it was Cathy Lynn. She was new to town. New to the job.

The regular coroner, Lou Fellows, was on vacation, giving the high-bun woman authority in his absence. There would be no autopsy, no toxicology screening, given the cut-and-dried nature of the accident. Head on, the onion truck skidding into the U-Haul at highway speed after crossing the line. She'd said all of this in a blur out in the parking lot but standing in front of those drawers in the icy, tiled room, all I could think of was, Ethan would have felt sorry for her. He would have tried to put her at ease. And the other thought: Why was Ethan on the highway in the first place? He should have taken the shortcut route through Kellogg.

"Ready?" she said in a somber voice.

I nodded, and she stepped up to the door marked E; the first one on the bottom row. E for Ethan, I wondered? The brain in shock does weird things. Thinks weird thoughts. The assistant unlocked the lock clumsily, keys jiggling in her fist. The sound of the handle turning echoed harshly. She opened the door and pulled out the gurney upon which lay Ethan's body wrapped in thick, white sheeting.

"You did all this by yourself? In only a couple of hours?" I said. In my experience, Lou took a day or more to prepare a body for identification.

The coroner's assistant tried to hide her self-congratulatory smirk, "As I told you, cause of death was obvious. No need to get the county ME out here."

Corinda folded over, hand to her mouth. "I'm feeling sick."

Kento took his hand off me and wrapped it around her heaving shoulder. He whispered, "Maybe you should wait in the car."

"I'll be okay," she said, between audible gasps.

Corinda and her drama.

"I'm ready," I said. I closed my eyes as the coroner's assistant peeled back the sheet. Ethan's face, how it looked that morning, a crumb of English muffin on his lip. The way he'd picked a blackberry seed from between his front teeth. I didn't want this mangled version to overtake that last alive image of him, but I had to witness it. I knew from the folks at Human Gifts Registry and from Grief Group, it was important to see a loved one's body in death. I was in the process of building a career around visual representation of death, crime, injury. Closure required physical proof. I forced my eyelids up.

What greeted me: purple hamburger covered half of Ethan's face. One eye hung from its socket. His beautiful face, his strong jaw, his head of golden locks—obliterated and replaced with fleshy rubble.

Corinda retched and the coroner's assistant snatched up a box of tissues and a plastic emesis pan from the shelf behind us.

"We have his personal things in the office," the assistant coroner said, in a tone that meant, *let's wrap this up.*

I bent down and kissed the cheek that remained. Noises roiled up my throat and burst from my mouth once again. Something between a keen and a groan. I straightened. Forced a deep breath.

"Do you have a pencil?"

The assistant coroner produced a pen.

I got to work.

I DRAW DEAD AND MAIMED BODIES FOR A LIVING. I'm currently the only forensic artist in the Silver Valley. If Ethan had been a John Doe, or had he died without identification on him, I'd have been called in to sketch facial reconstruction. Or, in cases like this, family might call me to draw what I see. Sometimes from a photograph, sometimes in person. For the eventual court case. It's not often that surviving family members immediately think to secure a visual record of accidental death for litigious reasons. The body decomposes so quickly, and loved ones are typically consumed with funeral arrangements, working through their shock, making banal decisions about repasts and guest books while their hearts are quaking.

I didn't have my phone on me, and Kento had left his in the car.

"Really?" he said, as I hammered out a sketch of my mutilated husband. He added, "I'm going to take Corinda home, then I'll come back for you."

Corinda, still dry heaving, hugged my back, and she and Kento departed, their echoing footsteps assaulting the peace I was trying to harness.

My brother's disgust was cumulative. I'd drawn both of our parents when they'd succumbed to their respective diseases. I had created a triptych of our mom, pen and ink. The first panel based on a photograph of her as a child, the third panel as a young woman, and the center featured her beautiful, freshly dead face. She was only in her forties when she died. Her hair had grown back when she refused further treatment, shiny and black as mica, framing her gaunt, heart-shaped face, her wide-set, gently uptilted eyes.

When our father died three years later, yellowed with cirrhosis, toothless, I chose watercolor as the medium. His distended, bulbous belly, his unclipped fingernails, his greasy combover—the reality of how he lived and died remains on my wall, despite objections.

The notebook hadn't been cracked open until this very moment, and the stiff, new paperness of it felt heavy in my hand. The pen was a cheap pen and left blotchy ink in its wake as I glided it over the page. Later, I would transfer the sketch to a proper backdrop, but in the hours following my husband's accident, my body took over. My greedy hand demanded that it capture the irreversibility of the moment.

In ancient Japan, there is a ritual called Kusôzu—the practice of capturing the beauty of a posthumous body's organic decomposition. It serves as a meditation on impermanence and transcendence. In college, I spent a semester abroad in London during an exhibit at the Wellcome Collection called *Forensics: The Anatomy of Crime.* The exhibit itself was a wonderland of brilliance, featuring artists like Goya, Géricault, Daumier and Sickert.

But I was immediately drawn to a series of nine Japanese water-colors painted in the 18th century. Delicate and beautiful, the series moves through a courtesan's stages of death and decomposition. Based on the Buddhist contemplation of Maranasati, these nine stages followed the body's posthumous journey from flesh to dust: dying; death; bloat; blood leakage; fluid purge; organ exposure; animal scavenging; skeletonization; total decomposition.

In hindsight, I wondered if my fascination with forensic art was a cosmic invitation. A way to prepare me for so much personal loss.

The coroner's assistant seemed unsettled by my insistence on un-sheathing Ethan, and my need to sketch his pre-embalmed corpse. She kept checking her watch, commenting on the temperature in the room. She didn't want to invite real time decomposition and stink into her vault. She was in a hurry to shove my husband's drawer back into its refrigerated compartment, hand off Ethan's ruined clothes, and file the paperwork.

"I hope you don't take this the wrong way," she said, "but I'm short-handed, and we need to go over some housekeeping details."

I kept my eyes on Ethan, gazing over his bruised chest, the patch of dried blood on his forearm. My hand worked on its own, deaf to the coroner's assistant's pleas.

# THREE

THE DAY KENTO AND I GRADUATED HIGH SCHOOL, a used Camry with an oversized ribbon appeared in our driveway. My father's arms spread wide for us, and his greeting, "You're all growed up now! Time to look for a job," was accompanied by the dangling of a scratched-up fob.

Our mother, not yet diagnosed, but suffering the daily bouts of shoulder pain that would soon reveal her stage-four ovarian cancer, stood behind our father, her index finger bisecting her lips. She knew about— and had, in fact, facilitated—our applications for financial assistance for higher ed. We'd had furtive celebrations once the acceptance letters came in. Kento had a partial ride to Seattle Pacific. I had been offered a meaty scholarship to Bard.

"Thanks, Dad," Kento said, grabbing the key. "This'll help get us to our summer jobs."

Our father, now on disability after injuring his back at the transfer station, grabbed the key back. "Ya gots to think beyond the summer, boyo. Now yer both eighteen and all, I imagine you'll be lookin' to move out soon. This here set of wheels? I'm paying the insurance 'til year's end, then y'all gonna take over. Clear?"

The ribbon was definitely our mother's idea.

"Let's take it for a spin," I said, snatching the key from our father's grip. He was much easier on me than Kento. Had I been an only child, he'd probably be fine with me living under his roof forever. Especially once Mom got sick.

I settled behind the wheel, Kento riding shotgun, a scowl marring his otherwise beautiful face. Our parents waved us off as I backed down the long, narrow driveway to the county road. I turned to my brother. "Where we headed?"

"Fuck him," he answered.

"We have a plan, remember? Three months from now, it won't matter what he thinks. We'll be out."

Kento craned his neck, taking in the blemishes of the car's interior. "Headrest all chewed up. Wet dog smell." He ran his hand over the dashboard. "And look at this crack!"

"Dude, we're going to sell this hunk of shit before we take off for school."

"Ha. If it doesn't completely break down before that."

There was a party at Morgan Taylor's house, and another one at Lionel Smith's. I wasn't in the partying mood though. My upper arm, covered in plastic wrap to protect the new ink, was itchy. Plus, I was achy with period cramps.

"Drop me off at Corinda's," Kento said.

She was a year behind us, and had barely passed enough classes to be considered a rising senior. I was leery about her neediness where my brother was concerned.

"You make sure you're protected when you fool around. I don't trust her," I said.

"Haze, mind your beeswax. Also, don't throw stones in your glass house."

What he didn't say, but meant, concerned Ethan. We'd first hooked up as sophomores after volunteering for Steeplejack's STARS program. The two of us, and our *Students Today Aren't Ready for Sex* posters, making the rounds and visiting Shoshone County's middle schools with our scripted abstinence lecture. Ethan, already sixteen and driving us in his beater Corolla, would pull off the road after our *Just Say No* sessions, a Pendleton wool blanket under his arm, a condom in his pocket.

Later, I'd confess to my brother—mainly, I admit, to brag and share the irony of the situation. Get a laugh. We were twins, after all. Best friends, for the most part.

Of the two of us, Kento, with his high cheekbones, glossy hair and thick lashes, was the more conventionally attractive. I took after Dad's side: pale, freckled skin with coarse, mud-brown hair that spouted cowlicks. A slight overbite that Ethan thought adorable, but I resented. In addition to his anti-college stance, Dad thought orthodontists were "money-grubbing quacks," and my pleas for braces were met with scorn.

I dropped Kento off at Corinda's, where she stood enthusiastically on the front porch of her family's manufactured home, not even trying to mask her glee, waving and giggling and bouncing like a five-year-old being handed an ice-cream cone. In a way, I envied her candor. She was incapable of pretense. I never quite understood why Kento bothered with her, but it may have had to do with her naked adoration—something he craved in the face of our father's disdain.

I drove on to Ethan's house, on the "good" side of town. Victorians that had been built with silver-mine money and had withstood the fire of 1910—a blaze that'd leveled most of the town. Ethan's ancestors on both sides were among the original white settlers in the Bitterroot Mountains, a fact about which Ethan's parents bragged shamelessly. Never mind the history of pioneers land-grabbing from the Kootenai. Ethan was their only child—the end of the line, so to speak—and they were less than thrilled that he was dating me, a half-Japanese girl whose father had a reputation as a penniless drunk.

I pulled up in front of the three-story house, all ornate gables and gingerbread trim. Mrs. Mackenzie was deadheading her flowerbox. She looked up as I cut the engine. I'd caught her looking annoyed before she had a chance to slap a smile on her face. Unlike Corinda, Ethan's mom was practiced at obfuscation.

"Hello, dear. I hear you are bound for New York. Congratulations," she said as I reached the pansy-lined walkway.

"Thanks."

"Ethan is getting ready," she said, hastily. "We have family friends coming over for his grad dinner."

Translation: he's unavailable for the likes of you.

"Do you mind if I visit for just a minute? I wanted to show him my new car."

She grimaced, twitched and bit her lip.

I held my gaze. "It won't take long."

Her eyes darted to my wrapped arm. "Another tattoo?"

A month earlier, my first, was a vine, wrapped around my wrist like a bracelet.

I nodded, pointed my nose at the plastic wrap. As a descendant of early settlers, I thought she might approve of the latest design. "It's just a few squiggles. An impressionist version of the mountains. The Bitterroots."

She sighed. "I wonder what you kids will do about applying for jobs. Aren't you limiting your career path by graffiti-ing your body?"

By *you kids*, Mrs. Mackenzie meant riffraff. Her only child hid his rebellion like a spy. He would eventually have a salmon inked on his hip, where his mother would never see it.

I tiptoed past her and bounced up the porch steps. "I'll just be a minute, okay?"

"Don't forget to remove your shoes," she chimed.

Ethan bounded down the stairs as I untied my thrift store high-tops. "Hey, you!" he greeted.

Already summer tanned, even in mid-June, Ethan could have been a sports model. Tall, muscular, blond. His only physical flaw was a branch-like scar on his chin that, down the road, marred any attempt at a full beard.

"He came through," I said.

"Who?"

"It's way used, with over 120,000 miles, but it works."

"A car?"

"Your mom says you have a dinner. I was thinking we could go to one of the keggers later."

Ethan's eyes widened; his finger shot to his lips. He harsh-whispered, "I'll have to sneak out. Mom's on the warpath again."

"What did you do this time?"

He smiled overly big. Irresistibly. "It's legal in Washington now."

He and the soccer team. Varsity initiation, Kento had told me last fall, was eating an edible after a winning match. Months after the season ended, they'd expanded the ritual. Most of the team members took turns procuring weed in all its glorious forms, over the border, in nearby Spokane.

"Only if you're twenty-one," I said, even though I knew Ethan had a fake. Then, in a quieter whisper, "You know your mom's somehow blaming that on me, right?"

Again, that smile. "What can I say. I'm a total mama's boy. Only child, last of the Mackenzies. At least, so far."

He winked at me.

AND NOW, TWELVE YEARS LATER, Ethan was inexplicably dead. No heir. No legacy. Barely out of law school.

His parents, who'd recently moved to a fifty-five and older neighborhood in Spokane, were driven in by Ethan's godparents and their best friends, the Millers. Skipper and Mac (I was never invited to call them Dad and Mom), clearly in shock, yet somehow lucid enough to counter every decision I made, accompanied me to the funeral home.

In his office, the director presented us with a binder full of caskets before stepping out, giving us privacy and space to "consider our options," which I appreciated.

"I don't see the need for a casket," I said. "Since he won't be buried, I mean."

"I don't know," Skipper said, her voice brittle as a frozen twig at the news that Ethan wanted to be cremated. "Is it possible you're projecting your own posthumous wishes onto him?"

"We discussed it," I said. "There's no doubt."

She pivoted away from me, her shoulders rose and fell. Quiet sobs. Mac, shrunken and feebler since the last time I'd seen him, comforted her by patting her overly sprayed helmet of a hairdo. With every pat, a waft of Final Net launched toward my nose.

She spun around, suddenly. "How the hell are we going to have a proper funeral—or a wake, for that matter—without a casket? Is it the cost? Because we'd be willing to loan you the money to pay for it."

I'd spent more than a decade allowing Ethan's mother the final say-so in my relationship with her son, inserting her opinion into every holiday meal, every visit, and I was damn sure not going to let her call the shots now that I had no more peace to keep. I flipped the plastic encased binder pages to the urn section. An array of receptacles dotted the page as glaring and colorful as menu options in a Thai restaurant. Ceramic, wood, metallic. A glass sphere covered in psychedelic ribboning caught my eye. Mostly, I'm loath to admit, as a way to fuck with my mother-in-law, I pointed to it and read the description aloud.

"This exotic rainbow orb holds cremation ash from your loved one, spiraled alongside electric ribbons of dichroic glass, making it a lovely choice for keeping your dearly departed close. This striking sphere will be breathtaking upon any sunny ledge or mantle, or feel free to purchase one of our optional cremation stands to create a memorial nightlight."

Her jaw fell open. She swallowed, then, "You are joking, I hope."

"Of course I am. Look, if we get two urns—tasteful ones—we can divide the ashes."

She shook her head. "How can you even think of joking like that? In the face of this horrible, horrible tragedy? You are such a cold person."

She wasn't entirely wrong. I could be cold. I could be odd. There were times when I caught myself blurting inappropriate things, wishing I could suck them back down my throat. Like that French phrase about the spirit under the stairs. Only, in my case, it was to retract a retort, rather than offer one.

"I loved—*love*—your son," I stammered.

Mac reached a hand in front of me and smacked the binder closed. "You're going to do what you're going to do, Hazel. All we ask is that you honor Ethan's life, his passing, by holding a service in his home church."

The words roiled out of me before I could swallow them. "Ethan and I, we're atheists. That's why the god we don't believe in invented a celebration of life."

My mother-in-law squeaked like a mouse in the process of being pinned to a trap.

My father-in-law's liver-spotted fists shook.

I breathed in, hard. Counted in my head, like the grief group said to. The grief group I joined when my mother died. It occurred to me that having lost three people in six years would elevate my status. Aside from Lucy Bartlet, who lost her husband and three kids in an avalanche a few years back, I was the group's biggest loser. It's so weird the things that occur to a person as they navigate the unthinkable. Sitting there in the undertaker's office with two people who loathe me, all I could think of was that the one person who tied us together was out of the equation. This negotiation would be our last. Or so I thought.

Skipper glared at me. "You corrupted our boy. Our only child. We will never forgive you."

IN THE END, I DID COMPROMISE. Whether due to guilt or just to get them—and their many friends here in Steeplejack—off my case, I agreed to a service at Steeplejack's Church of Christ—one of many increasingly evangelical organizations in the Panhandle. There was no casket, however. Ethan's ashes were split into two plastic bags. I bought a beautiful teak and metal box for my portion.

When I handed the Mackenzies their baggie of Ethan, his mother murmured, "As if he's a bag of dog poo."

Kento and Tom flanked me in the church. We sat in back, rather than in the typical widow's front pew, and I'm sure the Mackenzies were secretly happy about that, but it did create a buzz. The very fact that my brother and his husband agreed to set foot in a building that condemned their marriage, their very *personhood*, while enduring sideways sneers from the parishioners, this was a testament to their love for me.

In the two weeks between the accident and the service, my brother had made the five-hour trip from Seattle three separate times to help sort through the myriad details and paperwork surrounding Ethan's death. Ethan's law firm in Coeur d'Alene, Beacon and Bright, where he'd only worked as an associate for a year, offered to file a wrongful death suit without charging me the customary thirty percent, but they'd cautioned me that the trucking company would hire private investigators set on digging up any dirt on Ethan that might mitigate his worth.

"If you need to scrub social media, better do it quick," one of the partners informed me.

"Excuse me," I said. "What do you mean by that?"

The lawyer sighed, as if conveying information to a hopeless Luddite.

After the service, one of the couples in the Mackenzies' tight circle of mutuals, offered a repast. Another *fuck you* to me—the uppity widow. Steeplejack's most revered and founding mining families opened their newly updated ranch house to the bereaved. Tables laden with segmented submarine sandwiches, pasta salads, whole not-quite-ripe pears, greeted the three of us when we arrived.

In the kitchen, a young woman perched on a bar stool, wept. I'd come in to refill my water bottle as she dabbed her tear-filled eyes. She pivoted toward me, her head shaking slightly. "You have no idea, do you?" she said.

I let the water run, my Hydro Flask brimming, then overflowing. "No idea?"

"He was going to leave you," she said.

My eyes locked on hers. "Who are you?"

She gathered herself, a snake, coiling, ready to strike. She sprung off the stool, and scampered through the swinging kitchen door.

It took a while to compose myself after that cryptic assertion, but eventually I rejoined the throng of those offering condolences in the main room. Folks balancing heavy-duty plates on one hand and side-hugging with the other.

"So shocking," they said, whispering their fears in my ear, lest the boogie man hear them and punish with similar fates.

I was one of the few mourners not dressed in black. I wore one of Ethan's favorite summer dresses. A spring-green shift he'd said, *flattered* my coloring. It didn't occur to me until this very gathering that his compliment was a microaggression. My coloring–just a bit too Asian, perhaps? And here I'd always thought of my whiteness as a curse. The freckles. The rashy-pink and perennial sunburn. But by August I usually tanned to a medium ochre.

The young crier who'd rudely hissed at me wore the acceptable charcoal-hued outfit. I spied her hugging my former in-laws before sidling up to Corinda.

My *former* in-laws.

Kento snuck up behind me, his arm encircling my neck. "You okay?"

"Who is that bitch talking to Corinda?" I said, pointing in her direction.

"Never seen her before," he said.

I didn't divulge the content of her venom.

"I can find out though," he said.

I wanted to tell Kento not to bother. I tugged my bra strap under the thin band of material that rounded my shoulder. What had I been thinking, wearing a sundress to my husband's funeral?

Kento gave me a side-squeeze. Said, "I'll be right back," then shuffled off toward his high school girlfriend.

What I didn't realize then was that my brother had another reason to be in Steeplejack, beyond the so-called celebration of Ethan's life. A reason that would soon impact our lives in a major way.

# FOUR

I KEPT OUR WEDDING PHOTO NEXT TO MY BED those early months after Ethan's accident. In the middle of the night, when I'd wake up sweaty, sticky with the patina of a nightmare, I'd clutch the framed photo to my chest like a lover. Our wedding was a spur-of-the-moment decision; we'd tied the knot guerilla-style at Yellowstone, in front of an emerald geyser. Fitting, we joked at the time. The gush of it all. Our witnesses were a random couple we met in the lodge, and the officiant was one of Ethan's soccer teammates, Wesley, who'd done the online now-I-can-marry-people course, rendering him an ordained minister with the Universal Life Church. We'd paid for his room at the lodge, and he'd brought some girl he'd hooked up with the week before. The "ceremony" was as no-frills as they come, but what mattered most was our decision to forge ahead with our bond despite his parents' objections.

In the photo—which was taken by Wesley's date—the faux jewels on my dark blue, beaded flapper dress reflected the morning sun, giving off sparkles that outshone the aqua water, gold thermophiles and hot spring steam behind us. Ethan, with his bolo tie and Stetson, his calfskin boots, his rodeo belt buckle—he was a walking ad for a dude ranch. Even his carefully shaped mutton-chops screamed Hollywood extra in a remake of a gold rush-era film. Along with our small entourage, we sashayed down the raised plank boardwalk with the nonchalance and arrogance of a couple who think they're untouchable.

Ethan. Oh, my Ethan.

Every time I woke up and found that spot next to me empty, the shock of his death reignited in me. For months, this went on. Misremembering my widowhood. The oozing pain of reacquainting myself with reality. I couldn't even summon the energy to attend Grief Group. The pitying looks. The *there-theres*. Unlike when my parents died, the idea of sharing Ethan's death with well-wishers felt like inviting strangers into our bed.

His parents kept calling. Asking how the lawsuit was going. Asking if I'd return the heirloom wedding ring, "Since there are no heirs." Asking if I'd consider marking the site of the accident with a cross, "For remembrance."

Envisioning a cross along the highway where Ethan's head shattered infuriated me. Had the accident occurred a few miles east, in Montana, the state would have stabbed a simple white cross in the spot. *Fatality markers*, they call them. A warning. But Ethan had died in Idaho, five miles from his home. His parents, who now lived eighty miles west, wanted a ghoulish reminder of their son's demise on the side of a road they'd seldom travel, and it felt like a rebuke, somehow. A way to punish me. There'd been a few not-so-subtle jabs.

"If only he'd gone to work that day instead of taking it off," and "I wish you could have dealt with your parents' estate earlier."

Most of the time I retrieved their pleas from voicemail, deleting their messages without response. Occasionally, in a fog, I'd answer, allowing them to hammer me with *if onlys* and their bottomless pits of requests.

I was not going to give back the ring. What would they even do with it?

THE SEASONS CHURNED ON AS THEY ALWAYS DID, and the attorneys worked out the settlement. Suddenly, I had money. Enough to build on our property. Betsy Jones sold our parents' house, and I gave the proceeds to Kento. He and Tom were talking surrogate. They wanted a baby. I was hopeful that they'd move back to Steeplejack, but it was a long shot.

Even as the new house took shape, I remained frozen. Inert as a slug during summer's drought. The folks at Grief Group had finally stopped calling, and one day, I woke up to the realization that if I kept pushing folks away, I would, soon, be peopleless.

And so, through the quicksand of who-gives-a-fuck, I forced myself to act. I began with a sober look at my surroundings. The stuff of early marriage, three-and-a-half years worth of starter objects: our first couch, a thrift-store oak table, and an antique secretary that squeaked when you lowered the fall front. We had our ongoing Scrabble contest results that remained magnetized to the refrigerator, complete with Ethan's obnoxious smiley faces when he tallied his winning scores.

I'd grown soft around the belly from my year of sloth. My mountain-biking quads, my upper arms, they'd reverted to wiggly flesh. A preview of old age. Hauling furniture chunks from the doublewide, down the driveway to the sandwich boards where I'd pasted FREE signs, took half a day, with me stopping to rub my muscles and catch my breath every few steps.

But it was progress.

Then, on one of the hottest days of the year, my brother showed up, unannounced. My first thought was, something bad had happened. Because *history*. And because, his beautiful eyes were darting around nervously as he stood at the screen door.

"Spill it," I said. "Whatever it is. I can take it."

"Let's sit," he said.

I ushered him in. Offered hours-old coffee. He declined, and got right to it. "I have a favor."

Did he need more cash? Nope. A place to live? "You're not divorcing Tom, or anything, right?"

"God no. We're solid."

"Okay."

"Hazel, you are about to become Aunt Hazel."

It took a minute, but after I filtered the title through my tired brain, the part of me that still acknowledged joy woke up.

"Damn, really?" I was sure that the favor had something to do with being named godmother or guardian in case something happened.

Then it occurred to me that two dudes could not a fetus make. "You go through a registry or something?"

Kento said, "I know you've been out of the loop lately. But things have changed this past year. For same-sex couples, I mean."

There had been some political shifts, certainly, but Seattle was as blue as they came. "Well, in this state, yeah," I said. "I get why you can't move back here, but c'mon, no way will Washington state go back to the Dark Ages."

"You really have been in your own world."

He didn't mean it in a mean way, but it still hurt. "Ouch," I said.

Kento's gaze surveyed the living room. "Got rid of that hideous sofa, I see."

He pointed uphill from the trailer. "And it looks like the new house is close to move-in?"

"Yeah, I might sell it," I said, surprised that my mouth uttered the comment, because I hadn't really acknowledged my indifference, even to myself.

"No. Ethan and you had a dream. Why would you do that? Where would you live?"

I shrugged. "I'm kind of one-day-at-a-timing it."

His eyes focused down, then they met mine. "Corinda," he said.

"Corinda, what?" I said.

"She needs a place."

"What?"

"She's finally getting divorced."

I hadn't seen her in a while. Didn't know that.

"You want me to—here?"

"Her husband is abusive. The youngest step-kid is in high school now, so she wants to make her break legal."

It didn't surprise me that Corinda's much older husband turned out to be a dick. But it seemed odd that my brother was still so invested in her life. I must have registered my puzzlement because Kento said, "When did you stop knowing what I was going to say before I said it?"

I shrugged, then turned from him. Stuck my mug of coffee in the zapper for the twentieth time that day.

Silence.

Then.

"She's agreed to be the surrogate," Kento called above the beeping microwave. "Our, uh, baby mama."

I froze. Ignored my burnt coffee and the beeps and pivoted. "Are you out of your damn mind?"

Kento's jaw stiffened. Evidently, I wasn't the only one whose twin Spidey-sense had gone on sabbatical. Clearly, my brother expected something more *encouraging.*

"She needs the money, and she's, well, she's a good friend."

"Kento, stop. She's still in love with you. It's not healthy."

"Is that my dear sister talking, or someone still so deep in her own grief she can't be happy for anyone else?"

I had a snappy retort on the tip of my tongue, but a bigger question intervened. "So, you want her to gestate here, have a kid, and then give the child to you and Tom? What about the anti-gay legislation in Idaho? Is it even legal anymore for a gay couple to hire a surrogate in this state?"

"That's the other part of our plan," Kento said.

It came in a flash, this other part. Our mind-reading ability. "No."

"It's the only way," he said. "We already have a history, so, the Nosy Nellies around here won't raise a fuss. They'll simply think I knocked her up. It's not like we need to pretend to be married."

"Does she truly understand her role? I mean, no offense, but Corinda doesn't have a track record in the good cooperator department. Plus—"

"She's in love with me. Got it. Look, with the new changes to the laws, there is no other way for Tom and me to become parents. Unless we moved to, like, Canada or the Netherlands."

My brother looked so defeated. So up against it. I crept up next to him, tossed my flabby arm over his shoulder. "I'm totally for you and Tom raising a child, knucklehead. You'll be terrific parents. It's her

I'm worried about. And, you know, all the homophobes in Steeplejack poking around."

"We found a good lawyer. And Corinda has signed away all parental rights."

My jaw fell. "You've already—she's already—"

"Confirmed last week," Kento said. "We're looking at an early spring baby."

SUDDENLY, MY OWN SITUATION WAS PRESSURIZED. I agreed to vacate the trailer house within a month so Corinda could move in. The new house was mostly built, but that last ten percent was true to the cliché of taking as long as the 90 percent that came before. I packed and hauled, and before long, I could once again see definition in my arms. I wasn't as winded traipsing up and down the long driveway. The last bit of relocating was when I peeled the Scrabble scores off the refrigerator. Ethan's mostly illegible handwriting was a boulder to my chest.

The day Corinda moved in was heat-dome hot. Triple digits, and record-breaking for fall. Tom's and Kento's shirts were sopping with sweat as they struggled under the weight of the furniture she'd pried from her ex. Still in her first trimester, she was clearly loving her new role as baby vessel, her feet on a loveseat-sized ottoman as she pointed to the spots where her oversized breakfronts and credenzas would take residence.

She was already duck-walking, palm to lower back, groaning when forced to rise from, or lower into, her chair. Kento had purchased a Vitamix, along with the requisite carrots and kale in hopes that Corinda's Diet Coke habit would abate. The carrots had already turned soft, the greens, now liquified in their plastic bags.

"Cravings," she'd reasoned, while stuffing a Taco Bell bean burrito in her mouth, washing it down with regular Coke, because, "I intend to take maximum advantage of my break from dieting."

When busybody Benjamin Kreutz from down the road stopped by with the lame excuse he was checking on the U-Haul, making sure it wasn't "thieves come by to clean out the premises, Hazel being a widow and all," Tom literally hid in the bedroom closet.

Corinda, having rehearsed this moment forever, grabbed Kento's hand, and waddled them forth in a grand show of fakery. "Well, hello there, Ben," she said, her free hand rubbing her belly. "What can we do you for?"

Benjamin's eyes darted around the yard, surveying the clot of items queued up for dragging into the already overstuffed trailer. "Y'all moving in?"

I intervened before Corinda could fantasize out loud. "Temporarily."

His gaze landed on Corinda's midsection. "So you broke up with Arthur, I hear?"

In Steeplejack, rumors began with speculation, and barged forward, irrespective of the truth—especially when suspected cuckholding was involved.

Corinda nuzzled against Kento's cheek before returning Ben's stare down.

"What of it?"

Ben shifted his eyes to Kento. "You moving back here then? Thought you was all settled in a fancy Amazon job over to Seattle."

The public script was purposely vague, but Corinda was already revising it to suit her fantasy. "Why Ben, you know Kento and I have been on and off since high school." She pointed to her womb. "This isn't anything new. This here is the product of a long-term relationship."

Kento struggled to remain neutral. His tell, a childhood left eye twitch, advertised his anxiety.

"We're all good here, Ben. Nice to see you," I said, waving him off with the back of my hand.

He turned and shuffled down the driveway, craning his head around every few yards, no doubt trying to catch sight of something untoward.

"That guy," Kento said.

"Olly olly oxen free," I yelled into the house.

Tom emerged, even sweatier. His dark hair was sopping, glasses slipping down his nose. He was the kindest person. So patient. But it was easy to tell that he wasn't full-on buy-in with this scheme. Corinda still had hold of Kento's hand. Her eyes narrow as a cat's with contempt for Kento's husband.

"Let's break for lunch," my diplomatic brother said. "I'll whip us up some salads."

Corinda made a face, as if Kento had just suggested she eat feces. She returned to her perch, dialed up the box fan placing it inches from her pilled easy chair, and wrestled with a lever until the chair committed to horizontality.

"I'm craving McNuggets," she offered as her eyelids slipped down. "Can one of you take a run to Micky Dees?"

# FIVE

THE NEW HOUSE OVERLOOKED THE RIVER TO THE WEST, and the Bitterroot Range to the south. I'd sprung for special order accordion glass after Betsy convinced me that I'd be committing a real estate crime by not taking full advantage of the unprecedented view. The glass was on backorder, as was the Bosch convection steam oven, and the Tesla solar roof I'd signed up for. When I moved in, my only real view was obscured by the knots in an enormous slab of plywood, and it would be 50/50 whether the roof would arrive before the rainy season. For now, my house was capped by tarps. Industrial strength, but still.

In a way, I was glad that the house was unfinished. The ugly swirl of survivor's guilt marred my ability to enjoy the luxurious details of a house built with the fruits of compensation. What had I done, after all, to deserve such a fancy home? And yet, I could feel Ethan's approval from the box of ashes I'd set on the live-edge wood mantel that graced the hand-built granite fireplace. Of the two of us, he was the one with the conventional "good taste." The subscriptions to *Dwell* and *Nest* and *Architectural Digest*—they were in his name, and continued to arrive monthly, rolled and stuffed into the womb of our battered mailbox.

I couldn't bear to part with Ethan's handwriting and the teasing smiley faces on the Scrabble scores. I Amazon-ordered fancy magnets in the shape of exotic fruits, and transferred the brag-sheets to the stainless front of my new sub-zero refrigerator.

I kept my distance from Corinda. At least at first. The "arrangement," as Kento had referred to it, made me queasy—even though it was Corinda, not me, who'd been plagued with morning sickness. Her divorce had turned contentious as soon as her ex realized she'd moved onto my property. The rumor mill painted me as some sort of lottery winner. Plenty of accidental deaths in a silver mining town; none resulting in a multi-million-dollar settlement. In town, folks whispered behind my back—which, given my background and quizzical ethnicity, was not, in and of itself, unusual.

But there's nothing that turns a community against a person like a sudden windfall. Envy, resentment. It's an ugly response, packed with self-loathing when you wish ill on a widow. Arthur, Corinda's ex, widowed himself, and left with five kids to raise, did not benefit from a well-insured trucking company. His wife had perished of a neurological disease, which had eaten their meager savings. And now the replacement wife had gone and got herself knocked up by an old boyfriend. A half-Jap old boyfriend, to boot. And where was she holing up? Over to the Mackenzie estate. That's what the townspeople decided to call my property. An estate. Uttered with disdain, lingering on the hard dental –ate. As if I'd chewed up and swallowed the land itself.

Arthur "just wanted what was due," he claimed on his drunken visits to the trailer house. I could hear their shouting matches from my new teak porch. I always had a hand on my cell phone, ready to push those three digits if it came to that. Domestic violence oozed from the Bitterroot Divide. Most of the time, it was kept quiet. Odd thing about Steeplejack, everyone up in everyone's grill, but when it came to what a man did or didn't do to or with his wife—or his guns—well, that was nobody's beeswax.

And yet, those same busybodies would give you the shirt from their kid's back when it came to what the folks around here called "God's will." Oh, how they loved a good God's will disaster. A fire. A downpour that swept your home away. A hailstorm that ruined your livelihood. Even before there was Go Fund Me, Steeplejack's stock of God-fearers emptied their egg money jars, cleaned out their pantries, in the name of Jesus.

One afternoon, Corinda almost four months along, Arthur's truck crunched up the drive, only he didn't stop at the trailer house. He kept right on driving up the hill, and skidded to a gravel-spitting stop behind my newly purchased Jeep.

I'd been working on a new piece. It wasn't going well. The paint was sticky hot, plasticizing within minutes on my pallet, and I kept getting distracted with contractor phone tag—still waiting on the roof, following up on a bid for a hot tub platform deck out back. Rich people problems, I had to admit. So foreign at first, and yet, quickly becoming ordinary.

I met him outside, moved my reluctant mouth into smile. "Hello, Arthur, what brings you to this neck of the woods today?"

He was a small man, but practiced at gestures that embellished his infrastructure. Head held high, back straight. He didn't reach a hand out for a shake.

"She's ripping me off," he said, by way of greeting. "Got herself some fancy-ass lawyer, thanks to your jackass wife-stealing brother."

I'd had a lifetime of handling entitled, angry men, given my father and his outbursts, and I could smell alcohol puffing out with Arthur's lament. I backed up a few steps. "I'm not sure what that has to do with me."

Now came the finger jab, pushing through the air, stopping short of my Pixies T-shirt. "You city transplant liberals gonna learn a thing or two about messing with the backbone of this town. I got friends, and my friends don't like outsiders taking what don't belong to them."

One of the things you learn when you have a childhood speckled with parental rage, is how to force calm into your voice.

"That sounds like a threat, Arthur. But I'm not taking anything from you. I have nothing to do with Corinda's private life, I'm just renting to her. I'm a landlord."

"I'm a landlord," he mocked, all sing-songy. "And my prow-nowns is *they* and *them* and *kiss my ass.*"

The other thing you learn to do when threatened by male anger is offer them a gift. Might not be courageous, but it's like DEET is to summer flies. Takes the energy out of their agenda. Makes them pause.

"Arthur," I said. "Why don't you take a seat on my porch, and cool off. I have some sun tea and cornbread in the house. Looks like you could use some refreshments."

Arthur's fists unballed. His head dipped, just a bit. He was deciding what to do. A few seconds later he shuffled up the steps to my mother's Amish hickory rocking chair—one of the few online purchases she made before Dad cut off her Amazon access.

As I stirred in the sugar, a shot of whisky, a wilted leaf of mint, it occurred to me that Arthur (and his ilk) were gasping like a caught trout. Their world was turning without them. They'd been raised to think themselves invincible. Their mothers fussed over them, their fathers alternately praised them and kicked them in their privileged asses. The rules were simple: win, work hard, win some more. Even my Ethan, a supposedly enlightened and progressive product of Steeplejack, had been treated like Lord Fauntleroy by his parents. I used to tease him, call him my Little Prince, when he took for granted the ease with which things came to him in this town. His interview at Beacon and Bright, a minute after passing the bar, was a formality. Stephen Beacon was a golfing buddy of Mac's. Ethan would have made partner in no time.

With a mixture of disdain and pity, I trayed up the refreshments and brought them out to Arthur, who was busy scrutinizing the porch railing. "Lee Jacobs do this work?" he said.

"M-hm."

He turned to face me, pointing out the flaws in my $4,000 custom job. "He used scrap for these here balusters."

The men of Steeplejack loved nothing more than the ritual of putting one another down. A rite of passage second only to Friday night poker games.

"The railing is fine, Arthur. Come, have a snack."

He chose to sit on the stairs, facing his truck. With the help of my ancient toaster oven, I'd baked corn muffins from a box mix the day before, and I handed him one, slathered with honey butter. I could hear him swallow his saliva as he reached for the plate. Judging from

Corinda's fast-food habit, it was likely he hadn't had anything home-cooked since the passing of his first wife a decade earlier.

"All's I'm saying," Arthur said around a mouthful of gritty crumbs. "Corinda and me is married still. And she done get herself knocked up. What the fuck this town gonna think, pardon my French."

"Your kids are grown, Arthur. And Corinda's a young woman. Let her go."

He took a swig of the tea, his eyebrows raised at the taste of the booze. He cleared his throat. "What is it about that wormy brother of yourn, anyways? He gonna ditch his life in Sin-attle, and settle back this away?"

"He can't make a living here, you know that."

"So, she gonna single-raise the kid, you think?"

The conversation was venturing into dangerous territory. I needed to poker face, and send Arthur on his way. "No idea, and it's none of my business. I'm just a landlord."

Arthur licked his fingers, and groaned to a stand. Fake tipped his ballcap. "It ain't right, all's I'm saying. Thanks for the muffin and tea."

I allowed myself a crumb of self-congratulations for diffusing his wrath, but countered that with self-loathing for, once again, putting myself in a situation where I was soothing the ego of an infant-man.

"And Arthur," I managed, as he traipsed to his truck, "try and hold off on the shouting matches. Voices travel, you know."

He flinched, and shrugged. Stepped into the cab of his Ford, and rumbled down the driveway without stopping at the trailer house.

I phoned my brother and got his voicemail. It was a weekday, so no surprise there, but I felt the need to let Kento know his "arrangement" was like an unpicked-up pile of dogshit that he'd left for me to step on.

"Yo, bro. Had a visitor today. Your baby-mama's husband? Maybe Corinda should bunk with you guys for the duration?"

He texted back a few minutes later. Coward.

Tried to get her to do that, but she declined. She thinks Seattle is Satanville. Sorry.

*Sorry.* Kento's all-to-familiar closing refrain of artful passive-aggression. A way to have the last word, via dismissal.

As much as it annoyed me when Kento shut the door on debate, I understood that, for him, it was a survival tactic. Being a so-called minority, and a closeted gay man in a redneck town, boundaries were part of staying alive. But I was his sister. Once upon a time we shared a womb. Of everyone on the planet, I'd known him the longest. I was him, in a way. And he was me. I tapped out, and then deleted, several responses before shoving my phone on a high shelf. What I needed was fresh air. A hike to the outcropping above the property.

IT'D BEEN MORE THAN A YEAR SINCE ETHAN'S ACCIDENT, and I'd put off the ash-spread long enough. There were several contenders for the spread, and I'd planned to dole out his charred remains a bit at a time. Beacon and Bright had boxed up his personal stuff and de-livered it when I moved into the new house, and boxes were stacked in what one day would be a breakfast nook. His clothes I'd given to the Red Cross already. His grooming kit and childhood soccer trophies—they'd been shipped to his parents in Spokane. But these last pieces of my husband. The Scrabble scores. The wedding photos. The ashes. The laptop and books he'd had at the office—it was past time to lay that all to rest. All I could handle on this particular day were the ashes.

Separating a fistful of cremains from the bulk is a gruesome task requiring gloves and something a bit more formal than a Ziploc baggie. After hunting for a bit I happened on a silk drawstring bag in my gift wrap bin. I pried the lid from the fancy cremains box and spooned Ethan's organic matter into the bag, stuffed it in my short's pocket, and set out.

Our land, located a mile-and-a-half from town and sitting at nearly 3,000 feet elevation, backed up to a trail system through state park be-fore merging with national forest. Despite the infiltration of mountain bikers and hikers, the area surrounding our acreage remained remote and relatively pristine. Ethan and I had spent most weekends wandering the trails, scrambling screes, bushwhacking through wild huckleberry bushes. A stand of cedars marked the edge of our property, and against those trees I ladled out the first spoon of Ethan. A winding rocky trail led up a steep incline to the first view-worthy outcropping of sheared argillite. Somewhere in the Beacon and Bright boxes Ethan's argillite arrowhead collection lay hidden. Bird points and side notches. He was into all that—vestiges from his upbringing.

By the time I'd ventured up another 500 feet of elevation, I was sweating, my heart beating like a hailstorm in my chest. My legs; jelly. Despite the physical aspects of moving, I was still somewhat out of shape. I'd forgotten how much hiking I'd done with my husband. Most weekends, at least in our first year of marriage, we'd ascend the hills with the same competitive gusto as our Scrabble matches.

"You're turning me into a sloth, Ethan," I yelled into the hazy air. "Thanks again for leaving me to my lazy ways."

Letting that out, it was a cork sprung from an under-pressure bottle. What came out next were choking sobs. I couldn't stop the gush. The release. "You motherfucker. You asshole. Why did you do this to me? Why did you leave me alone like this?"

My lament echoed back to me, boomeranging off granite boulders. A battle started up in my head. Anger, guilt, shame. Sorrow. All the players. I screamed myself hoarse, my lungs and stomach burned with fury. It wasn't until I heard the rustle of branches that I realized I wasn't alone. A young couple—college age, maybe—burst out of the woods, and scampered up.

"Are you okay?" said the woman.

My head was already throbbing in post-weep ache. I'm sure my face was streaked in ugly-cry tears. My cheeks, bright red from exertion and sun. I hadn't even thought to bring a water bottle, and I was parched.

"I'm fine," I said, my grief instantly replaced with embarrassment.

The man, all dread-locked and tan, said, "We heard you screaming. It sounded like you were being attacked."

His tone was more accusatory than concerned.

"Sorry," I said, my brother's dismissive retort springing forth.

"Are you alone?" said the woman.

I nodded.

"Shouldn't hike alone," she added.

"It's fine," I said, pointing down the trail. "My property is just a half mile down there."

"Okay," she said. "But what made you so upset?"

This was turning into an inquisition, and I was not in the mood. "I'm here to spread some ashes. So—"

The couple exchanged a glance. Now it was their turn to be embarrassed.

"Oh," said the man.

"Excuse our intrusion," said the woman.

At this point I was standing, my position on the rocks, overlooking the view and therefore the endpoint destination, impeded their own agenda, but I wasn't about to cut my business short. They could damn well wait until I was done doing what I came here to do.

They picked up on my reluctance to move and turned around, heading back whence they came, leaving me somewhat ashamed, but mostly vindicated. As I watched their flannel-clad backs recede into the woods to light their celebratory spliff, or make out, or whatever, my mood lifted. Was it agency? Was it absurdity? The anger and sorrow I'd just spewed into the canyon, was out of me. I'd drained myself of wrath and rage, and in their place came light. And then came laughter. Before I knew it, I was convulsing in mirth, like a switch had been flipped.

I dug the silk bag of Ethan from my pocket, yanked open the drawstring, and fluttered his ashes in an arc as a gentle breeze carried them off the rocky ledge.

"Farewell, my dear," I whispered.

I stood there, on the outcropping, until the last particle of my husband left my view, and then I headed back down the trail to the house he would have loved to call home.

# SIX

THE POUNDING ON MY DOOR blended with my dream. In a half-asleep daze, I fought my eyelids. It wasn't until I heard Corinda yell my name that I finally snapped awake.

She stood on the porch, her face streaked with tears. Or maybe it was rain. An unforecasted downpour, complete with thunder and lightning, accompanied her sudden appearance at my house.

"Come in, my goodness," I said, as I pulled my robe closed.

She waddled in. Five months along, and she was looking nearly full term, complete with moaning as she stepped.

"What's going on?"

"I think something's wrong with the baby," she sobbed.

"What do you mean?"

She patted her stomach. "I went to the bathroom, and there was blood."

I didn't firsthand know much about pregnancy, but I'd seen enough movies and television to know that blood during a pregnancy wasn't a good sign.

"So, was it like, rusty brown blood, or bright red?"

"In between."

"A lot or a little?"

Corinda wailed, "Am I going to lose this baby?"

"Let's go to the hospital, okay? To the emergency room. Get it checked out."

She sob-nodded. Sniffed. And we made our way to my jeep.

The ER in Coeur d'Alene was packed with vomiting people clutching their stomachs, and babies coughing like seals. Fairly normal for the wee hours in November. At least that's what the intake person told us. Her name tag said B. Goodman, and she took Corinda's insurance info, and told us to take a seat. Told us we were priority since potential miscarriages were heavily scrutinized these days. The state had outlawed abortion a few years earlier, and pregnancy complications involved a slew of extra paperwork. Something that needed to be handled before shift change at 7 a.m. or a whole new group of healthcare folks would have to be involved.

B. Goodman didn't spell it out, exactly, but there'd recently been an article in the local paper about the new law, with a headline that read, *Idaho Heartbeat Bill a Drain on Healthcare*. The reporter and the editor of the paper were both fired a week later. Apparently, truth in journalism was a punishable offense these days.

Corinda had me get her a Coke from the machine, but I wasn't about to lecture her on proper nutrition given her state. As I trudged back with the soda, an attendant was ushering her into a room. "She a relative?" the nurse asked.

Corinda nodded. "She's my sister-in-law."

Her declaration shocked me. Well, maybe *shocked* is too strong a word. It was a warning that Corinda still held out hope that Kento would stop being gay, and they'd raise the baby together, but I made myself shift from that particular red flag. For my sanity, and for expediency, I decided her lie was just a shortcut way for me to be allowed to accompany her, and I followed them into a curtained cubicle.

"How far along are you, Mrs. Blair?" the nurse asked, after Corinda had changed into a hospital gown and had taken a seat on the gurney.

"Twenty weeks five days," she snuffled.

Her precision jolted me. Another red flag.

"Let's get you comfortable," the nurse, said, fisting a thin pillow. "I've put in for the ultrasound, so sit tight."

Corinda's lip pouted forth. I handed her the Coke.

She popped the tab, slurped a fizzy mouthful, and burped.

I pulled a chair up next to the gurney. Placed a hand on Corinda's leg. My fingernails were raggedy from the day's toil. Stains on my hand from a charcoal sketch I'd started in the afternoon. I'd yanked on sweats, hadn't had time to brush my hair, and a puff of breath when I spoke reminded me, I'd put garlic in my salad dressing earlier. There were so many other places I would have rather been. In bed asleep topped the list.

Corinda was half finished with her soda when a technician rolled in the machine that would apparently tell us if her baby was still alive. It'd started kicking a few weeks earlier, and when the intake nurse had asked her about it, she'd said she wasn't sure if it'd been gas or the baby.

"Can you call Kento?" Corinda whined as the tech rubbed some sort of ointment on the wand and hiked up the gown to reveal her mountain of a belly.

"Let's see what's going on first," I said. "It's four in the morning."

She shoved the half full can of Coke my way, and it sloshed on the cuff of my hoodie.

"Okay, can you take a deep breath and hold it?" said the technician, all business, no smile.

I craned my neck to view the monitor as the wand slipped around Corinda's belly. A black-and-white triangle appeared, then the *wah-wha-wha* of a heartbeat before the fetus came into view.

Corinda's eyes were squeezed shut. "Is the baby okay?"

"It looks good to me," I answered, then looked to the tech for confirmation.

The technician didn't answer, she simply said, "Doctor will be in to discuss." She pressed some buttons, and a long strip of paper emerged from the machine, photobooth style. She snapped the tongue of paper out of the dispenser and clipped it under the spring of a clipboard. She handed Corinda a tissue to wipe the goo off her belly, but Corinda still had her eyes shut, so I intercepted and wiped the stuff off myself.

"Leave the money on the dresser," I muttered as the tech wheeled the machine out of the room. "Wonder what got her panties in a wad,"

I said, once the technician was out of earshot.

"Speaking of that, I have to change my pad, if the doctor's gonna look up there," Corinda said, squeezing her legs together in a sudden display of embarrassment.

I helped her off the gurney, and she grabbed her purse with one hand, and held the back of her hospital gown closed with the other and then shuffled off to the bathroom on the other side of the nurse's station. I took a sip of Corinda's soda. The fizziness hit my nose and I sneezed.

"Bless you," said a voice. It was the doctor. A Korean woman. I always felt at ease when meeting an Asian person for the first time—mostly because there wasn't the obvious wheel-spinning, the unsaid and sometimes said—*Where are you from*? As in, Where are you *from*, from? As in, Where did your family move here *from*?

I didn't look as Japanese as Kento, but an astute phenotype assessor could tell I wasn't part Hawaiian, or Chinese, or some mixture of Pacific Islander, though that didn't keep some folks from musing out loud.

"Doctor Yun," she said, holding out a crooked arm. She looked me up and down after we bumped elbows. "You're clearly not the patient. Where is she?"

"Ladies," I said.

"Ah," she said. "Are you partner?"

"Just a—friend? I'm Hazel."

"Hm. Okay." She held the clipboard with the photo of the fetus. "You think she wants to know the sex?"

I shrugged. "Mostly, I think she wants to know if she's miscarrying."

"Am I?" Corinda said, as she stepped back into the cube.

"Hop on up here," Dr. Yun said, patting the gurney. "Let's chat."

I helped hoist Corinda back up on the metal bed, and the doctor began her spiel.

"You have a naughty placenta," she said. "It is in the wrong place."

She pulled the ultrasound photo from the clipboard and fluttered it in front of Corinda. "Hard to tell here, but the placenta is under baby, covering cervix. *Placenta previa* is the technical term."

"Can you fix it?" Corinda said, her voice melodic and seeking, like a kid hoping for a treat.

"Sometimes the placenta moves back to the uterine wall as pregnancy develops. But you are twenty, um, twenty-one weeks along, so should have resolved if it was going to."

Corinda instinctively placed a hand on her crotch, as if trying to prevent the placenta from falling out her vagina.

"The bleeding," Dr. Yun said. "Is it spotting, or period bleeding?"

"I think it stopped, actually," Corinda said. "It was like, last day of a period kind of bleeding, but now, nothing."

"That is good news. However, as a precaution, I think bedrest is in order, and then a recheck with your OB in ten days."

"Bedrest?" Corinda said. "But who will make food and do laundry and all that?"

A little acid worked its way up my throat. *Not I, said the cat.*

"Baby's father, perhaps?" said Dr. Yun.

"He—he lives in Seattle," said Corinda, her voice now taking the tone of the kid who was denied a treat.

"We'll figure it out," I said.

"Good," said Dr. Yun. "Now, for the better news. Your baby looks fine. Growing well. You want to know boy or girl?"

"Oh!" Corinda said, bouncy now. "Can you write it down on a paper? Fold it, so's I can't see it. We want to do a gender reveal." She craned around and looked at me. "Maybe you can know, and put the answer in a cake!"

Then, back to the doctor, "We haven't discussed this before."

"I will leave the answer in an envelope with the nurse," said Dr. Yun. "Meantime. Bedrest."

She twirled away, then, twirled back, and handed Corinda the fetus snapshot. "If you want the gender to be revealed, don't look too closely in the nether regions," she said.

IT DIDN'T TAKE MUCH CONVINCING to install Corinda in the big house, where I could wait on her hand and foot. At least until the weekend when Kento agreed to spell me. As for the gender reveal nonsense, I subbed that out to my brother as well, despite Corinda's plea for me to be the sole holder of the baby's sex. Fat chance I was going to embark on the gender reveal cake recipe Corinda texted me. The "secret" stayed in its envelope, but any moron could tell there was a penis on that fetus photo. I slapped the printout on the refrigerator next to the Scrabble scores, fastening it to the stainless with a star fruit magnet.

I gave her the primary bedroom because that was currently the only actual bed in the house, and immediately pressed send on an order for a bed-in-a-box. Nothing like a health crisis to light a fire under a procrastinator's ass.

I'D AGREED TO A FEW GIGS DOWN at the police station. Facial reconstruction based upon victims' recollections. Forensic art assignments were far more lucrative than medical text sketching, and the pay was more immediate, but with my new status as a rich person, money ceased to be an issue. The present motivator was time away from needy Corinda and her cavalcade of demands. I set her up with sandwiches and sodas as well as a few more nutritious items like grapefruit sections and a Cobb salad—which I knew would remain untouched, but still.

"You'll be home in a couple hours, right?" she whined from her princess perch in my king-sized bed.

"I think you'll be fine. I'm only a text away," I said, even though the job required a shut-off phone and intense concentration.

Kento and Tom were due in later. Corinda was already copping an attitude about Tom accompanying my brother, but Kento and I had decided to double down on reality since Corinda's imagination had leapt into dangerous territory along with the bedrest plan.

"BETTER TO NIP IT IN THE BUD," I'd cautioned on the phone earlier.

At the station, they were talking potential hate crime. The victims, Marcia Smith and Leona Katz, were the town's most vocal gay activists.

They'd been an out and proud couple for more than a decade, and despite Steeplejack's don't-ask-don't-tell attitude, they were tolerated. Not loved, but tolerated. In that nice-to-your-face way, though nobody invited them to potlucks.

But now that so many progressive federal laws had been challenged in Idaho, Marcia and Leona had been openly targeted. Graffiti, slashed tires, a bag of shit left on their porch, and, most recently, the front of their home shot up with pepper bullets.

Furious, Leona had stormed out of the house, and caught a slinking figure running from the scene. The figure had turned slightly. Enough for Leona to catch some vital descriptions, and that's why I'd been pressed into service.

I hadn't been down to cop HQ, as Ethan and I used to call it, since his death, and as I walked through the hall, it was like parting a sea of condolence-givers. Hats came off heads. *Sorry for your loss,* mumbled in my wake.

I was offered bad coffee and shown to the interrogation room where Leona and Marcia sat calmly at the table. Nobody had offered them coffee.

"Hey," I said, as I sat down with my sketch pad. "How are you two?"

We exchanged niceties. They'd attended Ethan's church service my in-laws had guilted me into, which had been a brave gesture.

I took out my pencils.

Warren Coulter, the detective on this case, hovered in the background. "Still doing this the old-school way," he said. "Thought the whole face recon was all digital these days."

I had the software, but rarely put it to use. For me, a digital product lacked nuance. Or maybe I was just a Luddite. "So," I said, ignoring Warren's thinly veiled insult, "let's start with the big stuff and then work into the smaller details."

The perpetrator was male, in the six-foot range. Thin build. Likely Caucasian, but Leona couldn't say absolutely since he'd worn a mask and a ski hat. It'd been dusk. The man had long hair though; some strands peeked out of the hat and reached his shoulders. Dark brown, probably.

I sketched a preliminary draft, and Leona said, "I just remembered something. His jacket. He'd rolled the sleeves up. Which was strange because it was one of those puffy numbers. Too small for him. Seemed like it was made for a woman."

Warren cleared his throat. "Maybe the perp was a tranny?"

Marcia glared at him. "Jesus Christ. No. This was not a trans individual. Also, *tranny* is pejorative."

"How do you know, Ms. Smith?" Warren said, his mouth twitching at the smack down. "You weren't even home."

"Because," Leona scolded, "this was a hate crime. You really think trans people commit anti-gay crimes? In this town?"

"Whoa!" said Warren, holding up a stop-sign hand. "We have not established this as a hate crime. Not yet. We need more information."

"More info," argued Marcia, the bolder of the two, "beyond the escalating evidence? A pink triangle painted on my Honda? I knew this shit would happen after the *don't say gay* law bullshit. The Nazis are trying to run us out of town. You know that group, the militia? Fuckers are moving here just to join it."

"Could be you had a beef with someone in town, and they're putting that stuff out there to derail the investigation. It happens," Warren said. The Coulters were descended from the early silver mine settlers. If there was a picture to describe the term "good old boys," Warren's mug would be featured. Also, designating a crime as "hate" meant more paperwork, and the feds coming in and pissing on Warren Coulter's jurisdiction.

Marcia pulled out her phone, scrolled through pictures, and placed the phone on the table. I leaned over my sketch to get a better view, and what I saw hit me like a two-by-four to the gut.

"Under the triangle, this. And we've seen this tag around town. Most recently on the steps of the women's health clinic and the back gate of the food pantry," Leona said.

The picture, a bit blurry, but still damning, featured three squiggly vertical lines underneath a horizontal line. I swallowed the excess spit that'd accumulated from a half-burp, half-gasp.

I needed to change the subject. "Can we get back to the description of the suspect?"

"That's what we're here for, after all," chimed Warren.

My hand began to cramp, and I loosened my grip on the shading pencil. "You mentioned rolled up sleeves on a puffy jacket," I said. "Can you remember the brand? The color?"

"It was getting dark," Leona said. "But the jacket had a tear. Now I remember. A rip in the back like it'd been slashed with a knife or something."

"And you don't have a security camera anywhere on your property?" I said.

Marcia burst in with, "We have one on order. Guess there's a shortage."

Leona said, "I don't know what is happening in this world. We've been living here peaceably for a dozen or so years. We never had a problem until the last election. God damn fascists taking over."

Warren's eyes narrowed. He straightened and sighed. Then, "Looks like Hazel here has done her sketch. We'll post it on the socials, give it to the papers."

I ripped the sketch out of my pad, handed it off for processing. It wasn't my best, but it was something. I shook the cramp out of my hand, then offered it to the ladies.

"I hope they get the asshole," I said. Typically, at this point, I'd issue my LLC, Bitterroot Renderings business card, along with the closing remark: *If you think of anything that might improve the rendering, be in touch.*

Today, I kept the cards in my satchel.

"How you holding up?" Marcia asked.

"It's an adjustment," I said.

"I hear you're helping Corinda out of her shitty situation," Marcia said.

"Speaking of Corinda, guess I'd better get back home."

"What do you mean?" Leona said.

I'd forgotten that the pregnancy was still hush-hush. I knew Arthur Blair was keeping it quiet. He wasn't about to advertise the result of his wife's infidelity. "She's a bit vulnerable at the moment," I said, hastily.

"Could have predicted that marriage was doomed," Leona said. "Girl was barely out of her teens when that shithead preyed on her."

Warren stood by the open door, my sketch fluttering in his grip as he gestured for us to vacate the interrogation room.

We took our time gathering our things. It was clear that Leona and Marcia's hate crime investigation was a low priority. Lower even than parking ticket enforcement, as proven by the neon yellow paper crammed under the windshield of my car that threatened to double the fine if I didn't pay within ten days. Apparently, my front bumper was an inch into a fire hydrant zone.

# SEVEN

On Saturday morning I awoke from the comfort of my new bed-in-a-box to the sizzle of bacon, and its accompanying pig lard stench. NPR on the radio, loud. But not as loud as Kento and Tom, who were narrating their culinary activities as if in a commercial kitchen of professional chefs.

Stuff like, "Behind you with hot grease!" and "Second pot of coffee coming up!"

I was overjoyed they were here for the weekend, and already lamenting their upcoming departure the next day. Through the variety of chatter, Corinda's voice pierced the air with occasional demands. She needed a Tums. She wanted another ice cube for her Coke. My nerves were stretched thin with her milking the bed-rest mandate. If only she weren't so squirrely about Seattle. It made much more sense for her to hole up in a clinging-to-blue, liberal city during her gestation. If the Steeplejack locals found out the real story behind her pregnancy, things could really backfire for Kento and Tom.

Also, there was the ever-present danger of Arthur's continued lurking in the background. He'd been semi-stalking Corinda. Several times in the past month I'd caught him in the driveway, parked in front of my car, just sitting there in his truck, blaring staticky country music.

"Breakfast is ready," yelled Tom, from the base of the staircase.

Corinda would be served in bed, of course. On a platter befitting her invalid status. I passed Kento on the stairs; he was balancing several plates and cups on our mother's lacquered Nashiji bed tray. "Seriously? That's an antique. Worth a couple grand," I scolded.

"Well, that's a fraction of what this baby's costing," he said.

"Touché."

"Tom whipped up a batch of huckleberry scones. Get 'em while they're hot."

"Aye, aye, Cap'n."

I found Kento's adorable husband taking off my mother's gingham apron, brushing it lovingly before hanging it on a hook in my deluxe butler's pantry. Tom was small in stature, but had the most excellent posture of any man I'd ever met. Blessed also with favorable proportions and long legs, Tom gave the appearance of a six-footer, though he was shorter than my five-foot-ten brother.

"I'd kill for this kitchen," he said, and then, realizing that a death had, indeed, occurred for its existence, he grimaced. "Sorry."

"It is a bit much," I said. "Especially since I'm more of a meal assembler than a cook. Ethan was the chef in the family."

"Was he though?" Tom said, putting his foot in his mouth for the second time in ten seconds. "I mean," he quickly amended, "I knew he was a foodie when it comes to dining. Just didn't realize he was into cooking."

Tom wasn't as harsh about Ethan as Kento, but there was no love lost between them. I held my tongue about it, and instead, closed my eyes and breathed in a lungful of competing aromas. "Rumor has it, there're some huckleberry scones lying about?"

From upstairs came laughter. Nobody could get Corinda as happy as Kento could, and, for the briefest moment, a warning bell sounded in my heart. Tom picked up on it and let out an audible sigh as I sat down to a plate full of delicious brunch food—the first proper home-cooked meal I'd had since the post-funeral repast. Nothing like crisp bacon, crunchy scones and local, free-range eggs whipped into a spinach and leek frittata. Not to mention small-batch roasted coffee to wash it all down with.

A plate of Nova lox, sliced red onions, and capers accompanied a basket of bagels. "You must have brought these from home," I said. "All we have here is grocery bagels that are basically circles of chewy white bread peppered with seeds."

"Steeplejack could use a decent Jewish deli," Tom said. "And an Asian market."

"Good luck with that idea," I said. And then, before I could stop my mouth it broadcast my latest dilemma. I offered the long-story-short version of Leona and Marcia, and the recent troublesome tagging. "It's my logo, Tom. Someone appropriated it and slapped it next to their homophobic symbols."

"The root logo? Shit. Has anyone called you on it?"

"Not yet, but now I'm tempted to rebrand. I mean, what the fuck?"

Upstairs, the laughter subsided, low murmuring taking its place.

I whispered, "Are you at all worried about Corinda's frame of mind? You *do* know she's still carrying a torch for your husband, right?"

Tom's face revealed his anxiety, but he shrugged. "She signed over the rights. She's taken the money. The law, thank goodness, is on our side."

"For now," I said, quietly. "Which is another reason you should push for her to gestate and give birth in your neck of the woods."

"We discussed it. But, you know, we have only two bedrooms in the condo, and we're knee deep in vision boards for the nursery already. I suppose we could give up our bedroom."

He paused, sipped from his mug, then said, "It's moot though. She's adamant that she wants to stay in Steeplejack, and, frankly, with her fluctuating state of mind, it would be unwise to uproot her. Don't you think?"

"Clearly, it's her call," I said. "I just wonder if she could be persuaded try it out for a month or two? Her ex is skulking around here, and there's the question of his volatility."

Kento's footsteps echoed as he trotted down the stairs. With the walls still bare and the rooms sparsely furnished, the acoustics were flinch-inducing. "Volatile? Who's volatile?" he said, slapping the empty tray on the counter.

"Looks like your baby mama's a member of the clean plate club," I said, waving off my brother's question. I really didn't want to get into the whole Arthur stalking with Kento. Not today, anyway.

"I wish she wasn't so addicted to Coke. The beverage, I mean," Kento said.

"Would you rather it were the drug?" I said.

Kento chuckled. We all did. The tension drained from the room, briefly.

"I'll clean up," I said. "Why don't you guys relax. You haven't sat still for a minute since you arrived yesterday."

They exchanged a look.

"What?"

"There's something we want to discuss with you," Kento said.

"Uh-oh. Should I be worried?"

"How would you feel about being named guardian. Just in case," Kento said.

My heartbeat picked up. "Isn't that a bit premature? I hate to invite Negative Nancy into the conversation, but she's not entirely out of the woods."

"It's just that," Tom interjected, "we need to have all the bases covered. Our attorney is a stickler."

Ethan and I had wanted kids. Ethan, more than me, to be honest. We'd even set a date to start *trying*, though I hated the term. It always sounded like attempting to take a shit when you were constipated. The date had come and gone, and then Ethan died, and the idea of motherhood died along with him. I tried to visualize the product of Kento and Corinda. And then I glanced at the envelope Corinda had pinned to the fridge next to the Scrabble scores. She'd tucked the ultrasound photo inside of it. She'd wanted to discuss the gender reveal idea with Kento before sharing the photo. It felt weird for me to know the gender before my brother and Tom.

I asked Kento if Corinda had discussed the reveal with him.

"No way," Tom said. "I draw the line at that."

"It's a small concession," Kento argued.

"I have to agree with Tom," I said. "The more you indulge her mommy fantasies, the harder it's going to be for her to take the money and, you know, run."

"And her knowing that Hazel is next in line if something should happen to us," Tom continued. "How is it going to work if she's plastering a fucking gender reveal video to her Instagram followers?"

"Look," I said. "I'll sign the form or whatever, only because I know it'll never happen—you both perishing—but I'm not going to participate in the *is it a penis or vagina?* parade. If you want to know the sex, it's right there, pasted to my sub-zero appliance."

Tom followed my outstretched finger and strode to the envelope.

"Stop," Kento bellowed. "Let's talk this over."

Tom began to argue, but his lament was cut short when Corinda suddenly appeared. Somehow, she'd managed to creep down the stairs undetected. I had to admit; I didn't know she had a stealthy gait in her elephant-stomping repertoire.

"Don't touch that!" she shrieked.

Tom froze.

"Let's do the reveal today. Before you leave, Kento," she pleaded.

CORINDA INSISTED ON BEING SHUTTLED to a nail salon, bedrest be damned, "for the close-ups when I slice the cake," she said. "And while I'm gone, you can bake it," she added, her pre-mani fingertip trained on my hardly broken-in Wolf convection oven, before rerouting toward my face. "But first you need to buy food coloring."

She was having a blast issuing commands. The way some women dream of their wedding (Corinda and Arthur had tied the knot at city hall), Corinda had logged her share of Pinterest time designing an influencer-level display of gender obsession. All this for a baby she was contractually obligated to surrender in four months time. The subtle warning bells in my head had become Fourth of July fireworks.

I didn't need Dr. Yun's hastily scribbled circle-arrow sketch to tell me that Corinda's fetus had a penis. As soon as the troops left for Nails and Much Much More, I set off for Safeway's bakery section. I was happy to see a random teenager behind the counter. A disaffected, acne-ridden adolescent, clearly disinterested in anyone over twenty-five.

"You know gender reveals are sexist, right?" the teen said when I asked if they had any ready-made blue cakes in the cooler.

Normally, I was grateful for the occasional woke Steeplejack citizen. If there was hope for our future, it lay with the kids. But I didn't feel the need to explain my situation to a stranger. "Maybe I just want to see what blue cake tastes like," I countered.

"We used to have a rainbow cake," the teen said, shaking her head, "but corporate discontinued it. *Don't say gay*, amiright?"

"I promise, I'm not with the morality police or whatever," I said. "I just need a blue cake."

"Hang on," the teen said with a sigh. "I'll check the cooler."

I watched the bakery clerk retreat to the back, and was practically jolted out of my skin by a tap on my shoulder. I pivoted. It was my neighbor, Benjamin Kreutz.

Fuck.

"Got company, I see," he said.

"My brother."

"I seen 'em driving off somewheres. Corinda, Kento, some other fellow. So is Corinda sheltering up to your new house now?"

Benjamin had lost his edge in the sly department. He was saying the spying part out loud. "We're, um, it's been a year, you know. Anniversary?" I stumbled over my lie. "Ethan's I mean. We're doing a family thing."

"A family thing, eh? Corinda part of your family now?"

"She's my—assistant. Um, my mentee. For the forensic work." The thing about lying is, once you start, you're committed. Like going down a black diamond single-track.

"Speaking of fer-in-sicks, I hear they got you on the alleged hate case. Leona and Marcia's claims?"

"You know I can't confirm or deny matters pertaining to my work with law enforcement."

In Benjamin's shopping cart was a twelve-pack of Oly, a head of iceberg lettuce, some cans of chili, a stack of frozen Totinos, a dozen Hot Pockets, and a family-sized bag of shredded cheddar cheese. It was a wonder he was still standing. His breath was chewing tobacco and his teeth had achieved a shade of mud not typically associated with a live human.

He reached a yellow-nailed hand to my shoulder. "Your papa, God bless him, he'd be happy you got that money. That's all's you need to think when you hear them jealous old biddies."

His touch was unexpected. Creepy, yet genuine. I was not in the habit of attending the modern-day quilting bee, aka school board meetings, and therefore had not put myself in the position of listening to whatever the so-called *old biddies* were saying, but I'd be lying if I didn't acknowledge that my feelings were hurt. Why would anyone hold the settlement against me? It was the insurance company that paid out, and insurance companies, the gristmill had historically contended, were profit barons.

Over the past decade, the right-wing political fear machine had convinced folks that insurance payouts were entitlements. A sort of welfare for the lucky. Ethan's untimely death had been morphed into an eye-rolling windfall. Not to mention the fifteen hundred dollars survivor's benefit that materialized in my checking account each month. I'm certain there was speculation on the amount, and I was also certain that Ethan's parents were feeding the gossip pipeline.

The real victims, according to Steeplejack's faithful, were Ethan's parents, and I knew, even though they now lived in Spokane, they were still part of the community in spirit.

The bakery clerk appeared just as Benjamin began squeaking his cart down the aisle, but he stopped and turned as the teen thrust a box my way. He definitely heard the closing remark, "Here's your blue gender reveal cake. Better eat it soon, it's about to expire."

# EIGHT

CORINDA HAD INSISTED THAT KENTO also get his nails done. Mostly, I suspected, so she could have his ear as the two of them sat side by side in the cushy massage chairs at Nails and Much Much More. As for Tom, he was sent off on errands. Balloons, poster board, streamers, markers. Corinda had actually suggested he drive all the way to the Spokane Michael's.

"You can download a coupon," she said. A coupon that might save three bucks while consuming twenty dollars' worth of gasoline.

While Corinda was wiggling into the new maternity dress she'd recently Amazoned, and my brother and his husband were puffing up balloons, I sliced into the cake to make sure it was the right color. The electric blue interior confirmed the gender answer, and I dabbed the brittle, white frosting over the crack as if shaping a clay pinch pot. One thing I had on my side was decent fine motor skills. I didn't even pretend that I'd baked it, and, once the fondant smoothing was finished, I plunked it back into its grocery bakery box.

In keeping with the baby daddy ruse, Tom, of course, would not be part of the video. Lately, young mothers-to-be were all the rage on social media. Becoming successfully impregnated and then advertising the stages of bump development with a Toby Keith song as background was the new right-wing Instagram craze, and Corinda was eager to get her verified checkmark. Plus, with Kento by her side, she had the added celebrity of a handsome partner to flaunt. Somehow, despite the growing

White Nationalism movement in the country, when it came to spawn creation in photo-forward social media, mixed race babies were all the rage. There were so many contradictions in racism.

Once Corinda was finally video-ready, and the backdrop view overlooking the mountains framed with an arc of blue and pink balloons had been adapted to Corinda's new iPhone's exposure compensation control, and once I'd positioned the cake on a platter and handed my brother our mother's ceremonial Kwaiken knife and server, the laborious process of filming and re-filming commenced.

Kento looked like a kindergartner on his first picture day, what with his artificially gelled hair, and his stiff, collared shirt. He sat next to Corinda on my Stickley leather sofa, all deer-in-the-headlights.

"Relax, okay," Tom prodded, making silly faces as I tested the light and sound in take after take.

The script consisted mainly of Corinda holding up a marquee board advertising her 21-week status, along with some bump-emphasizing profile shots, and Kento looking adorably up at her with a zombie smile plastered on his face. We rehearsed right up to the actual slicing, with Corinda acting as both performer and director.

She whined, "Can you maybe look at me, more?" Then, adjusting the angle of Kento's chin so it pointed at her instead of the camera, she implored, "And maybe you can make your jaw less stiff?"

After an hour of this, I reminded the production crew that we were losing daylight, and we'd soon have to drag lamps and crap into the living space.

"I have to pee again," Corinda said, for the umpteenth time.

Finally, though, we arrived at the money shot. Kento's wobbly hand (his fine motor not as blessed as his twin sister's, it must be said), and then Corinda's manicured hand atop his as I zoomed in.

"Wait," she cried. "This knife! I don't want to use it. Can we have a normal one, please?"

I intervened. "Are you fucking kidding me? This is an antique, and it has inter-generational significance."

Corinda sprang her hand off the handle. "I don't want to have this in my video. This weird Japanese relic! Can you dig up a normal knife?"

Kento, caught in the middle, tried to calm her escalation. He held the knife aloft. Explained its importance to our family. "It belonged to my mother, and the fact that it survived so many generations, I think it's good luck."

Corinda recoiled. "No! I recognize that knife. Your mother threatened me—"

It was that moment, as Kento brought the knife closer to Corinda for her inspection, that the front door slammed open.

Corinda's horrified face was the last thing I filmed as the shots rang out.

# PART TWO

# NINE

THE BULLET FROM ARTHUR'S RIFLE had miraculously missed essential organs, but Kento's blood loss had been the main worry, and because both he and I are AB negative, the rarest and hardest to find blood type, I'd donated all they'd let me in the same tiny, local emergency room that Corinda and I had shuffled to just a few days earlier.

Kento needed surgery and more blood, so after they declared him stable—after the local EMTs restarted his heart and replaced some of his blood—they transferred him by air to Seattle's Harborview Trauma Hospital. Tom rode with him in the chopper, and I broke all speed records on the 90 driving my way there. He was still in surgery when I arrived, and Tom was pacing in the surgical waiting room along with parents of a child who'd fallen out a third story window.

Tom grabbed my arm and led me down the slick, empty hall. He filled me in as we wrestled packages of Peanut M&Ms from the stingy vending machine.

"He was only four. *Is* only four," Tom said, in a shaky voice.

"I don't know how kids survive past their toddler years with all the dangers in our world," I said. "I mean, my mother used to put Kento and me in harnesses whenever we went to the park, or a crowded store."

As soon as it was out of my mouth, I wished I'd held my tongue. The fear on Tom's face. The terror. I knew I was doing the thing I do when I'm traumatized. I'd flipped my switch to keep from breaking down. Nonsensical, inappropriate anecdotes were my Xanax. I shoved the bag of candy into the pocket of my hoodie and placed my arms around my brother-in-law. He relaxed into me, his back jiggle-stuttering with poorly suppressed sobs.

"Shh," I soothed, patting his dried sweat-infused shirt. "Kento's going to be okay. He definitely, definitely will make it."

"This is going on hour eight in surgery, though. What are they doing to him?"

"Let's head back to the waiting room. He's probably already in recovery and we don't want to miss the doctors when they come to give us an update," I said.

"Yeah, I don't know if I can go back in there without losing it," Tom said, still clinging to me. "Those parents. Those poor parents. Their kid, they showed me a picture of him. All dressed up like a T-Rex for Halloween. That was only a week-and-a-half ago. The kid probably still has Smarties and Almond Joys hidden away in his room."

I pushed him out of the hug. We were the same height, and when I looked into his eyes, they were bright red from crying.

EVERYTHING HAD HAPPENED SO QUICKLY back at the house. One minute, the cake slicing, and Kento holding the knife up in the air before the big announcement, and the next, Arthur busting through the door, firing off a hunting rifle. Corinda screamed. We all screamed. Kento instinctively slapped a hand over his wounded side as blood oozed out in spurts.

Arthur, drunk and rage-fueled, pulled Corinda up off the sofa by her hair, and dragged her out the door, spitting as he yelled, "You fuckin' Japs, go back where you belong. Don't touch things that you're not entitled to!"

Corinda's yelping echoed against the walls as she struggled to free herself, but in her awkward, pregnant state, she was no match for Arthur's concentrated wrath, and he succeeded in taking her with him.

Tom was already calling 911 when Arthur's truck peeled down the driveway. Tom's voice hysterical, "Ambulance! Gunshot! Come now!"

Minutes later, sirens split the air. Four blood-soaked dishtowels lay in a heap next to my brother, and I'd stripped off my shirt to try and stem the unending red stream. Kento was in shock, his lips blue. He was uttering crazy non-sequiturs.

"Bridge. Mom. Guns." With the tiny bit of strength he had, he pulled me on top of him. "Warm me. So cold," he gasped.

The EMTs set to work saving his life. He passed out, and they were worried about his blood pressure and pulse. The next hour was consumed with assessments, decisions, and emergency treatment. Police reports would have to wait.

A GREEN-SCRUBBED SURGEON was talking with the shaking couple when we returned to the waiting room. We lingered just outside the door, not wanting to breach their privacy, but it was clear the boy had not made it; the postures of the parents, their beseeching expressions, the quiet delivery of the medical grim reaper. I was too familiar with all of it, and I froze. Uninvited memories crashed my brain. A series of images: My mother's emaciated body as she drew her last, rattling breath, my father's ugly, protracted demise, lying in his feces and urine because he wouldn't let anyone near him. The words, "He's gone, I'm so sorry," coming from the state trooper's mouth the day of the accident.

I'd wanted those images out of my head, and the sketches I'd drawn following their passing had offered a place to purge them. To store them outside of me. Make them Kusôzu-worthy. But now, as I awaited the status of the human I was closest to in all the world, I forced a different image into my consciousness, Kento's happy face when the stick line read: pregnant. His utter joy at impending fatherhood.

Right then and there, I swore to myself and the god I did not believe in that if Kento survived, I would make sure his dream of a baby—the little boy growing in Corinda's uterus—would fulfill that dream.

Shortly after the awful exchange between the surgeon and the dead child's parents, Kento's surgeon approached us. Tom's red eyes went big and round. I could almost feel his pulse quicken beside me, but when the doctor smiled, we both collapsed in happy tears.

"High confidence that he will make a full recovery," the surgeon told us, "but we'll keep him in the unit for a few days to monitor, and watch for signs of infection. It's protocol when a person is under for as long as he was. The bullet was deep, but we were able to excise it and repair the immediate damage. His tissue will take a while to heal, and he'll probably have intermittent nerve pain for quite some time, but the bullet missed his lungs, his liver and kidneys, and his main arteries, so, he's a lucky man."

"Thank you, doctor," Tom gushed. "Can I hug you?"

The doctor backed up. "Uh, no."

"Sorry," Tom said. "I'm just so—"

"You can visit him tomorrow," the surgeon said. "Why don't you go home, get some sleep. He's in good hands."

It was three days before they upgraded Kento from critical to good and moved him to the non-dire part of the hospital. Tom and I took turns sitting next to the machines, the beeping, and Kento's battered, but healing, body.

Since he'd been under anesthesia so long, his brain wasn't tracking all that well, and he awoke from his nightmares often, once so out of it with terror, he ripped his bandages off. Tom had been the one to see him through that episode. Later, over a bowl of steaming pho, he let his guard down, hyperventilating as he recounted the horror of watching his husband dissociate. "He had this far away zombie look as he was screaming. Hiding his head with his hands, yelling out, 'Daddy, don't! Don't hit her!' I mean, I know your father was an asshole, but was he really that abusive?"

I knew the episode that had played out in Kento's night terror. Knew exactly. Our father had been demoted from his garbage hauler position, relegated to the cleanup crew at the transfer station—a horrible job that involved wading through discarded plastic bags, and picking them off the blades of the waste separation machinery.

He'd come home stinking like rot, steaming with anger. Our mother asked him to take off his clothes and shower before dinner, and he lost it. Told her it was her fucking turn to bring home the bacon. Kento and I, first-graders, had been coloring our worksheets. Our teacher, Mrs. Graves, was a fan of worksheets, and if we didn't color in the lines, we had to redo it. I'd had no physical problem outlining and coloring in the teacher's prescribed way, but even at age six, I found the method restrictive and depressing, so I added my own sketches to the worksheets. No outlines. No boundaries. I guess you could say I discovered cubism and abstract art at a young age, and got sucked in.

Anyway, as our father's temper tantrum escalated in volume and physicality, Kento abandoned his worksheet and hid under the coffee table. I, on the other hand, doubled down on my task. I hummed to lessen the sounds of my father's rage, and pushed my crayon into the page so hard it snapped in half and tore through the paper.

When the slap sounds began, punctuated by our mother's high-pitched shrieks, Kento emerged from his hiding spot, begging our father to stop as he squiggled his way in between them. He was slammed against a low cabinet for his trouble, our father redirecting his anger, his stinking work boot, still covered in garbagy slime, kicked my brother in the jaw, dislocating it.

Kento's suddenly crooked face, his cries of pain, stopped our father's tirade, and he stormed off, leaving Kento crumpled and broken and our mother frantic. Bruised herself, she bundled Kento up and ran to the neighbor's house. Next thing I knew, the kindly grandma-type lady next door was hugging me, telling me it would all be okay. That my mommy and brother were getting fixed at the emergency room, driven there by a man we called Grandpa Fred.

I clenched the half crayon in my fist until they came home. All three. Mom, Kento, Dad.

It was never spoken of in our house again, and our father stopped drinking for a whole year after that, and was reinstated to his route. A whole year of peace. No apology, but peace nonetheless.

"Yeah, it was a low point in our childhood," I told Tom.

"Wow," Tom said. "He never mentioned it. Even after I shared some of my own shitty childhood memories."

I wasn't sure how to address Tom's feeling of betrayal. Part of me wanted to challenge him to a *whose childhood was shittier* contest. But, in all honesty, I understood. As wonderful as my brother was—generous, loving, creative—he was also closed off emotionally. Secretive. The whole fiasco with hiring Corinda—the ruse he developed, pretending to be her boyfriend, his semi-closeted status, even after marrying Tom—I could see how it would be hard to navigate an honest partnership with someone like Kento.

Our mother, lovely as she was, enabled the ongoing lie. The shame-driven self-loathing she'd inadvertently passed on to her son propelled him into a life of false narrative. Our mother was pathologically protective of the boy named after her own father, beholden to some sort of inter-generational mythos. Whereas I, subjected to a weird quid pro quo that branded me with my paternal great-grandmother's name, was mostly ignored. Until our mother got sick, and my status improved enough to grant me the role of caretaker.

As KENTO HEALED, the reality that he'd narrowly escaped murder slowly dawned on both me and Tom. The felonious aspects, that is. And Corinda, pregnant with Kento's child, had been kidnapped by her—well, her husband. They were still legally married, and in Idaho, that fact made our situation more complicated.

I would need to return to Steeplejack soon. I was being deposed as a witness to the attempted murder, but now it seemed that Arthur, out on bail, had claimed self-defense. Detective and confirmed Luddite, Warren Coulter, had phoned me several times.

"No," he said, "we can't do this over Zoom. You need to get back here and do this in person."

"Are you kidding me?" I said, sipping disgusting Keurig coffee in my brother's and Tom's minimalist kitchen. "Self-defense?"

"He was wielding a large butcher knife," Coulter offered. "Your brother, I mean. And holding Corinda captive against her will."

"Ludicrous," I said, and then hung up and dialed Beacon and Bright. An associate there informed me that if the detective was stupid enough to spill the beans of this bullshit version of events over the phone, we might be looking at an internal investigation. "These small-town cops can really gum up investigations by leapfrogging protocol."

Apparently, I was no longer a pro bono case, and instead of a partner, one of the grunts would be handling the lawsuit in my behalf. The quarter-hour billing meter was ticking away, so I cut to the chase. "What do you suggest I do?"

"First, let me ask you what the status is regarding your brother."

"He should be released tomorrow. He'd on the mend."

"Hmm," the lawyer said.

"Hmm?" I said.

"Sorry. It's just that he'll likely need to return to Idaho for the trial, and if he's fit as a fiddle, to be blunt, that might not work in our favor."

"What are you even talking about? Corinda was kidnapped by that asshole. Surely she can clear up any false accusation."

Silence.

"Hello?"

Sigh.

"What aren't you telling me?"

"You haven't been reading the local news? Checking the socials regarding the case?"

"I've been sitting in a hospital room with my brother. So, no. I haven't."

"I'll have my secretary send you some links. We'll talk after you've, uh, digested the current wacky alternate facts swirling around."

# TEN

THE FIRST LINK BROUGHT UP a headline in the *Silver Valley Times*: "Steeplejack Woman Survives Harrowing Ordeal." Good, I thought, at least someone interviewed her about her recollection of events. But instead of detailing the horrific account of her armed kidnapping by her ex-husband, Corinda is quoted right from the get-go, praising Arthur for rescuing her from the clutches of the degenerate Zapf family.

I had to cover my mouth to quell a shriek as I read further:

> Mrs. Blair, married to long-time Steeplejack resident, Arthur Blair, disappeared from the family home in September, citing marital difficulties. "Something wasn't right about it all," said her husband, accused of shooting Seattle area resident, Kento Zapf Saito. "We got along just fine, and suddenly she up and leaves?"
>
> "I was brainwashed," said Corinda, breaking down in tears. "They convinced me to help them have a baby. Told me they'd pay me. But once I felt this little sweetheart kicking, I knew it was God's will that I keep this baby from being victimized by a depraved lifestyle."

I had to click off the article lest I be moved to put a fist through my brother and Tom's fancily plastered accent wall.

Tom ran into the room, freaked out by my screaming.

"You won't believe—" I started.

"Oh dear. You saw them then?"

"You know about this?" I said, shaking my iPad in trembling hands.

He nodded. "I was hoping to break it to you over lunch. Look, I got some sushi. And then we can discuss how or if we tell Kento."

There was the slightest bit of *I-told-you-so* schadenfreude in his tone.

"I haven't even checked the other links the lawyers sent me," I said. "I can't believe Corinda would throw us all under the bus like this. Jesus. What we've done for that bitch—"

Tom raised a hand. "I know. But listen, they won't get away with it. You have that video, right? The aborted gender reveal?"

Did I? Or did I erase it, now that the whole charade was moot? I couldn't remember, so I grabbed my phone and began to scroll through the pictures and videos. The outtakes were there. The balloons in the background. I'd recorded Corinda's animated fakery, and Kento's reluctant glances. Then there was Kento holding up the knife just as Arthur slammed the door open.

If you didn't have context, Kento's face could be interpreted as menacing, but in reality, his expression telegraphed total surprise at the mad man appearing in front of him with a rifle. After that, the video featured only the ceiling, due to my dropping the phone. The gunshot blast. The screams.

I couldn't listen to it anymore. I clicked the side button, crammed the phone into the pocket of the hoodie I'd worn twelve days straight.

"How could she," I muttered as Tom led me to the kitchen counter where he'd spread out a variety of Japanese finger foods: sashimi, spider rolls, edamame, wasabi crackers.

I could barely bring myself to eat. It'd been nearly two weeks of hell, with my stomach in perpetual upheaval. They say a twin can feel the pain of the other. I never believed that until now. I pinched an edamame pod into my mouth. The salty seed of soy—at one time my favorite food—tasted like tears. Rocky, crunchy sea tears.

Early the following morning, I dropped Tom off at Harborview, and then drove north to Belltown, and installed myself in a coffee shop booth with my iPad until Kento was officially released. I needed space and clarity to figure out my next steps. Was my brother, nearly shot to death, really being accused of kidnapping? Of rape?

It occurred to me that I hadn't asked or known how the pregnancy occurred. It was unlikely they'd gone the costly and time-consuming clinic route with all the protocols and hormone shots. Corinda wouldn't even get a COVID vaccination, siding with the QAnon folk and their suspicions about lasers and government overreach. But I couldn't imagine Tom buying into "the old-fashioned way" of creating a child. Armed with ear buds, a perfectly frothed cortado and a gooey almond croissant, I took a deep breath and entered the nefarious world of search-engines.

It didn't take long to assemble the myriad lies Corinda had been spreading over the past couple of weeks. In addition to *The Silver Valley Times*, her bullshit was splattered all over the internet. She'd even, just yesterday, been featured on *Good Day Idaho*. I had to buy my way through the paywall of the right-wing media tool for access to the video of Corinda sitting primly on a Naugahyde sofa, a gleaming silver cross around her neck, the manicure Kento paid for still fresh.

The host, bearing her own oversized religious pendant, wasted no time. "So you're accusing your former boyfriend of coercing you into having a child that he and his homosexual partner would then raise? Why did you agree?" She then looks directly into the camera, "or did you, in fact, agree?"

Close up on Corinda's crumpled face, tears glistening her eyes: "The radical left has so many tricks. Such a big agenda. To think they used me like that. As a—as a—"

She broke down in tears and, magically, the host produced a Kleenex. "Take your time," said the soothing, off-camera voice. The view was all Corinda and her sobbing. A money shot.

"I'm so sorry. It's just, I trusted him. I really didn't think he'd turned *gay*, you know?" She'd whispered the word gay, as if it were something that might get bleeped out.

My hand was clenched around the croissant, and greasy flakes of pastry peppered my hoodie. How could she? What the hell had happened between the demand for a gender reveal party and this performative nonsense?

"The man you claim held you hostage is recovering from a gunshot wound in Seattle. This is a tough question, but I have to ask it."

"Okay," Corinda whined.

"Your husband, he shot that man, with the intention of killing him, I'm guessing. Was it provoked?"

Oh, my fucking God. They were feeding her talking points.

She tightened her jaw, and nodded her head.

"So the claim is that your husband, Arthur Blair, acted in self-defense? He was trying to rescue you? Do I have that right?"

Breath caught in my chest. My hand poised to shut my device down. But I couldn't look away. I needed to prepare for war.

"He, he, had a knife. A big, fancy heirloom knife."

"Heirloom knife?"

"His Asian mom's knife," Corinda seethed. "Pretty scary weapon, and I was surprised he chose it to cut into our—my—." More sobs.

After blowing into the Kleenex, her hand in the *Hold on, I have more to say* position, she continued. "Somewhere there's video. *She* has it. The video. It'll show how he turned toward me with that weapon, essentially. He could have stabbed me."

"She?" the pious faker asks.

"His sister. His sister, Hazel. She was in on it. She's a real piece of work."

In on it? I slammed the croissant down on the plate as the host introduced the most unflattering photo of me. It was my high school mugshot. The height of my Goth period. Ugh.

"Tragically, she lost her husband, but she got a nice settlement. You should see the house she's building now," Corinda yammered, miraculously tear-free.

The host reached an arm out to Corinda's wrist. A not-so-subtle move to keep her focused on the food for prurient viewers. She said,

BITTERROOT: A NOVEL | 77

"Getting back to the scene at the house that fateful day. Were you afraid for your life?"

Corinda had a momentary look of confusion. Her newly threaded brows veeing downward on her forehead. "I just want to have my baby. Raise my baby. Here in Steeplejack where guys still open doors for ladies. Y'know? That's the thing about Hazel. She's one of them *me-too* people. Wouldn't be surprised if she switches teams herself, if you catch my drift."

She lowered her voice to a whisper, "Rumor has it, her hubby was gonna leave her 'cause she didn't want kids. Can you imagine? I hear he'd turned to a more, um, suitable gal. Someone more God-fearing, you know. But, then, tragically, he perished and she got all the dough."

It was baffling, all this resentment. Had I been blind to it? And Ethan cheating? Planning to leave me? What the hell was she talking about?

"And she's got pictures of dead people everywhere," Corinda continued, her voice now returned to her normal nasal whine.

"Dead people?" said the host, leaning in.

Corinda pointed upward. "Hanging on her walls. Skeletons. Satanic, is what I think. That whole family, you know? They basically chained me to the bed when I had some spotting."

"Chained you?"

"Well, they made me have bedrest. It was that Chinese doctor in town who came up with that. I think she was in on it, too. Why can't we have more American doctors, you know? Just regular American boy doctors."

My mother's words clanged in my head. *Keep that girl away from our Kento. She nothing but trouble.* And then, another memory. That weeping girl at Ethan's repast. Who the fuck was she?

My phone dinged with a **We're ready** text from Tom. I slugged the foamy remains of my cortado, shoved the offending iPad—harbinger of bad news—in my tote, and walked toward the tangled web masquerading as my life.

# ELEVEN

TOM AND I AVOIDED—ACTIVELY AVOIDED—catching Kento up on the hell that was snowballing our way. The attending physician who'd okayed his release had done so with the caution that we minimize exposure to emotional stress while Kento recovered from all the trauma. There were warnings about PTSD, about depression.

"It's not uncommon for patients who've endured protracted anesthesia to lose themselves in funk."

Funk, eh? He'd actually written that on the discharge notes.

Then there was the warning about opioid addiction. A number to call should Kento need more intensive counseling.

Tom had taken a leave of absence, and Kento had had to quit his gigs as an independent contractor for big tech. They were surviving on the money from our parents' house. I added to their nest egg and wrote a sizeable check in prelude to the announcement that I needed to return to Steeplejack and have some face-to-face with the junior attorney who'd been assigned to my case.

Tom and I rehearsed the conversation while Kento dozed in the next room. We had to hint at the fact that there was a whole conspiracy circulating. A civil suit against him that could escalate into criminal charges. A victim-blaming circus that had ramped up while Kento was lying in an ICU bed because he'd been shot by the very fuckwad who was calling him a kidnapper.

We took turns being enraged. Calming the other down as we settled on a step-by-step approach. Kento had already asked about Corinda. The baby. If she'd been liberated from Arthur's clutches. All we said was, as far as we knew, she was safe, and still pregnant.

When he asked why she hadn't contacted him if that were the case, we sidestepped. Told him she'd been working out her own trauma. Somehow, we'd managed to keep him from the news and the pundits and the toxic chatter around Corinda's bullshit.

But there was no putting off my exodus, and after Kento awoke from his oxy stupor, I approached him. "They're calling you a miracle, you know."

His face was so tense. I stroked his cheek, and launched into an *I don't* scenario. "Okay, you have a choice between a hunky actor who will build you the house of your dreams and then dump you, or a balding accountant who shares your taste in pinot and adores you, even when you have garlic farts."

"You're leaving, aren't you?" he said, fluttering those pleading, generously lashed eyes.

"Tom and you need some time together after this. And I need to get back to all sorts of unfinished projects. Work."

He sighed. "Any way you can talk Corinda into coming this way. I mean, we have such better medical care and—"

I pressed a finger to my lips. Our mother would hush us this same way when we went on one our childhood wish campaigns.

"I know, I know. Rest, rest, rest," he said. Another sigh. "Is he in jail yet?"

"We have plenty of time to sort that out once you're stronger."

"That's a *no*, then. God damn it."

"He'll get what's coming to him. I promise you. But for now, I need to go back. I'll call you in a few days. Give you updates. Promise. First things first, okay?"

A third sigh sealed it. There was no way we'd keep him from finding out the truth, and law enforcement or a tabloid would soon approach him. Part of me wanted to stay. To mother both of them—Tom, Kento— they needed support. But I knew I'd reached the end of my *there-there* abilities. I needed space. Also, I had a long drive ahead of me that involved a bitter pit stop at Ethan's parents' in Spokane. They'd sent me an urgent email. Cryptic, but peppered with a smattering of hard-to-ignore exclamation marks.

Since their lives now revolved around Fox News and game shows, I had a hint of what I'd be in for. I kissed my brother on the cheek and set out.

I HAD NEVER CALLED MY IN-LAWS Mom and Dad. And they never suggested it. In fact, they were happy with the honorifics Mr. and Mrs. Mackenzie until our engagement, when Ethan suggested to them that their Steeplejack nicknames, Mac and Skipper, might be a more appropriate way for me to address them.

Old habits die hard, and, for a while, I continued to refer to them as Mr. and Mrs. Mackenzie. It was sometime before Ethan had been dead a year—months fraught with the ugly side of adulting—that I made the decision to level the playing field. Partly it had to do with their badgering about the ring and the funeral they insisted upon. Then there were the other, more nuanced stabs at my character and background. The classist, racist, putting me in my place interactions pushed me toward agency, and it dawned on me, why should I give respect to someone who doesn't respect me?

They recoiled, of course, when I finally unbent the knee, tossing around the *Macs* and the *Skippers* both to their faces via Zoom, and when in conversation with their friends. They never said anything to me, but with their expressions at my unprecedented casualness, the slapped-across-the-face flinching, it was clear they would never think of me as a peer.

As I drove over the Snoqualmie Pass, already glistening with overnight snow, Corinda's claim, *Rumor has it, her hubby was gonna leave her 'cause she didn't want kids*, bounced around in my head. I recalled a holiday trip a couple years earlier. Ethan at the wheel. Me, aching with period cramps. The set up for the worst argument of our marriage. Fight, actually. We'd decided not to give in to the divide-and-conquer holiday visits that our families hinted would make them most comfortable.

Instead, we forged a united front and did a couple of days with Kento and Tom, and were switching to the Mackenzies on Christmas for another few days, before heading back to Steeplejack for New Year's Eve. We'd agreed that, if we were to have children, our relatives would need to get used to the reality of a package deal. We would be a family, whether our family-of-origin liked it or not.

Christmas Eve dinner, we'd driven over to Tom's parents' apartment in Beacon Hill. It was one of those step-down assisted living places where, in return for all your money, they will place you in increasingly heightened care as you devolve into senility and ill health. Ethan called those facilities geriatric warehouses. His fear, I suspected, was that his own parents were slowly traveling down that path.

The trouble began after Ethan, tipsy on multiple helpings of Tom's mother's glögg, regaled us with his latest courtroom prowess. Kento, to his credit, endured the initial anecdote, but when it was followed by more chest-beating tales from litigation, my brother interrupted him with a tasteless lawyer joke.

"You hear about the one involving a corpulent lawyer? He was so fat that, when he died, the undertaker couldn't find a coffin big enough to hold the body. So, the undertaker gave him an enema and buried him in a shoebox."

Tom's Swedish mother, not a small woman herself, put a handkerchief to her chin, dabbing it for stray crumbs. Tom tapped Kento on the shoulder, gave him a subtle head shake. But my drunken husband happily jumped into a spar.

"That's a good one, Kento!" he growled. "Too bad there aren't any gags about country bumpkins in the big city. Oh, wait—I got one. So this dude, we'll call him Jethro. He's the first in a long line of hillbillies and bumpkins to attend schooling beyond the eighth grade. After his first day of high school, the whole family is bursting with pride to see him swaggering up the driveway. His father says, 'Jethro, come tell us about that fancy high school! What'd you learn up there today?' Jethro says, 'Pa, they taught me some al-gee-bra.' His father is dumbstruck. 'What is al-gee-bra, boy?' Jethro says, 'I ain't too sure. I think it's a math language.' His father says, 'Well, speak some of that fancy al-gee-bra for us!' Jethro says, 'Pi R Squared.' Everyone in the family stops smiling. Jethro's father shakes his head. 'No, boy. Pie are round. Cornbread are squared.'"

Ethan slammed his mug of glögg on the table, causing some to slosh out, and fake-chuckled maniacally.

Tom's Japanese father, feeble with Parkinson's, stood up with the help of a cane, and left the table, making his way to the kitchen to fetch something to clean up with. I scooted my own chair back and rushed to the kitchen to help.

"Let me get that, Mr. Saito," I offered, intercepting his slow, amble back to the dining room, sponge in hand.

He pulled his arm away from my grasping paw, and threw me a seething glare. "No respect," he muttered before shuffling back to clean up my husband's mess.

In the car, Ethan couldn't let it go. It wasn't just the lawyer joke, either. I saw shades of his parents in the way he grit his teeth while enumerating the, what he referred to as, slights against his chosen profession. He then started in on Tom's parents, and their "hovering and persnickety passive aggression." The lavish place settings that "smelled of old lady perfume." The cramped apartment stuffed with "tacky tchotchkes."

I asked him to pull off at the summit rest stop. I needed to change my tampon and refill my water bottle so I could swallow some ibuprofen.

As he screeched to a stop in front of the restrooms, he turned his anger on me. "If you'd let me put a baby in you, you wouldn't be bleeding right now."

My hand trembled on the door handle. He'd never yelled at me like that before. He knew my history. He knew my father could turn into a missile of venom at the snap of irritation, and how my brother and I had to walk on eggshells when he was in a mood.

"Well if you gotta go, go," he said, tersely.

In the restroom I took my time. I even thought about calling Kento to pick me up and bring me back to his and Tom's townhouse. Maybe, I thought haltingly, it would be best to reinstate our separate holidays tradition. Placate the in-laws and keep the peace. But, in the end, I decided to buck up and endure. I returned to the car, where Ethan had calmed down, and we drove to Spokane wordlessly, listening to canned Christmas tunes of the American Songbook variety. Nat King Cole's chestnuts. Eartha Kitt and the sultry teasing of her Santa Baby. Balm. By the time we pulled into the driveway of the Mackenzies' picket fence encircled tract home in the quiet, 96 percent white Liberty Lake neighborhood, my husband was whistling.

This time, arriving on my own, I immediately noticed the changes. The once-pristine lawn had browned, an icy crust swathed the tangle of weeds that had replaced grass. The travel trailer they'd purchased to accompany their golden years lay fallow and rusted in the driveway. The slanted light of early December emphasized chipped paint on the front gate, and when I pushed against the latch, the gate pulled away from its hinges, and dragged across the walkway.

Mac greeted me solemnly at the door. Barely met my eyes. From the stoop, I saw a sliver of Skipper, fully reclined in her TV room chair. The house smelled of warm grilled cheese. Mac said, "Wasn't sure you'd come."

I followed him into the room where they likely spent most of their waking hours. The outsized, flat-screen television, the focal point. Neither of them offered me a seat, so I stood there, trying to hide my shock at the degraded condition their lives had taken.

Into the uncomfortable silence I said, "What did you need to see me about?"

Skipper stared into the rancid air. She said, "Sounds like you've made a mess of things. You and that brother of yours."

Fox News was on, but muted. Closed captioning messaging the usual nonsense. I shifted, instinctively impeding Skipper's line of sight. Whatever they wanted to say wouldn't be bolstered by their allegiance to the gods of right-wing media.

I said, "Can you turn that off, please."

Mac grabbed the remote and clicked the off button in an exaggerated gesture.

Skipper pulled the lever on her recliner and sprung herself upright. She had shrunk a bit, and was wearing a stained tracksuit—another step in the spiral of decay.

"You and I both know," I said, "that the self-defense story is bullshit. Arthur Blair shot my brother in a premeditated act of rage."

"Really?" Mac said. "Corinda tells a different story."

"*Story* being the key word," I said.

"You know what? Mr. Mackenzie and I might just call that reporter back. He's dying to know more about your family. Your character," Skipper said, sliding her palms together in a that-takes-care-of-that motion.

"*My* character?" I couldn't stop an ironic chuckle from gurgling out.

Skipper extended an index finger and leaned forward. "Did you ever think maybe *we* should have gotten some of that payout? Living on a fixed income, what with the cost of living going up, up, up every month."

So that was what this was about.

"Last I knew, you guys had made a shit pile of dough on your house in Steeplejack. Sold at the right time, before the housing crash. What happened?"

My former in-laws traded glances.

Mac said, "You made out like a bandit after our son died. He was hardly buried before you started building that disgrace of a house."

I didn't bother correcting them about the buried part.

"He was our only child. He would have provided for us in our old age," Skipper said with a cracking voice.

"So you'd like me to give you money? Hush money? To prevent you from slandering me and my brother? Do I have that right? Sounds like extortion to me," I said.

"Your brother is a degenerate, and you're a—a common golddigger," Skipper growled.

Years of bottled-up resentment roiled in my belly. My chest. I swallowed something sour. Bile. Acid. These people were horrid. Before I could think it through, I pulled a checkbook from my handbag and scribbled a five-figure number on the first available check before releasing it to the cheesy air and pivoting toward the door before it had fully fluttered to the carpet.

# TWELVE

I'D NOT BEEN IN BEACON AND BRIGHT'S office since the settlement concluded, and was shocked to see how much had changed. It was as if they'd hired an Extreme Makeover designer. Where once a client was greeted by a matronly, pearl-wearing receptionist who held court behind a standard horseshoe-shaped desk, now that same client would be met with a coltish supermodel clad in a neon-bright, low-cut jersey. In place of veneered pressboard, the reception desk was composed of granite blocks arranged like a game of Jenga. Behind the greeter (whose name was Francesca, according to the badge on her boob), a built-in terrarium filled with orchids jutted from a plastic, turquoise wall.

"Welcome," said Francesca, extending a manicured hand. "How may I help you?"

"I'm Hazel. Hazel Mackenzie. I have an appointment. With—um—Simon, I think is his name?"

"Of course. Why don't you make yourself comfortable and I'll let him know you're here."

The waiting area furnishings were arranged under a tubular circle of light. After I took a seat in a leather and walnut lounge chair, the irony of this office facelift hit me—how Ethan would have loved coming to work here now. What with the sculptures and museum-quality art studding the interior. Not to mention the overly hot "greeter," who was now sashaying my way, bearing a glass of water with cucumber slices floating in it.

"Mr. Aaronson will see you now," she reported as she handed me the water. "Follow please."

She led me through a hall of panels until we arrived at a glassed-in cube where a man stood, slightly hunched, behind one of those standing desk contraptions. "Mrs. Mackenzie for you," she purred, and then floated away.

Simon Aaronson was a fish out of water in this fancied-up office. His off-the-rack suit didn't fit him all that well. His belly protruded over a cracked, worn belt. He needed a shave and a haircut. But his smile put me at ease. His eyes crinkled up in the corners, and his voice was warm and reassuring when he invited me to sit on yet another expensive lounge chair.

"Are you new here?" I asked right out of the gate. And then, before I could rethink came, "Did you know my husband?"

He cocked his head to the side, like a puppy. I knew this gesture. My training in forensics included musculature traits as they related to personality and psychological profiles. Tension in the jaw, over time, manifests in TMJ and swelling. Pronounced foreheads are often paired with uncorrected nearsightedness. Often, not always. Which makes my work susceptible to generalized assumptions. That said, with a fair amount of certainty, I read Simon's cocking as a stalling device. Clearly, he *had* known Ethan. Just as clearly, he hadn't liked him.

Finally, he said, "His passing, um, sorry for your loss by the way, hit us hard. I had just been relocated from Missoula. After the merger."

"Merger? What merger?"

"Oh. You didn't know?" he pointed outside his thick glass wall to the raised lettering on the panel facing his cube. BB&A it read.

"I didn't notice that in reception. Or on any emails or letterhead. Guess I'm losing my observational powers."

"Quite understandable with all you've been through," he said.

"So, the A stands for?"

His puppy dog demeanor accelerated into mensch-dom.

"Yeah. That would be Aaronson," he said.

I pointed to the letters, then to him. I could feel my face contorting in confusion.

"I get that a lot," he said, pointing to his own round cheeks. "Cursed with the baby face."

It wasn't his lack of cheekbones or wrinkles that were incongruous to his position; it was his posture. His lack of alpha characteristics. The messy suit and cheap belt. No jewelry, no gleaming Rolex. His tie, even. Something you'd find on the sale rack at Macy's. Also, if this man was a name partner, the office upgrade was a conundrum. Brand inconsistency.

I decided to put my confusion aside and get down to it. "Arthur's claim is ludicrous. You do know that, right, Mr. Aaronson?"

"Simon, please," he said. "Yes, I'm well aware. I also believe that his wife, his putative wife, I guess, was likely coerced. It's her testimony that we can pick apart. Full of holes."

Corinda was the least of my worries. She was the definition of an unreliable witness.

"Arthur is a calculating monster," I said. "My brother is still recovering, and the guy who pulled the trigger is not in jail. Why is that?"

"Bail. Friends in court. The hills here are alive with conspiracy spreaders. That's why I'm hopeful that we'll settle before this goes to a jury."

"That whole self-defense crap? He shot Kento with the intent to kill. He dragged Corinda out by her hair. There are several charges against him. Don't you think the evidence supports a guilty verdict? I don't see how a jury could reach any other conclusion. Fuck settling. Sorry. But fuck." I was heating up. Thinking about how my only living relative almost bled out in my living room. A room I had yet to return to thanks in part to the yellow-taped, on-going investigation.

I took a sip of cucumber water. Bitter.

Simon typed into a keyboard, and scanned his monitor. He turned to me. "I'm going to put a couple of associates on this. We need to get ahead of the *frénésie médiatique.*"

"Sounds expensive."

"That's where the civil suit part of this comes in."

I was pretty sure nothing would come of suing Arthur. He didn't have a pot to piss in, and this meeting alone was likely to run me a thousand bucks. I would likely need to give Francesca my plastic before I left today. Then I remembered the conversation with Mac and Skipper. I summarized the extortion attempt, leaving out the projection of Ethan providing for them in their dotage.

"That's interesting," Simon said, cocking his head again. "We'll look into it."

Something about the way he narrowed his eyes. I had to ask. "You didn't like Ethan much, did you?"

He neutralized his expression. "What makes you say that?"

"Call it a professional hunch. I'm trained in corporeal revelations."

"Corporeal revelations. I like that! Ethan. Well. I barely knew him. Seemed like he was pretty ambitious though. Billed a lot. Maybe more than necessary?"

I was stunned to hear that intimation. Ethan had always been scrupulous and painstaking about our own budget. He even had a mason jar into which he'd stuff five dollars every time he popped a can of beer. His "checks balances accountability jar," he called it.

"Do you think your brother will be healed enough to give a depo in the next couple weeks? I mean, we can do a remote one."

"Not according to the local sheriff," I countered.

"Coulter? Don't worry about him. We participate in remote depositions all the time."

"You do remember that it's almost Christmas," I said, reaching for an excuse. I really hoped to keep Kento away from all of this shit until his body and mind were further along in the recovery process.

"Ah. The grand, organized, perennial, commercial, idolatry pageant. Yes. Things are pretty slow in the courts during the holidays. Much like August. But with snow!" he said, raising a finger to his personal circle of tubular lighting.

"Ooh," I said, "don't let the good people of the Panhandle hear that cynicism. They'll run you out of town."

His finger pivoted from the ceiling to me. "Good point." And then to his lips. "Shhh. Mum's the word and all that."

He handed me a sticky note after scribbling on it. "It's my cell. Use it in the event of emergency."

I left the Extreme Makeover offices of BB&A and ventured out into the first flurries of the season. I'd had to temporarily move back into the trailer house, and was not relishing the lack of insulation, and annoyed that I hadn't stopped at Costco when I passed through Spokane. I needed to up my onesies game. It would be a long, long winter. One that required the props of hibernation.

# THIRTEEN

"I HEARD," LEONA SAID when I answered my phone. "The fuckers."

It hadn't been the first time she'd called that day, but I'd slept through the others. I'd taken an Ambien and snoozed like a grizzly in winter. "You heard? Heard what?"

"Did I wake you? Sorry."

"It's been a wild week," I said.

"I'll say. I hope I'm not catching you at a bad time, but my neighbor got some footage on his security camera, and it's something that might interest you."

"Me?" I was still groggy. Ambien fog is the worst.

"Going back to the incident. The hate crime. Well, there might be a connection between that and the situation at your place."

"Situation? You mean the attempted murder?"

"Can we meet?"

A HALF HOUR LATER I'D FOUND A TABLE at Helen Michael's bakeshop. It wasn't the season for her huckleberry pie, I was disappointed to find out, but she made up for it with some mead-soaked gingerbread. I do love me some alcohol-infused baked goods. Leona came bustling in a few minutes later, her nose red from the cold. She ordered tea and chatted Helen up—as one does in this town—before taking a seat across from me.

"How is he, your brother?"

"Recovering. Thanks."

"Those fucking shitheads," she said.

"Want a bite?" I said, sliding my half-eaten treat her way.

She held up a hand. "Gluten intolerant. But thank you."

"So—whatcha got?"

Leona extracted her phone. "I downloaded the footage; it'll take a second."

I took out my notebook as Leona's phone screen went through its download cycle. The Internet coverage wasn't great on this block, and Helen refused to get Wi-Fi. "Then the zoomers will take up my tables all the dang day," is how she phrased her reasoning. I couldn't disagree.

We hovered over Leona's outdated iPhone screen, and I was surprised at the clarity of the footage. Also, the tall, masked man in the torn jacket who was featured placing a plastic bag of shit on Leona's porch, and then leveling a pepper-box revolver at the door before firing it, was very close to her initial description. She paused the video when the guy turned around and yanked his mask down.

"Damn. That's one of the Blair kids, isn't it?" I said.

"Yup. That's Patrick."

"You show this to Coulter yet?"

Leona shook her head. Sipped her tea. "Wanted you to see it first. I don't trust the cops in this town. You heard how dismissive he was."

"I've hired an attorney," I whispered. "Someone new in town. Maybe we can take this to him? At the very least, it'll prove that family has some issues."

"I'll send you the link to the download," she said. "But Hazel? What is the deal with the logo used in the tagging? That's yours, right? Your business?"

"Does the footage show him slashing and tagging?"

"It didn't cover that area, unfortunately. But there's something else."

I waited. Leona pivoted her head, scanning the bakery. She crooked her finger for me to get closer.

"Before she passed away, the former Mrs. Blair, Constance, she was Marcia's patient."

"Her patient? You mean Arthur's wife went to therapy?"

Leona shushed me.

"Sorry."

"Obviously, there's a code of ethics and HIPAA, and all that, but between us, there was a lot of shit going on in the Blair house."

"Do you think Patrick's targeting your house has anything to do—?"

"I guarantee it does," Leona said. "If you recall, his mother's death was anything but clear-cut. They claimed she died in her sleep, but there was no autopsy."

Again, I waited for her to expound. She didn't. But she did say, "With this video, at the very least, they'll bring Patrick in for questioning."

I paused. Why would they use a version of my logo in their tagging? "Do you think they want to frame me?"

She shrugged.

I crammed the last few bites of gingerbread in my mouth. "I have to go," I said. "See if the investigation still has my house behind yellow tape. Thanks for this."

I DIDN'T SAY ANYTHING TO LEONA, but in addition to the dead woman's therapy connection, Patrick interned for Ethan the month before the accident. He seemed like a kid headed in the right direction, despite his fucked-up home life. He'd gotten out of town. Was home on summer break from BYU (the default for the Mormon kids who made it out of Steeplejack). He was studying criminal justice. He'd even come over for dinner one night. Ethan really seemed to like him.

Back on the property, the caution tape was gone. Apparently, I could now return to the big house, but then I'd have to confront the horrific shooting all over again. Not to mention, the mess. I imagined Kento's blood, the cake; everything would still be in disarray. I couldn't face it. Not yet. Instead, I called Kento. I needed to give him the heads-up, but more than that, I wondered if Corinda had tried to contact him.

Tom answered. "He's just getting out of the shower," he said.

"How is his state of mind?"

There was a pause.

"What?"

"He knows."

"Shit."

"I had to check in with my folks. My dad's Parkinson's is getting worse. I was only gone a couple hours, but he went online. Checked his email."

"Fuck."

"It really upset him, Corinda's lie. The whole baby thing. But we're working through it."

I hadn't thought too much about the surrogacy, and how it seemed now that Corinda was backing out of the deal. I was more freaked out about the self-defense bullshit, and I said as much to Tom.

"Do you really think they'll get away with it?" Tom said.

My hands were freezing. The trailer sucked during cold snaps. I put the phone on speaker and jammed my fingers into the fleshy cavern of my armpits. I didn't answer Tom, because, truthfully, I didn't know the answer. Also, I heard my brother in the background asking who was on the phone.

"Hey," Kento said, adding his sad monotone to the conversation.

"Hey yourself. I hear you're well enough to surf the web." I tried to sound light. Hopeful.

"It's a fucking nightmare," he said.

"We'll get through it, bud. And as for Corinda, you know she'll never hurt you. She'll come to her senses, eventually."

"Never hurt me? Do you even hear yourself?"

He was agitated—and who could blame him. I forced balm into my tone. "She hasn't tried to call you or email, has she?"

"As if I'd talk to her after what she's done."

"How well did you know her step kids?" I said.

"Matthew, a little. He was a freshman when we were seniors. Why?"

"What about Patrick?"

"Who?"

"The younger boy. I think he's twenty-one, twenty-two?"

"Vaguely. Why?"

I told him the short version: That he'd been implicated in a hate crime at Leona and Marcia's. That there was video evidence of him shooting up her house with a pepper-box gun.

"Those fuckers love their guns," Kento muttered.

"If she does call you, Kento, do you think you might be able to talk to her? To find out why she's lying?"

"I think she's all turned around," he said. "You know she lives for attention, right?"

I wanted to say, *finally!* complete with I-told-you-so glee. What I did say was, "I'll talk to her. You're still recovering."

We hung up, and I contemplated my options. If I called her, I'd likely get intercepted by her asshole, felonious husband. Then, it occurred to me. There was a magnetized appointment calendar on the fridge in the big house, right next to the Scrabble scores. Her follow-up appointment with her OB-GYN. I thought it was soon, maybe even the next day. I loathed what lay ahead. More drama. Funny how, in a snap, a person's day is ruined. I pulled on my parka and trudged up the hill.

The detectives had left an enormous mess. Clods of boot-dragged mud dotted the new carpet; fingerprinting dusting powder coated the furniture. I'd been warned that several items had been bagged for evidence and whisked away. Oddly, though, they'd missed the Kwaiken knife, which I found underneath the couch. Sloppy detective work, gifting me with the main piece of evidence. I picked it up with a paper towel and carried it to the sink before grabbing more paper towels, a pan of soapy water, and a sponge.

Kento's blood had stained the sofa, and I had to breathe deeply to keep from vomiting. A dozen or more discarded EMT gloves were soaked in blood as well, and scattered about the room. And the cake. The *it's-a-boy* blue interior of it lay in golf ball-sized clumps on the coffee table. The platter it sat on, smashed in the fracas, now shards of confetti-sized pieces sprinkled in a pattern that almost seemed deliberate. The violence of the scene was too much, and I gagged. Dry heaving, I ran to the kitchen sink and retched, but nothing came up.

My chest tightened and I had the odd feeling that my head was filled with cotton. That I was floating above myself, separated from the physical version of me. I hadn't felt this way since Ethan's death. That separation from reality that the grief group called the phantom soul. The horror, the absolute horror of the shooting grabbed me and squeezed me, and I bent over the sink again, this time puking greenish-yellow fluid.

Other than the rich, boozy gingerbread, I hadn't eaten today.

I crumpled to my newly installed slate tile, and lamented that I hadn't chosen a soft vinyl. The cold, rough stone punished me, but in a sense, it helped bring me back into my body, and the heaving ceased.

From the floor, I looked up and scanned the refrigerator, and, sure enough, Corinda's gestation calendar mocked me with its circled dates. A red-inked circle corralled tomorrow's date, and in the square the time: 11 a.m.

Now, I just had to hope that her anti-vax, anti-conventional medicine asshole of a husband would allow it.

# FOURTEEN

I PARKED A FEW BLOCKS FROM the doctor's office, and hid behind a Dumpster like a fucking stalker until Corinda waddled up the walkway. She was alone, which didn't surprise me. She'd likely lied to Arthur about where she was going.

It was a relief that he wasn't with her, but I knew she'd freak out if I approached, so I waited until 11:15 before heading up to the office waiting room. There, the usual array of women sat flipping through dog-eared Hollywood gossip magazines. A few were obviously third trimester, their enormous bellies summiting out winter coats. There was only one man sitting amongst the ladies. His hand resting on the knee of one of the most pregnant of the group.

I was taken by surprise when a heaviness thrumped in my chest as I stared at the two of them, so unaware of the heartache that undoubtedly would one day overwhelm them. I hated feeling that way—anticipating doom. Tragedy. But my life the past five years had been nothing but loss, and it was hard to escape the filter of it. Everything corroded by grief. It'd made me so cynical. Only Kento's joy at becoming a father had given respite. I'd allowed myself a few weeks of optimism, despite my anxiety about Corinda, and now even that had gone to shit.

I settled in the chair nearest the door, and grabbed an *Us* magazine with which to hide my face. A face that had been smeared all over national television and social media as the "sister of the kidnapper" or "victim" depending on the political leanings of the source.

Corinda finally emerged sometime after noon. She looked unfocused. Her hair, uncombed, as if she'd just rolled out of bed for the appointment. I still had the *Us* in front of my face, but peeked around it as she passed through the room and made her way out the door.

I followed her from a half hallway's distance, and closed the gap between us before she reached the outer door to the parking lot. "Corinda!" I said, steeling myself for a dramatic scream for help.

But she surprised me.

"Took you a while," she said.

I reached out to her, and she recoiled.

"Don't think you're going to manipulate me," she said.

"I just want to talk."

"No way I'm giving up my baby to you people. You guys are perverted."

A flash of rage welled up, and I clenched my fists. Fists that longed to smack her. Instead, I forced out the talking points I'd rehearsed all morning. "Is the pregnancy okay? Are you okay? Has Arthur harmed you?"

Her lower lip wobbled, but she recovered. "At least I didn't have some chink doctor giving me shit. I'm off bedrest. My proper American *male* doctor said everything looks okay. Considering."

*Chink?* Jesus. Did she even know who she was talking to? Kento and I called it Asian confusion. We were all *chinks* to racists. Whether our heritage was Japanese, Korean, Thai, Vietnamese, Filipino, Chinese, or a combination. *Chinks.* But I couldn't react. I tried reaching for her arm again, and again, she lurched away.

"You don't have to stay with him, you know," I said in the most soothing tone I could muster. "You left him for good reasons, and now he's gotten you mixed up in a very dangerous situation. The truth will come out, and you don't want to be on the wrong side of it."

"Truth? There's nothing *truth* about you and your brother."

Where had this about-face come from? My balled fists were twitching. "All I'm saying is, Arthur shot Kento. Nearly killed him. And he kidnapped you. Those are the facts."

"Kidnapped? Let's talk about—about coo-*er*-jun. That sicko had me believing he gave two shits about me, when all's he wanted was to rent my ute-truss."

With that, Corinda bashed her palm against the ADA button and the exterior door yawned open.

"You're making a huge mistake," I said as she lumbered into the parking lot, and then out of sight.

IT TOOK ME THE WHOLE DRIVE HOME to realize I had completely missed the opportunity to bring up Patrick and the hate crime. If there was one thing (or five things) Corinda resented, it was Arthur's children, who, as the young stepmom, she'd had little-to-no influence over. She particularly disliked Patrick, who she'd put in the *uppity* category. When on bedrest, she'd regaled me with snooty Patrick stories. How he insisted on a vegan diet. The way he chastised her for wearing leather. Apparently, he was an animal rights advocate. I would think with her mindset she'd be eager to hear that he was implicated in a crime, hate or otherwise.

I had a 2 p.m. appointment at the fancy BB&A office, and I'd hoped to have favorable news to report to Simon. All I had to share was the footage from Leona and Marcia's house, which had little to do with our defense and countersuit against Arthur. Discouraged, I called to cancel. Why get billed for an hour of nothing?

"That's short notice," the secretary said.

"Sorry," I said. But I wasn't.

"Okay, but be aware that if, in the future, you don't give—"

I cut her off. Said, "Twenty-four-hour notice, yada yada. Got it."

I clicked *end call,* and rolled up my sleeves to tackle the detritus left by the crime scene.

A few minutes into my cleanup mission, there was a knock at the door.

"Hazel Mackenzie," said the unknown fellow before handing me notice of a subpoena.

I'd been expecting the deposition, but not so soon. Someone had pulled strings to get this fact-finding exercise on the docket before the holidays. And it wasn't my side that'd wangled it. Arthur's attorneys were from Boise. The same attorneys who'd made headlines by winning a high-profile, anti-affirmative action case at the state university last year. The firm, Hunt & Lawrence, was backed by right-wing corporations. Oil money. Several years ago they'd managed to take a case against the Environmental Protection Agency to the Supreme Court. It had been just after the famous stacking of conservative justices on the high court, and they won their argument, thereby setting precedent for blocking the government's ability to regulate industries and businesses that produce greenhouse gasses.

How Arthur was able to land the firm wasn't a mystery. Corinda's appearances on Idaho's morning show circuit likely piqued their interest. I imagine someone from Hunt & Lawrence approached Arthur, not the other way around. I called BB&A to reschedule.

# FIFTEEN

ON THE DAY OF THE APPOINTMENT, the supermodel greeter was not Francesca. Her replacement was an equally polished transplant from the Bay Area (she'd let me know straight away) and her all-caps nametag read A O I F E. "It's pronounced EEF-uh," she declared, un-prompted. "Irish for radiant."

"I see," I stumbled, deciding whether or not to encourage her obvious compliment fishing. We held eye contact for an awkwardly prolonged interval before she led me down the hall.

Simon was even more unkempt than the last time, but I welcomed his shlumpily tied tie and half-untucked shirt as it mirrored my own disarray.

I was wearing one of my branded hoodies—Bitterroot Renderings with my now-compromised logo silk-screened along the side. I hadn't even consulted a mirror since attending to the cleanup in the big house. Likely, my hair—gathered hastily in a thin, produce rubber band—was frazzled and cowlicked. You'd think the two of us were planning on attending a Panhandle livestock auction rather than consulting on an important—and expensive—legal matter.

Even odder, was the small poodle lounging attentively in a dog bed next to Simon's desk. "She's hypo-allergenic," he said. "In case you're sensitive."

As if confirming her status, the dog yawned and stretched before shifting her eyes to her guardian for acknowledgement.

"Good girl, Greta," he said, and plunged his hand into his pants pocket for a cookie bone.

"Going to get her nails trimmed later today; she's overdue."

"I see," I said, oddly comforted by the care in his voice. I handed him my subpoena. "Thoughts?"

He scanned the document before laying it on his desk. "That's next week. Gosh."

"You saw the letterhead?"

"Oh, don't worry about them," he said. "They're beatable."

His dismissiveness unsettled me. "I haven't confirmed this, but I'm guessing Kento received one too. He's in no condition to drive all this way for what will likely be a stressful meeting."

Simon raised a finger. He seemed addicted to pointing at the swirling tube of light above his desk. "It'll work in our favor, actually. To have him less-than healed. Especially since they want to video tape this."

"Well if they want to tape it, why can't he just stay home and be deposed remotely?"

"I suppose he could, but it's better for our case if he does it in person."

I'd participated in dozens of depositions as a hired illustrator. I understood the strategy. The psychology behind flesh-and-blood and how a jury might read the body language of an innocent person set up for a bogus crime. But, having Arthur, Corinda, and Kento in the same room so soon after the shooting might trigger my brother, and it was hard to know how he'd react. I told Simon as much.

Greta sniffed the air, and let out a piercing squawk.

Simon gave her a stern look and made a lip-sealing gesture.

He turned to me. "Or," he said, "Mrs. Blair might very well be confronted by the error of her ways."

"Doubtful. When I spoke to her today—"

He interrupted me by lurching backwards, eyes bulged, hands in stop sign mode. "When you *spoke* to her? You mean to tell me you made contact?"

"I did."

"Let me make this crystal clear, Hazel. You are not, *not*, to engage with the plaintiffs."

BITTERROOT: A NOVEL | 105

That the Blairs were considered plaintiffs, not defendants, enraged me. Why had their side rushed to depositions, while the criminal case sat in a queue of quicksand? I asked Simon that very question.

"Civil suits involve rewards. Criminal ones only gunk up the system and the prisons," he said, nonchalantly, rubbing thumb to forefinger in a gesture of money-grubbing.

Greta must have agreed, because her tuft of a tail began wagging furiously.

"Then why aren't we counter-suing?"

"In the works," he said. "But let's back up a sec. This exchange with Mrs. Blair, what transpired, exactly?"

"Well, besides her levying a racial slur, she twisted everything. She's radicalized. Or whatever you want to call it. Corinda is an attention-seeking opportunist, and she's getting a lot of positive reinforcement spreading Arthur's lies."

"Where did this conversation happen? Witnesses?"

I shook my head. "Outside the doctor's office."

"You confronted her at a medical facility? After her high-risk pregnancy diagnosis?" Simon's eyes were round, unyielding, accusatory.

"Whose side are you on?"

"You know this is going to come up in the depo, right?"

"It's not like I shoved her down a staircase," I said. Then, quietly, "even if I wanted to."

Simon's gaze became unfocused. He had that staring into nothing look that folks get when they're spinning their wheels. The silence stretched. I waited it out, but my mind ticked off the minutes. His pondering was racking up fees. I cleared my throat.

Finally, into the tense air between us, he said, "I need to see the contract between your brother and Mrs. Blair."

"Stop calling her *Mrs*. Blair. She doesn't deserve an honorific. Call her Corinda the Cunt. Okay, sorry. Didn't mean that."

"Have your brother email the contract to me, can you do that?" His voice took on the quality of a closing remark. He turned to grab a sparkly leash from his desk and Greta sprang from her bed. His tone changed as he directed his next comment at the poodle. "Let's go get that mani-pedi."

I felt the heaviness of my footsteps as I left the granite Jenga reception desk and pouty Aoife behind, my fury now replaced with defeatism, given that we'd just squeezed past the solstice, and it was already dark. As I drove home though Steeplejack's quaint neighborhoods, the sagging Christmas lights meant to resemble icicles mocked me with their hellish blue illumination. Blow-up lawn Santas and neon crèches struck me as absurd. The streets had iced, and wending my way around the clot of Amazon delivery trucks was a treacherous feat akin to a life-sized game of Pachinko.

*If-onlys* battered me with regret. Why had I returned to Steeplejack? I'd had a boyfriend at Bard. A job offer in Poughkeepsie. And yet, I'd returned to my hometown to help my mother die and re-embrace an area where I'd always be an outsider, even though I was born here.

Kento had fled, and stayed fled. But the pull of this place sucked even him back, eventually. Gotten him tangled up with a woman who'd born out our mother's warning.

In Seattle, while Tom and I waited out the week from hell, unsure if or how Kento would recover, he'd shared, maybe overshared, the specifics of Corinda's impregnation.

"She obviously didn't want me involved," Tom had said. "But the contract was very specific, and she needed the money to escape her marriage."

"Specific?" I said, wincing.

The details unfolded.

"We treated her to a week at the Four Seasons, commensurate with her cycle. A luxury suite, room service, massage, the whole bit," he said.

I pictured Corinda donning one of those fancy Four Seasons bathrobes, drawing herself a bubble bath—probably replete with candles like in a romantic comedy, her ovulation predictor sticks lined up, bearing darker and darker double lines.

"Of course, as partners, we wanted to experience something akin to bonding," Tom said.

"The getting of the goods?" I said.

He nodded.

"So, the deposit?" I said, tentatively, "Was it a combo?"

Tom gave me an if-I-tell-you-I'd-have-to-kill-you look.

"Oh boy," I managed, guessing that Corinda had no idea that she'd shot herself full of double-magna cum laude.

"Anyway, we'd asked Corinda to go take a walk in the gift shop. We gave her a credit card. And then we, uh, got busy."

"Was there really a turkey baster involved?"

"Williams Sonoma," he said. "Top of the line."

"I'm guessing she wanted Kento to do the deed?"

Tom pointed to his nose, then me.

"So, what did she buy at the gift shop?" I asked.

"A ring, of course. An opal. And a pair of garish stud earrings that promised to bolster fertility. Elaborate ears of corn that hung down past her earlobes."

I'd seen her wearing them. Turquoise and silver shaped like daggers. They looked more like vampire fangs than corn.

As I rumbled up the driveway to the big house, my back-end fishtailing on an icy crust, I remembered that Corinda's crap was still in my bedroom. Despite my overwhelming desire to toss it out the upstairs window, it occurred to me it would help my case if I photographed evidence of my displacement. I'd given up my room, my bed, my dresser—all so she could play queen during her bedrest mandate.

But I kept hearing the scolding voice of Simon in my head. I decided to call for permission first. Resentfully, but with as much spare dignity as I could muster, I rang him on his cell.

Before it even rang, his voice picked up. "You've reached Simon Aaronson's mobile message box. Leave a brief message and have a lovely day."

"Who says 'message box,'" I said, after the beep. Then, "I just wanted to clear something with you before doing it. Trying to be a good client after all."

I dialed up the heat on my fancy Nest thermostat app, then stomped up the stairs and tossed the phone on my rumpled bed. The room still smelled of Corinda's lotions and potions, and I felt a gag erupt.

What did Kento see in her, anyway? Why did he think she was mentally stable enough to be his surrogate? Years ago, when he told her he was gay, she'd threatened to kill herself. She cast about for someone to blame, and landed on me—an easy target.

"You went to one of them fancy New York schools where they encourage all sorts of unnatural behaviors, and you put the idea in his head," she accused.

I'd laughed in her face, thinking, surely she must be joking. First of all, Kento went to school in Seattle. Even though his university, Seattle Pacific, had quote-unquote Christian affiliation, you couldn't get much more liberal than the Emerald City.

Secondly, I was a dyed-in-the-wool heterosexual. Cis-gendered, the whole deal. My tattoos and fondness for flannel often gave folks the wrong idea, but during my four years at Bard, including my semester abroad, I'd had a series of boyfriends. Senior year I'd almost said yes to moving in with one of them. Tony was a physics major, super nerdy. Came from a tight-knit Italian family whose generosity and heart you could sense the moment you walked in their humble New Jersey row house. Their radical acceptance, their warmth, the way they welcomed me with a plate of macaroni (never call noodles pasta or anything other than macaroni in an Italian-American kitchen), seduced me—even though I felt shame for not being more attracted to Tony himself.

It was Ethan I wanted. Ethan, and the way my chin tucked so easily into his clavicle. Ethan's deep voice, the way he raised that very chin to get the full-on view of my overbite, kissing all around my lips, the tip of my nose. Senior year of college, I had a choice to make. Tony had been accepted to Rutgers to pursue a master's in computer science and wanted me to follow him to the cement confinement of a tiny one-bedroom apartment in New Brunswick. Poor, nerdy Tony, his hands shoved in his pockets deep, when I didn't say yes immediately. "Can I have until the end of the week to decide?" I said.

"What's to decide?" he said, his forehead wrinkled, his glasses halfway down the bridge of his nose.

I called Ethan, who had just received favorable LSAT scores and was out partying with his frat brothers.

"What do you want me to tell you?" he slurred with the background beat of rap punctuating his words.

"I just—do you think there's any chance—"

"Hold on," he said before the ambient noise turned to muffled chaos. I thought about how Tony didn't celebrate when he got the nod from Rutgers. Instead, he went to church.

Ethan resumed our conversation without the background ruckus. "What were you saying, Haze?"

"Never mind," I said. "I think I got my answer."

I was all set to alter my life's path. Instead of returning to Steeplejack and hammering out a living as a silk-screener or working in one of Coeur d'Alene's notorious tourist traps during the season, I would find work as a junior graphic artist in one of the close-but-not-in the city agencies and spend weekends in Elmwood Park learning how to stuff cannoli and press dough into perfect pizzelle snowflakes at Tony's Ma's.

I arranged to meet my boyfriend for dinner at an Indian place. Over dal and naan, I planned on making his day.

But then Ethan phoned me back.

# SIXTEEN

WHILE I WAITED FOR FURTHER GUIDANCE from Simon, I scrolled my phone. I was still on the email list for Grief Group. An all-caps subject line announced that, given the holidays and its relationship to suicide, there was an extra meeting tonight. I hadn't been in six months. In fact, I'd only been once since Ethan's accident. And that was to a potluck in the park. It was time. More than time.

Outside, icy rain spat at me. I'd yet to swap my regular tires for snows, but Grief Group was only a couple miles away, in the basement of one of the more liberal churches. One where the priest was a woman who moonlit as an herbalist. I slalomed down the drive and down the narrow streets to town, avoiding blown-over trash bins and tree limbs. The winds were picking up.

Grief Group had been my mainstay after my mother's death. A revolving door of the recently bereaved shuttled in and out, but there were lifers, as well. Amy Miller, for instance, who had been widowed a decade earlier. And the Mortons who'd lost their only child to an aggressive cancer. A handful of folks who'd lost siblings, parents, best friends. We liked to think we were the anchors of Grief Group—we'd even formed a team in Coeur d'Alene's bowling league, the team name, RIP, embroidered on our shirts thanks to Amy.

After my father died, my attendance became spotty. I had a wedding to plan, a house I was supposed to clean out. Betsy Jones, the pesky realtor, teamed up with Ethan, the two of them badgering me about putting the house on the market. I quit the bowling. Backed off the weekly meetings.

As I inched my way toward tonight's meeting, it dawned on me that one reason I'd avoided the group after Ethan's death was shame. A memory of a conversation with my husband a week before he died, swooped in. It was this conversation that led me to ordering the Dumpster and signing a contract with Betsy to sell my parents' house. It was, ironically, a tipped domino that resulted in Ethan being at the wrong place at the wrong time.

"You're stuck in the past," Ethan had said. "At some point, you have to live for the future. If we ever want to have children, ridding yourself of your childhood home, at long last, is a necessary first step."

That our parents' house legally belonged to Kento further enraged my husband, who'd drafted an agreement that mandated a 50/50 split and forced my brother to sign it. Which he did, happily, but Ethan's distrust and legal maneuvering had further soured the in-law relationship between the two most important men in my life.

Ethan had never come right out and scolded me for my protracted grieving, but his dismissive attitude toward the self-help world, the support group world, was obvious. He believed in self-reliance. In action. Instead of launching his opprobrium at me, he focused on Kento as proxy.

"His sentimentality is getting in the way of our lives," Ethan had said when Kento showed hesitation about selling the house.

"Can we just wait another year?" I'd argued. "He's not ready."

It was the one time Ethan stormed off during an argument. His clear-headed, pragmatist façade trampled by a show of frustration. When he returned home, hours later, he apologized. But it was a half-hearted apology, negated by the excuse that he only wanted our lives to blossom. That it was time for me to discontinue birth control, sell my parents' house, and put energy into building our dream home and getting pregnant.

I felt ashamed, but I didn't realize that my avoidance of Grief Group was connected to that shame, and to Ethan's frustration, until I pulled into the parking lot of the church.

I was late, and the group had already done their intros. The place was packed, which shouldn't have surprised me. Grief multiplied as soon as Christmas lights emerged. I took a seat at the rear, surveying the hunched and be-jacketed backs in front of me for familiar postures. A small space heater was the only source of heat, and it was placed near the front of the room, so I was the only person in the back row.

The leader was someone I didn't recognize. An older, frail-looking woman with straw-like gray hair that jutted out a ball cap. She addressed the room. "Would anyone like to share how their week went? How it's going?"

There was the usual hesitation. Nobody relished kicking off the sharing part of group. The leader scanned the room, and finally, a hand shot up, near the space heater. It was one of the old timers. Someone on the RIP team—a balding man. Bent over. I'd forgotten his name, but as soon as he stood, I remembered.

"Hello, my name is Ned," he began.

The group chorused, "Hi, Ned."

"As some of you know," he said, "I lost the love of my life, Ingrid, a few years ago. Alzheimer's."

As Ned trotted through the backstory, I had to admit, I felt Ethan's cynicism kicking in. As I recalled, Ned prefaced his sharing this way every week. His wife had passed six years ago, and at every meeting, he related her slow, horrific demise. The insidious plaques, and how they took over her brain month by month. I found myself checking my phone for the time as he rattled on.

The straw-haired woman at the front of the room had evidently heard his diatribe a few times herself, and I marveled at how compassionately she moved him along. She wandered over to him, placed a hand on his shoulder, brought him in for a side hug, unsuccessfully quelling the "last stages" part of his spiel. The end-of-life care he gave her. During his well-rehearsed litany, he rattled off the laborious tasks: changing her diapers, administering rash cream, and when he reached the summit of his martyrdom: feeding her pureed bananas, straw-hair interjected, "Thank you, and bless you. Who's next?"

A be-shawled woman stood up. A newbie, I guessed, claiming to have driven all the way from Sandpoint. She was here after losing a beloved pet. It became clear that she'd been kicked out of her local group because, "Can you believe it? They said the loss of a cat isn't worthy of community support."

Again, I consulted my phone. Maybe it had been a mistake, coming here tonight. What did I have in common with a crazy cat lady, anyhow?

She sat down amid murmurs and *there-theres*, and then the next jacket stood up. A jacket I'd just seen in a video: too small, ripped in the back.

"My name is Patrick."

"Hi, Patrick."

"I haven't been here in a bit. As some of you know, I lost my mother several years back. There've been some recent developments in my life. In my family's life, that've pointed to some unfinished business. Call it grief, call it anger—that's a stage of grief, correct? Well, I'm past the run-of-the-mill anger, and I can't get to acceptance until justice has been served."

Patrick's voice was punctuated with sniffs. Cocaine, I wondered?

He went on with his cryptic story, his voice escalating at times as he turned around to engage the entire room during his lament, his face turning redder and redder, and when he sat down, the room sighed collectively the way you'd expect if a shooter had barged in and leveled a gun at the crowd, but then revealed they were only holding a water pistol.

My gaze followed Patrick as he lowered himself back to his chair. His arm flung over the shoulders of the skinny woman next to him. She turned her head toward him, pecked him on the cheek. I caught a glimpse of her profile. The same profile I'd seen in that post-funeral kitchen, only then it'd been bowed in sobs.

I had to decide whether to bolt, or to hang out until the end and then confront him. And her. As the minutes ticked away, it seemed I was staying put.

The leader closed down sharing time with a passage from a new book called *The Joy of Grieving,* which was oddly calming, and stepped hard on the whole mindfulness component. My heart thudded speed-ily. The muscles in my legs spasmed—I had been tensing them for a sudden escape.

I planned my strategy in the closing minutes, and snuck off to the parking lot before the grand exodus. Whatever I was going to say—however I planned to confront Patrick and that hussy—it had to be done with people around. Witnesses. As clots of grievers disgorged from the basement door of the church, I stood near the top of the steps. Patrick was one of the last to emerge, and he was flanked by two women, the straw-haired leader and the woman who'd been fucking my husband.

They were engaged in conversation, and it seemed somewhat tense, so I backed off, and followed them at a distance. I caught stray words: temper, community, aggressive. Apparently, Patrick had crossed a line. His posture was subdued. He walked haltingly, as he had in the video. His spidery legs, out of proportion with his wide shoulders, gave him a martini glass appearance.

The leader parted ways, and the homewrecker on Patrick's other side crooked an arm around his. She was bundled in a fashion-forward puffy coat. I hustled, and caught up with them just as they reached their car.

Smoke billowed out my mouth and into the frozen air as I called out his name.

He turned sharply, and the thieving whore was briefly caught off balance, slipping on an icy puddle. "God damn it!" she cursed as she righted herself.

"Can I have a word?" I said.

Patrick blinked a few times, as his brain registered who I was. Then, "What the fuck are you doing here?"

I planted my feet wide, met his eyes. "I'm a widow, remember?"

His arm candy was still brushing slush off her expensive coat, but at the sound of my voice, her head shot up.

"I heard you've been stalking Corinda," Patrick said. "And now you're here. You got a problem with our family?"

This didn't seem at all like the man who'd interned for Ethan two summers ago. I'd only spoken with him a couple of times, at company functions. A picnic by the lake.

"You have a lot of nerve showing up here," the bitch said.

"Where do you get off accusing anyone of kidnapping," I said, trying to ignore the smart-ass comment from a woman who was the very definition of nerve. "Your father shot my brother for no reason, and now you're all twisting this to feed your lie? What the hell?"

"Lie?" he said. "Funny word coming out of your mouth. You and your brother, both."

Before I could stop myself, I shot out, "We have proof that you committed a hate crime by the way, so get ready. The law is coming for you. I can't believe Ethan put his neck out for you."

"Get in the car," he ordered, addressing his companion, who was still brushing the last of the muddy ice from her ass. "And you," he said, launching an index finger toward my chest, "stay away from my family."

His words hung in the frozen air between us. Sharp. Combative. The few remaining stragglers from Grief Group had turned our way. We'd created a scene. Patrick wrenched open his truck door and leapt inside, slamming it shut. The engine roared to life, and I stepped back, just out of range of the spray of gravel that spurted from his tires as he sped out the lot.

I shuffled to my own car on the far end of the lot, where I'd unfortunately parked next to the crazy cat lady. She was sitting behind the wheel of her Lincoln, weeping. I paused before clicking my fob. All I wanted to do was get in my car, blast the heat, turn on some mind-numbing tunes, and head home. Instead, I knocked on her window, and she lowered it.

"You okay?"

She nodded, then shook her head, then sobbed, gulping.

Fuck.

"You shouldn't drive all the way to Sandpoint in your condition," I said, reluctantly.

"Got nowhere else," she said. "Where's a woman to go in this icy town?"

# SEVENTEEN

"I WISH I COULD OFFER YOU SOMETHING to eat, or some tea," I said as I helped Inge—aka Crazy Cat Lady—haul her overly large "emergency kit" into the big house. "I'm recently returned from out of town, and haven't managed to shop."

Inge, puffy-faced from crying, but now smiling broadly, said, "Not to worry, I always travel with provisions. Would you like a glass of Maker's Mark?"

I pulled a couple jelly jars from the cupboard. They were the only glasses I'd unpacked, and a wave of embarrassment bowled through me. I shrugged it off.

Inge yanked open my freezer and pulled out the ice bin. She pointed to Corinda's gestation calendar. "Uh-oh, you're not pregs, are you?"

"That's not mine," I said.

"'Cuz, drinking while pregnant, well, I've seen the results in the NICU."

"Seriously, I'm not having a baby. I'll take a double of that bourbon if you don't mind."

Inge filled the jars with ice and poured the liquor. "Thirty years I worked with preemies. Fetal alcohol syndrome ain't a walk in the park. I have rice crackers if you want," she said. "Got Celiac. Wheat's the devil."

Over the last few days I'd barely eaten anything, and just a whiff of the bourbon would be enough to make me light-headed. "I do have peanut butter," I said. "Rice cakes and peanut butter sounds like a good dinner."

"Horrid," Inge said as she handed me a jar of booze. "I have some salami. And olives."

Inge was a round woman with a large bosom, dressed like a childhood favorite character of mine, Pippi Longstocking—her graying red hair fumbled into wiry braids, her calves encased in colorful knit leggings. She rummaged through her bright orange backpack and held up a penis-shaped sausage with triumphant glee. A gust of wind knocked against the window over the counter, accompanied by the shrill clickety-click of ice pellets. I flinched. First winter storms of the year always caught me by surprise. After thirty winters, you'd think I would be desensitized.

Inge smiled, "Take a nice, big sip there, Mavis, calms the nerves."

"Hazel," I said. "Good thing you didn't start that drive north."

"Good thing," she chimed. "And I'm so grateful to be here in this beautiful home." She turned on her boot heel, surveying the half-assed cleanup job around the sofa. "You have a party recently?"

"So, you don't watch the news?" I mumbled after taking a swig. "I'm infamous, apparently. Flavor of the frickin' month."

Inge was now opening drawers. "You have a knife? For the wurst?"

Unpacked boxes were stacked on the periphery. I had cutlery in one of them. Inge spied the Kwaiken in the sink. "Ah! This'll do."

"No!" I screamed. "Put that down right now!"

Inge dropped the knife, and it clattered as it fell to the enamel basin.

"Sorry," I said. "It's just, there was a situation here recently. I can find something to cut that salami up, just give me a sec."

"Whoa, girl. Are you okay?"

I hadn't realized how hungry I was until I started stuffing my face with Inge's emergency foods. I was on my third refill of Maker's Mark before I began divulging my hellish situation. The deaths, the shooting, Corinda—it all spewed out as I sipped myself into a sloppy state of drunk.

Inge sat straight-faced, leaning in toward me, rubbing my upper arm as I described the last couple of weeks: My worry for Kento. My anger at the Blairs. The polarized politics in Steeplejack, and how much worse it had become in recent years.

I had no idea where Inge lived, politically. Sandpoint, like anywhere else in the Panhandle, appealed to extremists on both the left and the right. But mostly, the right.

Finally, once I took a breath, she said, "And people wonder why I prefer cats."

Cats. Right. I'd nearly forgotten.

"Sorry for your loss," I said. "So, do you have family?"

Inge whipped out a phone from her calico pinafore. "Not anymore. Well, Bella, my Abyssinian, she was my family." She pushed her phone across the table to show me a photo of a strikingly beautiful cat, sitting regally on a swath of black velvet.

"Bella was eighteen. An exceptional mouser."

She'd hardly gotten the words out before another round of sobbing.

I'd never had a pet. My mother had been allergic to dander. Like many folks during the pandemic, Ethan and I had gone through shelter photos with porn-level addiction for a bit, but after losing out on several lotteries during the height of the pet adoption craze, we lost interest, and poured our porn time into interior decorating sites, following designers on Insta, clicking videos of farmhouse kitsch, which we ultimately decided didn't appeal to us.

"Maybe I should get a cat," I said, mindlessly.

Inge's forehead wrinkled. "If you do, do not declaw, and do not let it go outside in this predatory environment. In fact, I can introduce you to an excellent builder of catios. You seem to have room here."

"What's a—never mind. Let me show you to the guest quarters."

The guestroom was actually the last room I slept in in the big house, so I slapped on some fresh sheets, and rustled up a towel. Inge, meanwhile, took over my kitchen, and soon the smell of something baking—something applely-and-cinnamony—wafted up the stairs.

I was hospital-cornering the guest bed when Simon phoned.

"Did you stalk another plaintiff?" he asked while I was saying *Hello*.

"If you're talking about my conversation with Patrick, he's not a plaintiff. He's a suspect. In another case altogether."

"Did I not make myself clear about the Blair family?"

"It was incidental," I argued. "I had no idea he'd be at Grief—"

"And yet you approached him after the meeting?"

I felt a bolt of anger slice through me, gut to chest. "Hey, Missoula guy, this is a small fucking town, and you can't spit without hitting someone you know."

Silence.

Then, "Fair. Okay. Here's what we need to do. If you haven't touched anything in that room you want to photograph, don't. I'll come over there tomorrow and take a look. See what's what. It's important to establish Corinda's intention, and I'd be interested to see what personal items she brought to your house."

"Great. I was planning on sleeping in there tonight."

"Don't you have a guest room?"

"Yes, I do. And it will be occupied tonight by an actual guest."

"You have company?"

"Is that also not allowed? How about you send me a user guide for clients caught up in bullshit legal trouble? The dos and don'ts"

"Okay, why don't I stop by right now. I'll take the photos I need for the case, and then you can enjoy your evening. Sound okay?"

"I guess," I said, half-heartedly. "Hope you have all-wheel, or studded tires. My driveway's iced over."

"Mind if I bring Greta?"

"Fine. Bring your poodle, your camera, whatever. Let's just get this done so I can reclaim my bedroom."

The telltale spinning of tires up my driveway announced Simon's visit just as Inge was taking the gluten-free apple crisp out of the oven. I'd given her a five-cent summary of the upcoming visitation, and it'd been met with raised eyebrows. She was happy that a pet was part of the entourage, however.

"Will your guest join us for dessert?" she asked.

"He's not a guest, and no," I said. "He's probably charging for this house call, and I'll be damned if I'm going to shell out more *dinero* while he's stuffing his face."

The spinning tire sound grew louder and more deliberate. Then, a thunk. A big thunk.

I peered out the front window, into the dark, swirling storm. Two figures emerged from the black as though escaping an ominous thundercloud. A man. A dog. Both bent forward against the wind.

I opened the door, just to have a gust force it closed again. I leaned hard into the solid oak of it, forcing it wide as Simon and Greta came through.

Simon was covered in sleet. Greta shook ice chunks off her fur. "Greetings," he said, sheepishly.

"Rough out there. You get stuck?"

His eyes met mine. "I may have skidded into that big car halfway up the drive."

"That would be Inge's Lincoln," I said. "Oops."

"I'm fully insured. Not to worry."

"Skidded? Into my car?" came a high-pitched voice from the kitchen.

Simon waved the open-close fingered salute of a child. This so-called lawyer was one quirky fellow. "I'm so sorry. Guess I should have put my snows on last week. This storm wasn't really in the forecast."

The tiniest bolt of schadenfreude speared me, serving up a modicum of glee—like when an authority figure farts while chewing you out. Inge rushed in, alarm on her face, but as soon as she caught sight of the dog, it melted away, replaced with a child's wonder.

"Who is this sweet thing?" she said.

It was love at first sight between the crazy cat lady and the poodle. As though they'd been long lost pals, reunited at last.

"Wow," said Simon. "Never seen her warm up to a stranger like that before."

Simon was dripping on my newly finished hardwood. "Can I take your coat?" I said, though the rod in the entry closet had yet to be installed.

He fumbled free of his outerwear revealing an ugly Christmas sweater. I didn't know him enough to assess the degree of irony, so I asked, "You come from a party?"

"Ho, ho, ho," he said. "Children's Hospital in Spokane. A little holiday party. I dressed as an elf. Left my hat in the car."

"Oh, Eastern Washington Children's Hospital? I worked there once upon a time," said my unexpected guest to the other unexpected guest. Her hand jutted from her own knitted atrocity. "I'm Inge."

"Simon."

They shook like colleagues, the car mishap evidently faded to the land of no-big-deal. Third wheel that I'd suddenly become, I retreated to the kitchen and refilled my jelly jar with Inge's bourbon.

I led Simon through the mess, beginning with the bloodstained sofa, followed by the crumbs I still hadn't vacuumed up, and then we went upstairs. Inge and Greta were rolling around on the living room carpet, and she'd already invited Simon to sample her apple whateverthefuck, but the meter, I decided, was off, given that my lawyer's car was stuck in a ditch, having locked bumpers with Inge's Lincoln.

Simon extracted a phone from his pocket. "So you haven't moved anything in the bedroom, correct?"

"Not since Corinda was hauled off to her cult," I said.

We surveyed the unmade bed, the pile of her clothing on the floor. On the new West Elm nightstand, now ringed with water stains, sat a stack of gossip magazines, and a dog-eared copy of *What To Expect When You're Expecting*. On the dresser, atop a tsunami of cosmetics, lay a receipt from the manicure place—though Kento had actually been the one to foot the bill.

Simon clicked away.

"I like portrait mode for clarity," he said. "Will be good to have hi-res slides of this stuff for the depo."

"I could have done this myself, you know," I said.

"True," he said. "But I'll be the one arguing on your behalf, and I find it easier to construct an oratory after experiencing evidence firsthand."

"Oratory? Aren't we fancy."

He stuck his tongue out at me. His ugly holiday sweater included a three-dimensional reindeer nose smack in the middle of his torso.

Nubby antlers flapped in the vicinity of his nipples. It was hard to unsee. It occurred to me, briefly, that Simon and Inge would make an interesting couple, though she had twenty or so years on him.

"Sure looks like she made herself at home here," he said.

"Inge?"

"Huh?"

"Sorry," I said, still mesmerized by the spectacle of Crazy Cat Lady and Simon as a couple. "Not only did she take over my life for more than a month before nearly getting my brother killed, but now she's planning on reneging on the surrogate situation."

Simon slipped his phone back into his pocket. Downstairs, the poodle and Inge were play-growling at each other.

"Greta really likes that woman," he said. He stepped closer to me, staring me down in an almost parental manner. He said, "I looked over their contract. It has standard surrogacy language, which is legal in Washington State. Idaho though? Different laws. Also, the public ruse your brother schemed up as a workaround? It's gonna bite him in the ass. An affair gone wrong, or gestational hijacking, take your pick. Either way, precedent favors Corinda."

"Gestational hijacking? That's a thing?"

"We live in interesting times," he said.

I wanted to point out that the consummation—if you could call it that—took place in Seattle, as did the signing of the contract. Corinda even agreed to pretend that she and Kento lived together in Kento's Lake Union townhouse. But I realized that Corinda would just dig in deeper with the lie that Kento manipulated her.

I had a thought. "What about following the money? Corinda was paid plenty for her surrogacy."

"Yup, that's where we're headed with this. Character arguments." He tapped his pocket. "The images here will paint the story of an extortionist. Someone who changes her story to suit her self-interest. Didn't you say you were involved in her medical emergency not long ago? Taking her to the hospital, I mean. Maybe we can subpoena the doctor for her impressions of Corinda's mental state."

I remembered the *chink* comment. Dr. Yun, if she lived in the area, she'd probably dealt with her share of racist White Nationalist patients. "My hunch is, she'd cooperate," I said.

He continued to stare me down.

"What?"

"Please, please, avoid interaction with anyone involved. Let justice do its job."

I raised my palms in surrender. "Fine," I said, and then, because it was hard to resist, I tugged the Rudolf nose on his sweater. "Just, please don't wear this in my presence again."

# EIGHTEEN

INGE'S GLUTEN-FREE APPLE COBBLER was surprisingly delicious. We were on our second helpings when a huge popping sound intruded, and the lights went out.

"Branch must have fallen on a wire, or someone smacked into the transformer down the road. It was bound to happen," I said. "I have candles. Somewhere."

Inge, who was not done sharing her scout-like acumen for being prepared, produced a head lamp seconds later. "Maybe this will help you locate them?"

I crammed the light onto my head and began rummaging through boxes.

Simon had been on hold with Triple A, and now his phone was in the red zone. Holiday hold music whined out his speaker.

I found some tapers and a striker in the third box, but no candle-holders. Once again Inge flung herself into the task, recruiting the jelly jars we'd drained of bourbon, with help from the foil with which she'd lined the baking tray. Soon the kitchen and dining room were glowing.

"No fireplace in this joint, eh?" said Inge.

"Part of my carbon footprint reduction agenda," I said, lamenting the holdup on the solar battery system I'd orchestrated by refusing the substitute panels the solar company suggested since the ones I wanted were backordered.

A crackly voice cut through Frosty the Snowman. Simon lurched toward his speaker. "Hello, hello?"

"Can I have your member numb—"

Simon's phone cut off. He gripped his skull. "Fuck!"

Greta yelped.

"Looks like I'm an inadvertent Airbnb," I said.

"I can call an Uber," Simon offered.

I pointed to his impotent device. "Not on that you can't. Besides, the roads are treacherous."

I pressed my forehead against the windowpane. The storm had not let up—in fact, it had grown. Sleet whirled, every gust sweeping frozen rain into nature-choreographed dances. I turned around. "I have blankets. A couch. Also, there's my humble trailer at the bottom of the driveway, although, I don't recommend schlepping down that grade with all this ice."

Nobody wanted to address the elephant in the room—the blood-stained couch I was suggesting Simon use as a bed. Simon offered a resigned sigh. Him and his goofy sweater. A lawyer version of Mr. Rogers. But unlike Simon, I was happy for this accidental slumber party. Bodies. That's what I needed. The comfort of bodies around me.

"I found a deck of cards," I said with the forced cheerfulness of a talk show host. "We could gather around a candle and play some poker? Gin? Old Maid?"

"I know a card game called Poo-Poo Head," Inge piped up. "It's easy to learn."

"I think I know that one," said Simon. "I prefer Polish poker, myself."

The storm raged on as we took turns dealing and winning and losing. The howl of gusts, the assaultive tinkle of chimes I'd hung the month before. Over the candle flame, Simon's and Inge's faces glowed in a way that conjured *The Little Match Girl*. Greta took residence on Inge's lap, her head draped down one side, her haunches down the other. A chorus of coyotes yipped in the distance, and Greta lifted her head, sniffed the air, then resumed her poodle dreams.

"My fingers are getting cold," Inge announced. "I think I'm headed for bed."

Greta hopped down, then followed her new favorite person upstairs.

Once they were out of earshot, Simon let out a breathy, "Jesus, that woman is an odd duck."

"Said the dude wearing the reindeer cardigan."

"Fair," he said. "But don't you find her a little—witchy?"

To be honest, I did. "She's resourceful, I'll give her that," I said.

Simon's face in candle shadow looked younger. It was a pleasant face, really. Full lips, a skein of whiskers, round, rosy cheeks. Cherubic, almost.

"Tell me a bit more about why you merged with Beacon and Bright," I said, dealing out another round of rummy.

He had long eyelashes. The kind mothers say are wasted on sons. Just as my mother had said about Kento. He grabbed the discarded card, slapped down his reject. "A story old as the hills," he said.

"Love gone wrong?" I said.

"Hm. Your turn."

I was meldless. Dealt myself a shitty hand. I picked up a card. "I'm going out on a limb, but, Greta, she was her dog, yeah? Or his?"

"*His*, huh? Is it the poodle?"

"I didn't want to assume."

"I'm divorced. The ex is definitely a woman."

I picked up another crappy card that matched nothing in my hand. "Sorry. About the divorce, I mean." I met his eyes. Those eyelashes.

"How long were you and Ethan married?" he asked, moving the inquiry artfully, the way lawyers do.

"I thought I'd grow old with him," I started. Then stopped. Simon slapped down a short run and discarded an ace. Always a gamble with aces, but he was down to two cards. "Well," I added, "maybe I didn't give it a lot of thought at all. Maybe that was the problem. I assumed. Took for granted. The usual sin of young marriage."

"I'm sorry I yelled at you for going to that support group earlier. It really wasn't any of my business."

"I shouldn't have gone. I was in a snarky mood." I pointed up the stairs. "I mean, she drove all the way from Sandpoint to go on and on about her dead cat. The tears. The whining. I sort of wanted to punch her."

"And yet, you welcomed her into your home. You're not a bad person, Hazel."

"Hm, I sort of am. But not as bad a person as Corinda. And Arthur. Good lord. I hope they get what's coming to them."

Simon picked up my discard. The two kings in my hand glared at me—twenty points of deadwood if I ended up with them.

"And what would that be, exactly?" he said.

"Duh. Justice? Kento gets a baby, Arthur gets locked up, and Corinda—"

"She's been in your lives a long time, hasn't she?"

"Ye old millstone around the neck," I said.

Simon chuckled. I drew another card. Nothing I could use.

"She and Kento have history. It's complicated and she has been living in a fairytale world. One in which Kento magically decides he's not gay."

"Kind of figured it was something like that," he said. "Ethan didn't care for your brother?"

The swerve threw me. I discarded. Shook my head.

"I have a question," he said. "And it's a tad intrusive, I'm afraid."

"I'm an open book. Maybe."

"Why'd you marry someone so homophobic?"

"Ethan? He wasn't homophobic. He and Kento just didn't like one another. It went back to their soccer days. High school."

I started to explain the whole state final fiasco, and Simon stopped me.

"Ethan's membership in Patriot Root, I'm talking about."

"His what?"

Simon set his cards down and stared at me. "You didn't know?"

I froze. The last candle was almost melted into the jelly jar. It flickered in time with my heart. "There's no way he'd be part of that cult. No way! Don't you think I'd know if my own husband was an anti-gay freak?"

Simon's forehead wrinkled. "You'd be surprised at what a duplicitous person can pull off without their spouse knowing. I speak from experience."

I hadn't wanted to bring Ethan's suspected affair up. One thing I'd gotten from my mother's DNA was shame. Better to look the other way than to admit you're not enough. But with Simon, the candlelight flickering, highlighting a sadness in his face, I took the bait. "So your wife cheated, too?"

"Charisma," he said, "the death knell of long-term successful marriage."

"Yeah. Ethan was Mr. Congeniality. Everyone's pal. But not yours, I'm guessing."

"I'm sorry. I shouldn't have said anything."

"You really think he was part of that group? What makes you—"

"Amanda. That's her name, in case you didn't know it. The firm hired her when they did all the fancy upgrades. She was fired a month or so before Ethan's accident, once they found out she was involved with the Root. And with your husband."

My stomach heaved. I covered my mouth to suppress a gag.

"Do you need water?" He was already up, looking for a glass that didn't have melted wax in it. He found a measuring cup and inched over to the sink. "What the heck?"

He recoiled.

"What?"

"That's some scary knife. Is that the—"

"It is. It's a ceremonial Kwaiken knife. The idiot detectives missed it."

I heard shuffling and clanking in the dark, but wasn't able to make out what Simon was doing.

He returned to our card game with my water and the knife, now wrapped in a dishtowel.

"I'm not sure what to do about this," he said, glancing at the bundle. "It's evidence."

"It's a fucking family heirloom," I said. "My mom's rolling in her urn right now."

"Why did you use this to cut a cake?"

I wasn't too thrilled with his sudden change in tone. "Look at what we're using as candle holders, okay? It's what was available. And—"

"And?"

I felt a well of sadness behind my eyes. Literal tears were forming back there. "Kento," I said. "Legacy, you know? Something from our childhood. From our mother. It just seemed right that the banal fiasco of a gender reveal party should include something redemptive."

Simon examined the dagger by the waning light of the almost expired candle. The hammered finish. The smooth, rosewood handle. He held a hand above it and I could tell he wanted to touch it. A devotee of form and function, my mother used it for everything: Chopping, slicing, serving. When Ethan and I were dating in high school, before my mother became ill, she explained the significance of the dagger to him. He'd listened, fascinated. Asked so many questions about her upbringing and her parents' internment, heard the stories of courage, and how this sacred knife had once belonged to her ancestors in Japan. I could still hear her voice: *My great-great grandmother once slayed an attacker with this knife,* she'd claimed. *They called it a bosom knife, and women of the Samurai class carried them for protection.* Ethan couldn't get enough of those stories—which, at the time, truly embarrassed me.

"There is no way," I said, taking the wrapped knife from Simon. "No way Ethan was affiliated with those White Nationalists. He was open-minded. Liberal."

"You really don't know then?"

I stared at the darkening form of him, daring him to hold his ground on his mistaken theory. I had plenty to counter it with. I was his *wife*! His high school sweetheart!

"We were in the midst of negotiating the merger. Ethan had been partner track, but once I found out he was affiliated with the Root, well, I didn't want any part of that. There was an ultimatum. And then, well, the accident, so—"

The last candle was only a wick floating in liquid at this point. I could no longer see the eyelashes, the slight stubble, the reindeer sweater. The card games were over.

"I hope the sofa isn't too hard on your back," I said before taking

my wrapped heirloom knife in hand and drifting upstairs to sheets
that smelled of Corinda's fruity bodywash.

IT WAS SOMETIME LATER—hours, minutes, hard to know for sure—
that the vandals descended. Into the calm, gray early morning, the
unmistakable sound of four-wheel mischief pierced the air and woke
me. Reflexively, I snapped on the bedside light. Still out. I reached for
the wrapped Kwaiken knife, then thought better of it, and shoved it
under the bed.

I leapt up, plowed through a pile of Corinda's clothes and sped
down the stairs. The front door was wide open, and I found Simon on
the porch overseeing his dog's morning shit. She was still squatting in
the snowy yard at the base of the porch steps. "Good," he said, turning
to me. "You're up. Sounds like your friends in town have paid you a visit."

"Did you see the vehicle?"

"Ford. One of those jacked-up, F-350s, I'm pretty sure. Think they
ran over your mailbox, did some donuts in front of your other house.
The one by the road. You have a plastic bag I can use for the poop?"

The storm had passed, but it was still below freezing, and the
ground was encased in a layer of hoar frost, topped with an inch or
so of snow. I ran back inside, grabbed my parka, pulled on my muck
boots and half-skated, half-jogged down the driveway, past Inge's and
Simon's hooked together sideways cars, to the mess left by the vandals.

Deep ruts scored the area in front of the trailer. A section of picket
fence lay flat and splintered. The mailbox and its pole were similarly
knocked to the ground. But most disturbing, a sizeable chunk of
granite wrapped in twine-fastened notepaper had been hurled toward
the trailer house, and jutted up from the snow like an errant pimple.

I was about to pull the note from the rock when Simon scooted up.
"Don't touch it!" he warned. "Fingerprints!"

He pulled out his phone to take a picture, not remembering it
was dead.

"I'll get mine," I said. "It still has some juice."

Together we shoveled the chunk of granite onto a plastic saucer sled. I pushed, Simon pulled, and we hauled it up to the big house.

I used tongs to extract the note, and by the time we brought it inside, Crazy Cat Lady was doling out apple slices and lamenting the lack of electricity needed to brew coffee.

The note was really just a sentence inked onto the paper with a strong enough hand that the marker had bled through. *YOUR DONE IN THIS TOWN. – THE ROOT*

"Ah, the usual illiterate troll scribble," I said.

"There was quite a lot of commotion this morning," said Inge, shaking her head. "And here I thought Steeplejack was a calm, loving community."

"Whatever gave you that idea," I said.

But there was something else. A smeared version of my logo, underneath the threatening language. The horizontal line, the squiggly lines underneath. The snow had washed away part of it, but it was clearly a botched imitation of my insignia. Someone was trying to send me a message. But why?

Simon took the tongs from me, the note still damply in its clutches. He examined it from various sides, holding it up to the window where the low winter sun now leaked through. "We'll get our handwriting expert on this. See if it matches anything the cops have found around town."

I thought of Patrick, and the sign-in sheet typically passed around at the beginning of Grief Group. But I kept that detail to myself. I didn't want another lecture from Simon on witness tampering.

Our ponderings were interrupted by the beep of the microwave. The power had been restored.

"Thank the Lord!" cried Inge. "Now we can be properly caffeinated."

"I don't know if I have any coffee left," I said.

Inge shuffled to her oversized handbag. "Not to worry," she announced, lifting up a Ziploc full of grounds.

The woman was like a Mary Poppins for grown-ups.

Simon spied my plugged in iPhone charger on the counter. "Mind?" he said, already shoving the cord into his device.

After a flurry of activity, after Triple A separated the cars and all the insurance info was sorted out, my guests departed and left me to ponder the unwelcome revelations. How well did I know my husband? What other secrets had he kept from me?

# NINETEEN

I SPENT THE NEXT FEW HOURS digging through Ethan's work boxes, which I'd stacked in the bedroom closet of the trailer house. There were a couple personal items: an 8 by 10 wedding photo of the two of us, smiling giddily, and a smaller framed snap of his parents dressed fancily for some event—clearly not taken at our wedding, since they were smiling. Most of the file boxes contained case law textbooks, but one smaller box was stuffed with notebooks, a grad tassel, and handwritten envelopes containing a variety of missives. I lingered on the greeting cards he'd never shared with me. Most of them from his parents' friends congratulating Ethan for graduating with honors from law school. A handful of cards acknowledged our marriage—two of these contained checks that Ethan had evidently deposited via the cloud.

At the bottom of the box, I found a fat, maroon data stick I recognized as one I'd been missing. My hand shook as I popped it into my laptop. Sure enough, the stick was loaded with my zip files. All of Bitterroot Renderings' vectors and design assets. Why would he have these?

I logged into Gmail, and typed in Ethan's username and password, and got an error message. He'd changed his password at some point. It had always been Hazelhazel77. Seven for luck. Double luck. That's what he used to tell me.

I slammed the laptop closed. What else didn't I know about my late husband? Why would he coopt my brand for such a disgusting purpose? Was that Amanda woman part of it? There had to be more to it, and the only folks who might give me a fuller picture had just vandalized my property.

I trudged back up to the big house, a box of ice-melting salt under my arm, when my phone pinged with a FaceTime call. I dropped the salt and connected to see Kento's and Tom's faces pressed together in the little window of my phone's screen, their eyes, round with fear.

"What?" I said as they glanced at each other, not speaking.

"We just got a call," Tom said.

"From a hospital in Boise," Kento said.

"Corinda," Tom said.

My ears weren't tracking with my brain. "What's she done now?"

"Apparently, there was a car accident. She's been life-flighted to Boise, and I'm somehow still listed as the emergency contact on her medical forms," Kento said, the delivery of this information so rapid-fire, it left him breathless.

"An accident? When?"

"A few hours ago. Her stepson, Patrick, was driving."

The vandalism. The timing. "Was he driving a truck?" I said.

"I don't know, but, apparently, he died instantly, and Corinda, along with some other woman, are in the ICU with a concussion and some broken bones. We don't know the status of the baby."

*Along with some other woman?*

Kento began to weep, and Tom took over. "Kento isn't cleared to travel yet. Do you think you could—"

"Drive to Boise?" I said. "What about Arthur? He *is* her husband still."

"She asked for Kento," Tom said.

*Fuck that*, I didn't say, but wanted to.

"So did you speak with her?"

"They put her on the phone, briefly. All she did was sputter and sob," Tom said.

What I'd just uncovered about Ethan, and knowing what I knew about Patrick, Amanda, and the note—it was all too much to digest, the crazy sequence of events this last 24 hours, beginning with my ill-fated trip to Grief Group. I needed to think.

"My lawyer has warned me not to interact with the Blairs," I said.

"We need someone there to represent the baby," Kento managed.

"In what world would I be that person?" I said. "Tom, you should be the one to go."

"He's not on the list," Kento said. "You and I are, apparently."

I was out of excuses, and frankly, shocked that I was listed as a close family member. Hadn't Corinda just bad-mouthed our whole family a millisecond ago? She'd been in Patrick's truck, doing donuts on my property, threatening me. But the fear and anguish in my brother's face. After everything, Kento still cared about that bitch, apparently.

"I'll call the lawyer," I said. "See what I can work out."

"ABSOLUTELY NOT," said Simon through the crackle of a marginal connection.

"Thought you'd say that," I said.

"I just clicked on the local news. That truck was the very same one that assaulted your property and lobbed the threatening hate note—it was Patrick Blair. He skidded into a tree a few miles from your house."

"Doesn't that change the game plan, though?" I said. "Fat chance they'll be suing us now. And the bullshit claim about self-defense? How can that possibly hold up?"

I did not reveal the part about finding potential proof that Ethan was a part of their sick cult.

"Corinda is no doubt traumatized. You'll look like an opportunist if you intervene."

"If I go, it'll be for Kento. He has always had a complicated relationship with her, and since he's still recovering—"

"From Arthur shooting him," Simon interrupted. "Look, I can't stop you, but if you do go, remember, Idaho is a one-party consent state. If you are part of the conversation, you don't need her permission to record any interaction you have with her at the hospital. So long as you use your device, and make it known that you are in the room and contributing to the conversation."

"In other words, I might be able to get her to admit Kento didn't threaten her with a knife, or force her to carry his baby?"

"Should we go over how to do that?"

"I don't want to delay driving down there. There are still a couple hours of daylight, and the roads are plowed and salted. Knowing Corinda, she's more apt to spill her guts when she's vulnerable."

I did not divulge my curiosity about Amanda, but I'd already decided I needed to confront her as well.

"Maybe I should go with you," he said. "At least for the drive. We can practice. But I think it would be best to set off in the morning, do the whole drive in daylight."

I wasn't eager to road trip six hours with Simon—and Greta, as they seemed to be a package deal—but I had to admit, I was out of my league, and had done nothing but fuck up with my impulsive confrontations.

In the end, I agreed. "Come meet me over here. I'll drive."

THE ROADS WERE TREACHEROUSLY ICY and slow, and it took a full eight-and-a-half hours to reach St. Alphonsus in Boise. We'd stopped only twice for short breaks—toilet, gas, and fast food—but I could hardly eat, my stomach was so churned up. Kento had alerted Corinda that I'd be coming, and through hysterics, she agreed to the compromise—though she clearly would have preferred Kento to me.

Arthur, apparently, was still in Steeplejack, despondent over the loss of his son. Admittedly, this was a favorable situation, and my gut turned over with guilt as relief flooded my nervous system. I felt a bit like a buzzard, picking the flesh of roadkill, as I practiced surreptitiously hitting the record button on my phone on my way to the ICU waiting area. With any luck, Amanda would be occupying a bed proximal to Corinda, but even as I thought this, the chest-squeezing vice of shame accompanied my scheming agenda.

"Remember to lead with compassion," Simon had counseled. "Try to channel Kento. She obviously considers him an ally now that the tables have turned, and she's the one in a trauma ward."

*Compassion*, I mantra-ed. *Kindness. Forgiveness.* But these were empty words. My heart didn't feel the truth behind them. Still, I muttered them under my breath as I strode down the Christmassy corridors of the hospital. A three-story evergreen commanded the atrium, bedecked with enormous velveteen bows, soccer-ball-sized gold orbs and glass angels. *Joy To The World* piped through hidden speakers as I made my way.

It was late. After visiting hours, the receptionist in the ICU waiting area informed me. I explained the long drive and the fact that Corinda wouldn't have any other visitors, and she was frightened.

"She's having my brother's baby," I said. "And he has also been recently injured and can't travel."

She made a call, and soon a Nurse Ratched type appeared, complete with grim face and brisk manner. "We have rules for a reason," she scolded. "Your loved one isn't the only patient in the ICU."

*Loved one*, I wanted to argue. *What makes you think she's a* loved *one*? Instead, I played to whatever grinchy heart lay beneath her immaculate scrubs. "She's so frightened, after the accident and the Life Flight, and being pregnant. I just wanted to see her for a minute or two."

Her sour expression lifted a tad, but her arms remained crossed. I decided to play the fetus angle. This was Idaho, after all, and there was a high percentage that this nurse belonged in the Save the Baby at All Costs camp.

"Wouldn't it be wise to do everything in your power to see that her pregnancy continues? Her mental state is fragile. I can help with that."

"Five minutes," she said.

I reached a hand into my pocket, and felt for my phone, engaging the record button before reaching her curtained off cubicle.

She was in rough shape. Tubes, monitors, casts, a weird contraption fastened around her head and neck. There were two heart monitors. One for Corinda; one for baby. I watched the jagged green peaks for a few seconds before announcing my presence.

Corinda's face, swollen, black-and-blue from airbag deployment, which likely saved her life. "Pssst," I whispered. She startled and moved her eyeballs in my direction. "Where's Kento?" she rasped.

"Not cleared for travel," I said, surprised that she hadn't remembered that she'd been party to a conversation divulging as much. I stepped closer to her bed.

"The baby," she said. "I might lose him."

"You're in one of the best trauma hospitals in the west, so—"

"Why are you here?" she said.

Why indeed.

"Kento," I said.

"That car. It came out of nowhere," she said. "And Patrick. He didn't deserve to die."

A tear rolled down her battered cheek. No mention of the third party in the truck. But the car?

"There was another car involved?"

"One of those boats. Big sedan. Wrong side of the road."

Maybe she was confused. She had suffered a head injury, after all.

"Corinda," I said, my voice steady, clear. "I know that you and Patrick and whoever that *woman* was paid me a visit right before the crash. You threatened me with the note tied to the rock. Why?"

Her lower lip trembled, but she remained silent.

Nurse Ratched peered in. "Wrap it up. We need to check her vitals," she said, and then snapped the privacy curtain closed.

I had to get a confession, and time was not on my side. "Help me understand what happened the day of the shooting. With Arthur. Why did you lie about Kento?"

"Because," she hissed. "It's unnatural."

"That's why you lied? Because you can't accept that Kento is gay?"

"He was going to propose, and then he went to that socialist college, and they turned him. I know he's a real man. I have proof."

"A real man? Corinda, what are we talking about?"

"Your husband even said that. The pressures in those liberal schools—it's a whole conspiracy."

"My husband? Ethan? Where did you get that idea?"

"Yes. Ethan. So you can go to hell with your liberal behaviors. Arthur may not be perfect, but at least he's not a sinner. At least he has normal impulses."

"Oh, really? You don't consider shooting someone in cold blood a sin? You don't see a problem with violence?" I scratched air quotes into the space between us. "That's a *normal* impulse?"

The drape peeled open, and the nurse hip-checked me away from the bed. "Times up. This little gal needs her rest."

I offered a cynical salute, and pressed the end record button on my phone. To Corinda I whispered, "We're not done here."

I stomped out of the ICU the long way around, peeking in the other cubicles for signs of my husband's erstwhile whore. Since the cunty nurse was busy with Corinda, I approached the nurse's station. "Excuse me, is Amanda one of the patients in here?"

The nurse, a dude with bags under his eyes, scrutinized me. "Amanda?"

"The other patient in the MVA flown in?" I thought using the acronym would give me some cred, but the tired nurse was unmoved.

"You related?"

"Yes," I lied.

"Close family?"

"Close enough."

"Wait in the family member room, Ma'am. Someone from social services will meet with you."

"Is she, uh, expired?"

Medical facility jargon was full of antiseptic euphemisms.

His face was stone. He pointed vaguely to his left, where the room for bad news awaited.

Luckily, I was alone in that space—a sterile, plastic-couched room with bad motel art mis-hung on the walls. A flurry of contradictory emotions meandered under my skin, or so it seemed. The predictable rage, sorrow, and grief, accompanied a twisted irony. The would-be husband-stealer was dead. Killed in the same manner as her lover—my husband. Had she been the one to pen the angry note? I pictured her as I'd last seen her: picking dirty ice chunks from a jacket.

Soon, a middle-aged woman with gray Brillo pad-hair shuffled in, her arm extended in my direction, but her eyes focused on the charts in her other hand. "Have a seat," she said, after we shook.

She remained standing, a little to the side so as not to appear an intimidating, hovering presence. "So you are a sister of Miss Adams?"

*Miss Adams.* Amanda Adams. AA. I vaguely remembered seeing texts from AA on Ethan's phone, and I wondered at the time if he'd been secretly attending Alcoholic Anonymous meetings.

I nodded. What else could I do? Lying was hard for me, especially when I was asked to confirm a falsehood via speech.

She made eye contact for the first time, her lids heavy, her gaze downturned, then meeting mine. "I understand she passed en route. Her injuries were too severe."

Again, the irony that my husband's mistress would suffer the same fate as he had collided with the more appropriate shock response. My emotions were all over the place. I pictured Ethan's name on her lips as she succumbed. A *star-crossed lovers together at last* bullshit fantasy. A bit of phlegm wiggled up into my throat. I gagged. The social worker extracted a tissue from a mysterious pocket.

I left the room sad and furious. I'd been denied the ability to confront Amanda—to get some closure around Ethan's betrayal. It was clear that she'd coveted more than my husband. I was certain, now, that she was behind the theft of my logo. The hate. The duplicity. Such a waste. I flashed on the memory of her at the repast after Ethan's service. What makes a person so entitled? So angry. It seemed connected to the whole mission of groups like Patriot Root. So afraid of change. Of progress. So worried that justice was a fixed commodity, and if others were granted it, they were denied it.

By the time I passed the overly optimistic Yuletide décor in the lobby, however, I'd softened. In my pocket was vindication. Corinda hadn't completely confessed, but I had enough on the recording to contradict the Blairs' claim of self-defense, though Simon had told me the deposition would now be cast into the distant future thanks to the accident.

Simon was walking Greta near the hospital's entrance. She yipped when she saw me, her paws scratching in the frozen earth. Simon shushed her, and she squatted next to his shoe. Simon directed his attention at the phone in my hand.

"That was fast. Did you record her recant? Is she of sound mind?"

"Her mind is no less sound than usual. As in, loony tunes. As in, she's a nightmare." I left out the dead Amanda part of the recon.

Simon extracted a plastic baggie and, in one swoop, disappeared Greta's turd pile. Holding the smelly sack aloft he said, "Let's get something to eat and we'll see what's what."

Simon was an enigma. In some ways, he seemed progressive and ready to take on the hate groups that'd multiplied in Idaho over the past few years, but in other ways, he was blandly suburban. Tentative and conservative. His goofy Christmas sweater, the poodle, his penchant for mall-anchor chain restaurants—Chilis, Cheesecake Factory, Red Robin, Idaho Potato Barn. Which is where we found ourselves—just in time for late night happy hour.

I ordered a glass of chardonnay, and Simon, after asking a shitload of questions about the menu, decided on a brandy Alexander. We chose the red potato flatbread pizza and a potato nacho to split.

"So," he said, once the server set our drinks down, "I got a call while you were in there with Corinda."

"A call?"

"Apparently, your house guest was involved in the Blairs' wreck."

"Inge?"

"She blew a one-point-six. Twice the legal."

"Wait, what? Are you telling me that Inge caused the accident? And she was drunk?"

"That Lincoln. Pretty heavy-duty car. She hardly had a scratch. Or, at least that's what she said."

"You spoke with her?"

"They have her booked at the precinct. One of our associates is seeing about bail since I'm out of town."

I flashed on that bottle of Maker's Mark in her purse. She'd left a half-hour or so after the Blairs hurled the rock at my house. God Damn crazy cat lady.

"Talk about small town coincidences. Jesus."

The food arrived, and I realized I was starving, and now a bit tipsy myself. Clearly, we wouldn't be driving back to Steeplejack tonight.

I played the recording for Simon, and he hunched over the phone, replaying the exchange several times, while I stuffed myself with potatoes and cheese sauce.

"Well?" I said, after the sixth replay.

"It'll help our case. But now that we have the Inge problem, it might get messier."

"I had nothing to do with Inge's drunk driving," I said.

"She left your house impaired," he said, all monotone and serious. The brandy Alexander foam on his upper lip contradicted his sober tone.

"Impaired with her own booze," I reminded him.

"We know that, but I'm going to be straight with you—there will be a serious wrongful death investigation, and it's not good news for you."

I ordered a second chardonnay.

"My ex-in-laws have a summer home near the Boise River. We can stay there tonight."

"You must have a better relationship with your in-laws than I do." I pictured Mac and Skipper, and our recent interaction when they extorted money from me.

Simon stuffed a potato-laden slice of pizza in his mouth and shrugged. After swallowing he said, "They like me better than they do their daughter."

"Ouch. What'd she do?"

"Let's just say borderline personalities are hard on loved ones. Particularly parents. But Lucinda is more than just a mentally volatile freak show. She's got a good heart."

My second wine came, and I sipped, waiting for more details. Finally, he offered a teaser. "After all the political turmoil here in the states—the crazies taking over congress and stripping rights—she moved to Banff. Joined a cult group involved in social justice issues."

"Ah. A warrior for the people. Well, at least she didn't cheat on you with a cult member."

"She's exploring her bi side, so I wouldn't say she didn't experiment during our marriage."

I thought of Corinda and the way she keeps fooling herself. And my willful avoidance, choosing to ignore the red flags when it came to Ethan. "In my experience," I said, letting thoughts percolate before slipping out unedited, "love can make a person blind to reality."

"Yeah," he said, wiping a smear of cheese grease from his lips.

"So she took off and left you with Greta?"

He nodded. "And the practice, well, after the split, I had to downsize. And, you know the rest."

"So her folks are all Team Simon, then?"

"Pretty much. Lucinda is their only child, and her parents are getting older. Her dad just got diagnosed with Parkinson's, and her mom has pretty serious arthritis. She abandoned them in their dotage. I do what I can, but they're not, you know, my parents, so it's hard."

I was curious. "Lucinda. Hmm. Does she go by Lucy?"

"Not on your life. Her folks called her that as a kid, but by the time we married, she had them trained to use her preferred name."

"And your own parents? Where are they?"

"Dead. COVID got them."

"I'm sorry. I know how it is to lose parents. Mine suffered for a long time before they passed."

Simon shook his head in the manner of palate-cleansing. We were done talking about unpleasant things. He played the recording again. "Good job," he said, and then we ate silently until the plates were empty.

SIMON'S IN-LAW'S HOUSE WAS THE SHACK in a neighborhood of otherwise impressive real estate. The moon was a toenail clip, the sky as dark as it gets, but I could still see the telltale signs of deferred maintenance. Like with Ethan's parents, there was peeling paint and gutters overflowing with leaves. Twigs and a few larger branches littered the path. The front door lock had been tampered with, but not successfully, and the key took a while to function.

"They want to sell," Simon explained. "But they live most of the year in Tucson in an assisted living place. Hard to handle all this repair crap from a distance."

Houses, I thought. They can be a mixed blessing. My own parents' house—it took years for Kento and me to face the enormity of cleaning it out.

Greta seemed perfectly at home here though. She raced from room to room, prancing and sniffing as if on a treasure hunt. The place was musty smelling, and at some point a windstorm had blown a chunk of glass out of a window. A pile of crispy oak leaves lay clumped against a wall. Greta squatted on the pile, relieving herself again.

Simon got the furnace working, and I cleaned up the leaf and dogshit mess, and then taped a cereal box over the broken part of the window. In a way, this was a familiar scenario. Growing up, there was always something out of whack in our house. Something that needed a temporary fix. Duct tape and a shop vac were never far from our grasp. And when Ethan and I bought the trailer house, we spent many a weekend patching, scrubbing, shoring up. After the tense few weeks I'd had, and the long drive, and Corinda's bullshit, putting things in order felt therapeutic.

I found a vacuum cleaner and started in on the carpets. As I pushed through the various rooms, liberating the floors from accumulated dust and dirt, I flipped light switches, and slowly the house quit feeling like an untended hovel, and more like a comfortable domicile. Welcoming, even. Childhood photos of Lucinda lined a hall. Her face contorted in a variety of poses. Her big eyes as buggy as a pug dog's; her grin big as Alice's Cheshire Cat. You could see the mania—it radiated off of her. She wasn't a very cute child, but in her teen years, her striking features settled into favorable bone structure, and sometime between the beginning and end of high school, the girl became stunning. Movie star stunning. Think Angelina Jolie crossed with Meghan Markle.

At the far end of the hall hung a wedding photo. Simon's cat-got-the-canary gaze at his bride told me everything I wasn't sure I wanted to know. His bride was not looking back at him. She had her eye on whatever came next.

Simon snuck up behind me and caught me off guard. I jumped and since my hand was on the wedding photo frame, it fell to the ground, shattering the glass.

"Damn! I'm so sorry," I said.

"That's an omen if ever there was one," Simon said. He was already picking up the pieces and transferring them into an ash pail.

"You looked—in love," I said.

"I imagine you felt that way on your own wedding day," he said.

*Did I? Had I?* I nodded tentatively.

"You think you know people," Simon said.

In the photo, Simon's hair hadn't yet receded, and his chin was still chiseled with youth. I asked him, "How long ago did you marry?"

He paused, his wheels spinning in math. "A lifetime ago?" he said.

"On the day he died, Ethan looked the same as he did when we said our vows."

"You guys were still newlyweds, no?"

"Three years. Married three, I mean. Together since high school. Mostly." I tried to conjure our own wedding pictures, but we hadn't framed any. On my walls, the framed art was death and decomposition. Kusôzu.

We finished cleaning and settled into respective beds—neither of us claiming the primary bedroom out of respect. Or maybe the weirdness of the situation. I called my brother, who'd left a half-dozen voicemails.

"About time," he said, breathing like a marathoner. "You got to her? How's Corinda? How's the baby?"

"So far, the pregnancy hasn't ended," I said. "And she's gonna live, I'm pretty sure. Banged up though, and still spewing hate."

"What about that placenta previa thing? Has that resolved?"

I'd forgotten the bleeding was the whole reason we coddled her in the first place. Was it only a few days ago that I'd cornered her at the doctor's office? "I think it's resolved. Or moved back up, or whatever."

I filled Kento in on the last few hours, all the players, the deaths, the note, before hitting him with the latest wrinkle.

"Let me get this straight, you invited some random person to stay in the house where the attack happened? Are you nuts?"

"The storm—" I started.

"How could you be that dumb?" Kento shouted.

I pulled my phone from my ear. Kento had never spoken to me like that before. "Whoa," I said. "Hold on, buddy. I appreciate that you're stressed and all, but we're still the victims here."

There was a muffle in the background, then Tom's voice took over. "Sorry, Hazel. He's coming off the oxy, and it's been *crazytown* over here. How about we all get some sleep and talk tomorrow?"

We hung up, and my head began to pound. A migraine on its way. Kento's desperate voice echoed through my nervous system, as it always did when I sensed the world ganging up on him.

A memory surfaced amid the pounding. Kento and I on the one Disneyland vacation with our Japanese grandparents before they passed. We were eleven, the last childhood year Kento was taller than me until he got his growth spurt late in high school, and I stopped growing. We hadn't invented "I don't" yet, but we played all sorts of twin language make-believe games. We'd been reading Charlotte's Web in school, and had just seen the Dakota Fanning film version the week before our trip. I had a Halloween spider decoration that I carted around with me, folding its bendable legs around my neck like a scarf. Kento had resurrected a pig puppet from our toy box, and pretended it was Wilbur. We recited the lines from the story, embellishing the part during the fair, when Charlotte tries to save Wilbur's life by writing messages in her web.

When our mother packed our suitcases, we snuck the toys inside of them, and brought them along on our very first plane trip. Our grandparents were old school. The type who dressed formally for air travel. Our mother had warned us that our grandfather, on his second pacemaker, would not be able to accompany us on the more adventurous rides. We were, she counseled, to remember our pleases and thank-yous. To not ask for extra treats or souvenirs.

"You are very, very lucky children to go to Disney," she reminded us.

Our thrifty grandparents, Jiji and Baba, had booked reservations at a nearby motel—one of those crappy rent-by-the-hour places. But we didn't care; we'd never stayed in a motel before, and this one had a pool and cable TV. We arrived the evening before the date of our Costco-purchased tickets for Disneyland, and immediately unpacked our Wilbur and Charlotte companions, hoping we'd be allowed to explore the motel with them.

Kento cradled his Wilbur in his arms, quietly murmuring loving sentiments. While our grandmother laid out our dinner—disgusting fish sandwiches she'd brought along in a carry-on soft cooler—our grandfather shot Kento scolding looks. I watched with trepidation. With every raise of our grandfather's eyebrows, with every grimace of his sour, downturned mouth, I knew an eruption was forthcoming. I hid Charlotte under a pillow.

"You, boy. Do not embarrass me. Far too old to play with a doll. You look—you look—*retarded*. I want more dignity from my namesake."

My breath caught in my chest. I couldn't bear to look at Kento's shamed face. Retarded? Did he just call my twin brother a retard? I wanted to punch my grandfather, but I was frozen.

Kento tiptoed to his suitcase, which our grandmother had already zipped back up and stuffed in the closet. When he re-emerged, there was no Wilbur in his arms. Our grandmother pointed to the small round table near the window and commanded us to sit where she'd placed our dinner on squares of paper toweling. Kento tried hard to keep from crying, turning his face away from us as he ate every bite of the awful fish sandwich in self-punishment. I refused mine, and was told I would not get anything else to eat for the entire night.

The pallor of shame stuck with us through our trip. Kento tried to hide his penchant for the Sleeping Beauty castle over our grandparents' choice—It's a Small World—a ride we stood in line for over and over

again, since it was near the front of the park and required minimal traipsing. Our tickets were good for three days, and our grandparents made
sure we were there when the park opened. At noon, we walked back to
the motel for liverwurst sandwiches and apples, and our grandfather's
daily nap. It was oddly cold and rainy in Anaheim during the trip, so
the pool wasn't an option. We were told to be quiet during naptime,
and color in coloring books our grandparents had brought along to
keep us entertained.

Why they thought we were young enough for coloring books but
too old for Wilbur and Charlotte remains a mystery. One afternoon,
during Jiji's nap, Baba took us aside.

"If Jiji sounded harsh, it's because if you lose dignity, they have won."

We pondered that, trying to grasp what she meant.

Baba shook her head. "Jiji was an infant, you know, during war
time. His family sent away to a camp in Northern California, after his
father was pulled into army. He was Nisei American born to Japanese
immigrants. They made him fight for a country that locked his wife
and baby away in a camp."

We had never heard the word *Nisei*, or how our grandfather's boy-
hood related to his disgust for our Charlotte's Web play-acting, but we
nodded as if we did.

After three days of It's a Small World, we boarded a shuttle bus
back to the airport, remembering our thank-yous, our practiced show
of gratitude. Six months later, our grandfather had his fatal heart attack,
and Baba moved in with us until her death a year later. I was glad they
were dead.

IN BOISE, ALL THESE YEARS LATER, in a child-sized twin bed likely
once occupied by Simon's ex-wife, I swallowed an Excedrin PM, and
waited for sleep to take me. The last thing on my mind before slipping
into dreams was the memory of Wilbur, stuffed in our kitchen garbage
can, covered in banana peels and wadded paper towels.

# TWENTY

I awoke to the sound of shoveling out the bedroom window. In the low-angled winter light, I spied Simon flinging snow off the walkway. It had dumped the night before, tapering off to flurries in a typical Idaho winter solstice pattern. There was at least a foot of the stuff on the ground. Greta gamboled beside him, puppy-bowing, tail-wagging. It would not be easy driving back over the pass.

To my great disappointment, the only coffee in the house was a teaspoon of Folgers packed against the bottom of a rusty tin, circa the aughts. In the cupboard, I uncovered a forgotten bag of English muffins, so green with mold they resembled hockey pucks painted for St. Patrick's Day.

My phone informed me that the closest Starbucks was two-and-a-half miles away. I would have to walk, but first, I needed to unearth my rubber boots from the emergency crap in my trunk.

Simon called to me as I walked toward my half-buried car. "Wanna give me a hand?"

"Don't talk to me before coffee," I admonished.

"Oh," he said. "You're one of those."

He grabbed Greta's trailing leash and dropped his snow shovel. "Where are you headed?"

He seemed so bouncy. So youthful. "How long have you been up?" I said.

"I'm a lark," he said, shrugging. "You seem to be an owl."

His upbeat tone felt like a spray of bullets hitting my ears. "Sorry for my crankiness, but you're right. I'm not a morning person."

"There's a mom-and-pop café a few blocks from here," he said. "And they allow dogs on the patio."

I pointed to the walkway he was half done shoveling. "Patio?"

"Seriously, it's covered and, if memory serves, they have heat lamps."

"If they have coffee, I'm in," I said.

A FEW BLOCKS TURNED OUT TO BE more than a dozen, and by the time we arrived at the Boise River Coffee Shoppe, my fingers were nearly blue with frostbite. The café was small, but they did have a warm outdoor patio, and the coffee claimed to be small-batch. Also, they had a case full of savory scones complete with bacon bits—my favorite.

The patio was half-full of other defrosting patrons. We sat at a wobbly table directly under an electric heater, and Greta was offered a ceramic bowl of water, which she lapped up immediately. My own beverage was served in a roughly textured clay mug, and I cradled it between my palms as my hands slowly thawed. Simon had ordered Earl Grey with almond milk. A disgusting combination, in my opinion.

"You want the bad news, or the worse news," he said between sips.

"And here I thought you would wait until I had a few cups of this stuff in me before assaulting me with reality."

"The judge denied Inge bail."

"What? That's crazy. Do they think she's a flight risk?"

"Turns out," Simon continued, "she has priors."

"Huh?"

"She's a felon."

The vision of her Pippi Longstocking braids, her handknit leggings, her crazy cat lady eccentricity, didn't align with my experience in forensics. Odd ducks like her were typically victims, not perps.

"She lied about driving down from Sandpoint. She's wanted in Billings and Salmon for theft. Been living in her car for at least a year."

"Thanks for the update," I said, glumly. "This is a two-scone revelation."

"I'm not done."

"Oh, boy."

"Blair's team of attorneys is trying to pin an aiding-and-abetting-a-fugitive charge onto their wrongful homicide case."

"What?"

"They found your dagger in her car."

"She stole—I'd hidden it under my bed. What the fuck?"

"Yep. The woman has balls. Not literally, of course."

My appetite fizzled, and I pushed the remaining bite of bacon bits scone out of my reach. The woman would have had to sneak into my bedroom, poke around. I wondered what else she'd taken.

"Out of conflict of interest, we—the firm and I—won't be representing her."

"No shit," I said.

"I'm sorry. I really didn't want to confront you with all of this until I had a game plan. Apparently, we're both being chased down for questioning. Our trip here may have been a huge mistake."

There are two words that, when they pertain to you, you never want paired: huge and mistake. "Witness intimidation?" I asked, already knowing the answer.

"Why didn't you tell me about Amanda Adams?" he said.

Fuck.

"I was planning to. I just didn't get around to it."

"Posing as a family member, Hazel? Getting information you weren't authorized to get?"

He glared at me, steam slowly fogging the lenses of his glasses.

"Well," I said, meekly. "She fucked my husband, so, um, two degrees of separation?"

"Not sure that'll fly in court. Anyway, the pass is closed today, so there's no easy way back to Steeplejack."

"Do they know where we are?"

"They know we're in Boise. They know we were at the hospital yesterday."

"I guess another Corinda visit is out of the question."

"I wouldn't be surprised if they've installed law enforcement there. The firm repping Patrick is a big one. At least here in Boise."

My anxiety leapfrogged into rage. Those fucking Blairs. First, Arthur shoots Kento and calls it self-defense, and now this. The gaslighting. The criming. The bullshit. I felt like a cage had been placed over me. Impenetrable walls, closing in.

Simon reached a hand toward me. "Hazel, we'll untangle this, I promise."

"But you currently don't have a plan, right? Is that what I'm hearing?"

I realized my voice had escalated. Some heads had turned our way. "Shh," Simon hissed.

"Fuck that," I whispered back. Then, "That bitch stole my Kwaiken knife? Really?"

AN INVERSION HAD SETTLED OVER BOISE, trapping the cold air in a freezing fog that enveloped the city. Cars were slipping and crashing all over the place, according to my traffic and weather apps.

"Buying us time," said Simon in a forced silver lining voice. He said, "I always think better when I'm moving. You up for a hike?"

I'd enjoyed winter hiking with Ethan. We'd gotten into snowshoeing in the backcountry behind our property. I rolled my wedding ring around on my finger—it'd become a nervous habit. I hadn't packed any hiking gear. My rubber boots were good for muck and short walks, but more than that would give me blisters. Simon read my hesitation. "I think you're about the size of my ex-mother-in-law. Let's find something that'll work."

Simon himself kept a stash of outerwear in one of the closets, and he emerged with puffy Patagonia jackets, earmuffs, and mittens. A worn but solid pair of Vasque hikers fit me like a Cinderella story. When he held up matching striped stocking caps, I couldn't stop laughing. The origin story of his hideous holiday sweater—solved.

The in-law house was situated near the edge of a wild space. A trailhead punctuated the dead-end road a few lots up. Simon located some hiking poles, and we set off. Greta, leashless, bounded along beside us.

The trail began flat, rolling over roots and rocks half-buried in snow, before abruptly shifting to an uphill scramble. I hadn't hiked elevation since spreading Ethan at the overlook, and my lungs and legs protested. Surprisingly, Simon scurried over the trail like a mountain goat. But he was a polite hiking companion, and doubled back when I lagged behind.

"I'm out of shape," I huffed. "Sorry."

"It's not a race," he said. "Take it slow. We don't want to be forced back to that hospital if you break a leg or suffer a heart attack."

"Did you hike a lot with your wife?" I said.

Simon tugged the tassel of his stocking cap, "As you may have guessed, her whole family was really into the outdoors," he said. "In a sort of goofy, suburban way."

I tried picturing his fancy ex-spouse in a reindeer sweater and Dr. Seuss cap, slogging along this trail with Simon. "Was she fast, like you?"

"She was an elite marathon runner," he said. "Part of her mental illness was about going beyond in whatever she did. Running, climbing, sailing, skiing, lawyering."

Ah. Lawyering. I'd forgotten that she was his business partner as well.

I paused to catch my breath and leaned a hand against the thick bark of a ponderosa. "It's hard to be a partner with a perfectionist," I said, mostly to myself.

"Ethan was wound a bit tight himself, eh?" he said.

"Yeah, well, I'm not sure what Ethan was, or wasn't, at this point. His parents treated him like their golden child well into adulthood."

"Noted," he said. Then, "His association with Patrick and Amanda is curious though. The Blairs are politically right wing, clearly, but class-wise—"

"Yeah, not a match made in heaven. The Mackenzies are total snobs. No way would they have been happy to hear their son was consorting with what they think of as trailer trash. Bad enough he married a half-Asian girl from the other side of the bike path."

"These are some crazy times," said Simon. "Unholy alliances all over the place. Especially in Northern Idaho."

I pushed away from the tree and continued the uphill trudge. We hiked in silence for a bit until reaching a clearing near a waterfall that had partially frozen. The fog still hugged the tops of the trees, but it was thinning. Greta found a stick too big for her mouth and was trying in vain to figure out how to carry it. She ran around each end, nipping at the frayed wood. Occasionally she'd manage to grasp a chunk of it, only to have it come away from the mother stick when she pulled.

"I can relate," I told her.

Simon belly-laughed. "No kidding."

"So, now that your blood is pumping, any revelations?" I asked.

"We need to change the narrative," he said. "The rock. And the threatening note. They'll be key. We'll have the handwriting analyzed, but I'm suspecting Amanda wrote the note. And also, Inge's statement, along with Corinda's semi-confession. Oh, and the contract she signed with your brother. We have the pieces; we just need to balance the defensive with the offensive. One thing is weighing in our favor, though. Inge's stealing the evidence that the sloppy detective work forgot to bag. They can't pin it on you hiding evidence, right?"

"I suppose. But she did yank it from under my bed."

"The bed Corinda last slept in, you mean."

"Ah. There's that, I suppose. I'd like to see those fuckers locked up, and that includes Corinda," I said, surprising myself with the veracity of the statement.

"That's a reasonable goal," he said. "But justice takes a while. Especially these days with all the QAnon-supporting judges, and the so-called 'jury of peers' in a state that's deeply red, all this adds a new wrinkle."

His words knocked into me like a stiff gust. The horrifying truth of them. I'd grown up in the shadow of racial injustice, never feeling directly targeted, but never truly accepted. As a young child, I'd adopted my mother's syntax, her accent. She'd dress me like a precious antique doll—complete with frills and bows—when the other girls wore Target jumpsuits and rompers, or jeans and flannel shirts. I stood out like a plastic orchid in a field of sunflowers. *Chink* was a common epithet—ignorant as my classmates were regarding the vast array of Asian identities. Kento, who wore normal clothes, but looked more Japanese, was bullied until he realized sports prowess was his in. He excelled at tennis and soccer, and by high school he became one of the most popular boys, especially after he and Corinda hooked up.

But over the past decade, things had changed in Steeplejack. Neighbors who'd once gently ribbed one another for their political leanings were now shunning folks on the other side of the ideological divide. *Chink* and *fag* and *homo* and even the N-word were no longer off limits. And on the other side, *QAnon crazy, anti-vax nut job, Nazi,* and similar labels were lobbed like snowballs in a never-ending fight.

Common sense, critical thinking, truth—all were swept under a carpet of religiosity, conspiracy theory, and fear. The cut-and-dry attempted murder of my brother, backed by evidence, had been twisted by the perpetrators of a senseless vendetta. I had zero confidence that, if our case went to trial, a jury would convict Arthur. And now with this accident, and Inge muddying the waters, who knew what outlandish gaslighting would be tossed into the litigation arena.

Greta managed to get her mouth around a skinny part of the stick, and dragged it to Simon, where he engaged her in a game of tug. I watched them play. The faux growling, the wagging puff of a tail. A contract between dog and guardian. My fingers were starting to sting from the cold, though, and anxiety began to grip my gut. "We should turn back," I suggested.

Simon let go of the stick, and Greta fumbled backwards with her prize.

We were halfway down the trail, when my phone, abruptly back in a service area, dinged with several messages and missed calls. Kento.

"Oh dear," I said as I listened to voicemail.

"What now?" said Simon.

I turned the screen around, and he read the succession of messages.

"That's a very bad idea," said Simon. "Can you call him? Have him reconsider?"

"He called from the airplane, awaiting takeoff, so, that air-ship has sailed. Or flown."

What was my brother thinking, coming here? Defying his doctor's orders, not to mention our legal strategy.

"We should head him off at the pass," said Simon. "The last thing we need is for your brother to derail our plan."

Not that we had actually hammered out a viable plan, but I held my tongue.

I TEXTED KENTO THAT WE'D MEET HIM at the hospital, cautioning against his impulsive decision to confront Corinda in the ICU before we had a chance to update him. By the time it took to hike back to the ex-in-law's house, dig the car out, and negotiate the icy streets, Kento had arrived, Ubered, and installed himself in the hospital's holiday-festooned lobby.

Kento was naturally lean, but with all the trauma and surgery he looked gaunt standing there, leaning up against a candy-cane ribboned pillar. I moved in for a hug, but he cautioned me away—his midsection still tender from his wounds. I realized that he'd never met Simon, and I introduced them, hoping they wouldn't immediately become adversaries. They shook hands tentatively, their expressions neutral.

Simon caught Kento up on the latest complication, and Kento's palm rose to stop him. "I know all about it," Kento said. "I'm actually here because Corinda reached out. I thought I made that clear in my message."

For some reason, my brother's brush with death had jarred loose a snarkiness in his normally sweet disposition. I wasn't sure how I felt about his new take-charge attitude.

"She's pretty erratic," Simon stated. "And vulnerable. I don't think we can trust her motives."

"I know her pretty well, Mr. Aaronson," Kento said.

"Simon," said Simon.

"One thing I'm pretty sure about is, she doesn't want anything to happen to the baby," Kento said. "And neither do I."

"I understand," said Simon. "But because of the legal issues, it isn't wise to make contact."

Kento's face registered pain. He shouldn't even be out of bed, let alone travel to another state in the midst of a winter storm.

"Kento," I said, "let's get something to eat and talk this out."

Kento glared at me. "There's nothing to talk out. I'm here, and I'm going to see her."

Simon opened his mouth to protest, but I preempted him. "Fine. But be quick. Don't linger or get her riled up. We'll wait here, in the atrium."

Kento struggled to walk; hunched and laboring, he shuffled down the hall toward a bank of elevators.

"I wish you would have stopped him," said Simon, his voice taking a wistful, almost childlike, tone.

I felt the urge to defend Kento, but Simon wasn't wrong. Every move we'd made regarding Corinda and the Blairs had tightened the knot of injustice. I realized that we'd listened to our better selves, our humanity, at the cost of common sense. We were prey. They were hunters. We kept stumbling into their traps.

"He might," I said, "manage to get through to her. If anyone can, it's him. Her bitterness and the lies are all because she loves him and can't have him. Maybe the accident knocked some sense into her."

Simon placed a hand on my shoulder. A tender gesture that caught me off guard, and I backed away. He stepped closer.

"Hazel, you walk around with rose-filtered glasses, and that's admirable. But some folks are irredeemable. I'm pretty sure the Blairs—including Corinda—meet that criteria."

I could tell he thought Ethan belonged in that category as well.

"I agree with you," I said. "But hate doesn't solve anything."

"No," he said, "it doesn't. And a jury will likely align with your compassion and fairness."

"And yet, I'm the town freak because I draw dead people in varying stages of decomposition. Forget that my renderings have resulted in criminal apprehensions and convictions, half the population of Steeplejack thinks I'm some kind of witch."

"But the other half thinks you're a hero, right?"

"Hero? Please. I have a few friends. Freaks, like me. But most of the artsy crowd fled Steeplejack after high school for the cities and never looked back."

"So I have to ask, why did you move back?"

"Believe me, I ask myself that very question daily. At first, it was because of my parents and their failing health, but then Ethan and I got back together, and I just one-day-at-a-timed myself into a life."

Someone had been asleep at the switch with the holiday music, but a shift change had likely occurred, and suddenly "Frosty the Snowman" echoed off the atrium rafters. "Ugh. This song is the worst" I said, saltily.

"Is it though?" said Simon, rhythmically tapping a boot on the overly polished floor.

"Frosty" bled into "White Christmas" bled into "Hark the Herald Angels Sing" and Kento was still not back. My spidey twin sense was stirring up some doom. I texted him for an ETA, and the message went through but didn't say *delivered*. They were a bit fussy about cell phone usage in the critical care unit. I wondered if that Nurse Ratched had made him turn it off.

"Should I go check on him?" I asked.

Simon met my eyes and shook his head, then, his eyes focused on something else behind the towering Christmas tree.

"Uh oh," he said.

I followed his gaze. Two FBI agents were headed in the direction of the ICU.

I texted Kento again, including a row of exclamations with my missive: FBI HEADED YOUR WAY.

"Why would they be here?"

"Hate crime," he said.

"The note on the rock? You didn't have time to…"

"I had my intern head over to your house and bring the evidence to the firm. I think they got the feds involved."

Simon gave me the ten-cent explanation: Since Patrick was involved in the crime against Leona and Marcia, the FBI had already been tracking his movements. Now Corinda was involved as a suspect, witness or corroborator, and part of declaring Patriot Root a domestic terrorist organization.

I felt a bolt of annoyance rush to my mouth. "How much of that did you already know? Didn't you think you should have shared those details?"

Simon grasped my shoulders and looked me piercingly in the eye. "The fluidity of the situation made it impossible to know for sure and I didn't want to rile you up. But those guys, if they are indeed headed for Corinda, that's good news, isn't it?"

Was it? "What about Kento? Remember the witness tampering warning you gave me?"

"Yeah, not ideal that he's likely at her bedside right now."

"Fuck."

Simon rubbed his chin in an odd, professorial gesture. "Your brother's visit muddies the waters," he said. "But she is carrying his baby, so I think we need to cite that as his motive for flying over here."

"Plus, there's probably phone recordings of her calling Kento, right?" I added, trying to convince the skeptical jury in my brain.

"Depends on what's on those recordings, and who called who."

"It's Beginning to Look A Lot Like Christmas" blasted out the sound system. "So much for honoring an other-than-Christian response to the winter solstice," I murmured.

"Yeah, well, this hospital does start with the word Saint," said Simon.

"Point taken," I said.

We found a bank of empty seats facing the hall where the agents had marched through. I hadn't realized how sore my legs were until we sat. The short hike through snow had worn me out. I was dying for an espresso, and I searched the surrounding area for confirmation that a café existed amid the Christmassy set-up.

"I need caffeine," I said, as I rose to follow what looked like promising signage at the far end of the atrium. "Want anything?"

Simon offered a complicated response: matcha latte with three inches of oat milk and a pump of almond.

"I'm shocked you don't have diabetes," I grumbled.

"Hey, hold on a sec," Simon called as I began my sojourn.

I pivoted to see Kento creeping toward us, his limp more pronounced, his mouth in full-on grimace.

"What the fuck?" he said, in greeting.

"Sit," I commanded, pointing the seat I'd just vacated.

"The FBI? Really?" Kento said, directing his verbal indictment at Simon.

Simon stood over Kento, imploring him to lower his voice via pantomime. He whispered, "Tell us what happened."

"I was getting through to her," Kento said. "I told her that we could start fresh, but she needed to own up to Arthur's involvement. She needed to recant her self-defense story. I promised we'd have our lawyers work out an abused wife defense. That's a thing, right?" He directed his plea to Simon.

Simon breathed in, hard. Now that I knew how annoyance and alarm registered on his face, I expected a barrage of scolds directed at my brother. But instead, Simon praised Kento.

"You're on the right track," he said. "Your impulses were solid. Unfortunately, your visit to Corinda might be interpreted differently by the agents."

"They barged right in, despite the objections of the nursing staff. They knew who I was, too, and tried to question me—"

"I hope you didn't say anything," Simon and I said, simultaneously.

"Well, seeing as you're not my attorney, and I didn't have one in my back pocket, I couldn't exactly demand—"

"What did you say?" I yelled.

"Shh," said Simon.

"I told them Corinda was innocent," Kento said, a question in his upspeak.

"What?" I said.

"I figured it was a perfect time to gain her trust. I mean, they were grilling her and everything. She was sobbing. I just wanted to show

her I had her back, so I told them she wasn't responsible for the vandalism. For the rock and the note. I told them it was all her vindictive
ex-husband and stepson."

Simon's face crumpled.

"Dude," I said, stepping between them, "I appreciate you trying to
help, but Corinda was guilty. *Is* guilty. And now, if she wants to fight
for custody for the baby she's carrying, you've just weakened your case."

Kento looked as though I'd just hit him in the head with that
very rock.

"The whole thing has grown more complicated because of the accident,
and Inge's drunkenness coming from your sister's house," said Simon.

"Silver Bells" crooned through the atrium. Silver fucking bells.

"So what do we do now?" I said, into the void.

"We need to get back to Steeplejack and prepare," Simon said. "We
leave first thing in the morning, and Kento, you're coming with us."

# TWENTY-ONE

THE DRIVE HOME WAS SLOW and fraught with closures, but despite the lingering foul weather we arrived safely in Steeplejack on Christmas Eve. We'd all agreed to keep our phones off while we navigated the snowy passes and the icy roads. Getting home alive was the main prerogative, and in service to that, we needed to have uninterrupted time to develop our plan. The last thing we needed was to let the chaotic new developments and their ensuing messengers of doom blast us off course.

As soon as we pulled into the driveway, Kento turned on his phone to let Tom know he was still in one piece. Tom had indeed called and texted several times, but when Kento phoned, it went straight to voicemail.

"He's probably at his parents' for their annual bitch fest," Kento said.

I shot him a look. What had happened to my docile, sweet twin? "I thought I was the snarky one here," I said.

"They haven't been all that supportive," Kento said. "To put it mildly."

Simon scurried out of my car and began scraping ice off his, which was still, in its slightly dented posture, parked diagonally near the spur to the trailer house. Greta leaped and jumped, so happy to be liberated from the back seat of my car.

"I know this is a lot to ask, especially given all you two have been through this past couple of weeks, but would you mind if I left Greta here for the day? I—"

"Not a problem," I offered. "You get going. I imagine there's a lot to catch up on at BB&A HQ."

Simon ceased his scraping and turned toward me. "You're a lifesaver. Thank you."

I left my car downhill from the house, as the last third of the driveway was a steep sheet of ice. Kento stood shivering between the car and the big house. His arms were tucked tight, his gaze pointed at the frosty ground.

"Well, c'mon then," I beckoned.

"I need a minute," he said.

A bolt of reality cut the air between us. This would be his first time here since the shooting.

"Maybe we could get you set up in the trailer house?" I suggested.

He nodded stiffly.

"And maybe I could hang with you down here?"

That idea relaxed him, and we got busy. A pipe had frozen, so there was that, and the pilot light on the propane heater was being its usual stubborn self, flickering and popping off every few minutes. But troubleshooting regular life stuff was preferable to perseverating on our legal quicksand. We'd leave that to Simon.

We continued in our respective tasks wordlessly. I heated a can of Progresso navy bean soup and cut the eyes out of a few potatoes before chopping them into a boiling pot of water.

"Wow, you learned how to cook? Sort of," Kento said after giving up on the heater and unearthing a box of outerwear—which included some of Ethan's adolescent fleeces—a perfect fit for my emaciated brother.

Ethan had been the foodie in our coupledom. Our divide-and-conquer life had been a bit of traditional gender reversal. I chopped wood; he carried water. As far as I was concerned, God created Grubhub for a reason. I found a dusty bottle of Veuve Clicquot left over from our wedding, and marched it outside to a small snowdrift. It *was* Christmas Eve, after all.

Back in the kitchen, Kento was stirring the boiling soup. The steam and his recent activity had pinked his cheeks, and he looked more like the brother I'd grown up with. His usually shorn and styled hair had grown out, and its untidiness complemented his youthful, hopelessly angelic, face.

"Should we find a secular holiday playlist on ye old music app?" I suggested.

"Something instrumental, perhaps?" he said.

I scrolled through my Spotify and commanded Alexa to ignite our air with Henry Smith's piano renditions of the same shit we were listening to at St. Alphonsus. But here, in our modest trailer house, "A Holly Jolly Christmas" via piano bar riff felt just perfect.

We Champagne-toasted, and slurped our soup-and-potato dinner at the small table that once graced our childhood home while the music wrapped its familiar, Pavlovian schmaltz around our brains.

After we'd helped ourselves to seconds, I brought up one of the elephants that had been sitting quietly between us. "You and Tom okay?"

One side of Kento's mouth curled up. His tell for *it's complicated*. "He's trying," Kento said, after a beat.

I sympathized. "Yeah, it's been a lot to ask of any partner. Not to mention the sheer financial impact what with paying Corinda and now medical bills. I—"

Kento knew what was on the tip of my tongue. I wanted to help. At least with the legal charges that were mounting. But even with my solid widow windfall, I'd be pressed to finish the big house and foot the various bills.

"I'm not here to screw up your life any more than I already have, Sis," he said.

"None of this is your fault," I started.

"Yeah, it is. You warned me about getting retangled with Corinda. I didn't listen. And that's become a bit of an issue between me and Tom."

"I'm so sorry. Who knew she was this screwed up?"

"I did. I dated her, remember? It's just, when you yearn for something so much, you trick yourself into deflecting any argument. I now understand how a person can thwart their own critical thinking abilities."

"Ergo, your enmeshment with QAnon Corinda," I said.

"Yeah, I guess."

Before I could rethink the boldness of my big question, out it came. "Why do you want to have a kid so bad, anyway? What is driving it?"

He paused mid-spoonful. "Do you remember what Dad said to me when I came out to him?"

I did not, but I did remember that Kento and Tom held hands at his deathbed, and the look of confusion on Dad's face.

"Told me that his only regret was he didn't kick my ass harder. Called me a pussy."

I hadn't heard him say that, exactly, but I didn't doubt it.

Kento cleared his throat the way our father used to, before going off on one of his tirades. "'I'm glad your lot will never have sons, so you'll never be as disappointed as you've made me.'" Kento's affectation of our father's gravelly voice was so spot-on, I got chills.

"So you want to prove him wrong? You're having a spite child? He's dead, Kento. That ship has sailed."

"Says the woman obsessed with drawing death."

*Ouch!*

I fired back. "What's that supposed to mean?"

"It's your way of proving they can't hurt you anymore. Listen, I've had years of therapy. At least, with Corinda, it's the devil I know."

"Why not just adopt?" I said, regretting the insensitivity as soon as I spoke it.

He got that I got the answer. His head cocked cynically. The country was tiptoeing politically right, election-by-election. All it would take is a Republican governor in Washington State, a few more right-wing senators, one more life-term Supreme Court justice on the side of fear, and adoption by a gay couple would be a Sisyphean climb, involving state-hopping and continual legal intervention.

I watched Kento methodically spoon soup into his mouth. Despite his recent weight loss, he was still so beautiful. The twin who got the looks, the bastard. I recalibrated my tone.

"Hey," I said. "We don't usually dwell on trips down Memory Lane, but if you had to pull a pleasant recollection from your hard drive, do any benevolent ghosts of Christmas past bubble up?"

He paused mid-bite again and stared at the wall behind me. "Hmm," he said. "How about the year they bought us matching banana seat bikes?"

"Those red ones they got second-hand?" I said, half-recalling their scratches and perpetually flat tires. "You actually have fond memories of that Christmas? Wasn't that one of the ones where Dad stormed out of the house, calling us ungrateful brats?"

Kento chuckled. "Well, after that, remember, he came home with two Hawaiian pizzas and a Costco tub of licorice?"

Our father's way of apologizing was treating us to foods we loved, but he hated. A sort of unspoken penance. What came to my mind about that particular Christmas was our mother's overcompensating for our father's tantrum. She offered to replace the tires on the bikes and buff out the scratches, and gave us beaters to lick during a baking spree. Our mother channeled anxiety by cooking excessively, and that Christmas the oven never turned off.

Unlike Kento, the red bike Christmas would not register in my fond memories bank. But there was another one. "The Christmas Dad was sober? The year before Mom's cancer diagnosis," I said.

"Junior year of college," Kento said. "That was a good holiday."

Neither of us could remember the gifts we exchanged or the meals, but we agreed that with the lack of drama and chaos, it had been the only peaceful family Christmas in our family of origin.

"And somehow," Kento said, "I was still on edge. Waiting for Dad to hit the bottle, and go on a drunken tirade."

"We actually watched 'It's a Wonderful Life' together, remember?" I said. "Mom and Dad held hands?"

"Maybe they already knew," Kento said. "About the cancer."

I refilled our Solo cups with bubbly, and we moved to the sofa, snuggling under a slightly moldy quilt, Greta curled at my feet. I found a channel that played "It's a Wonderful Life" on a loop until our lids grew heavy and we dozed off, our heads leaned against each other.

# TWENTY-TWO

I AWOKE TO THE SOUND OF MY BROTHER'S arguing voice.
I tried not to eavesdrop, but with Kento, I was programmed to react
whenever I sensed something awry. He was on the defensive, and clearly
upset. The words from his side, *I'm doing the best I can*, and *Why won't
you support this,* and *I don't understand*. No I love yous. No Yuletide
blessings.

The janky front door tried to slam behind him, but the cheap hollow
core of it prevented a satisfying bang. By the time I stumbled off the
couch in futile search for coffee, Kento had left the property on foot.

I knew a domestic argument when I heard it, and my heart hurt
for him. I was halfway pulled together for the rescue operation when
Simon roared into the driveway.

I popped out to intercept him, Greta bouncing along at my heels.
I imagined Simon would guess we were in the big house, but, to my
surprise, he had Kento with him. Better than that, Simon was carrying
a tray of coffees from the miraculously open Starbucks.

"Ho, ho, ho," he chanted, holding out the cardboard carrier of caffeine.

"Life saver," I said.

Kento begrudgingly took one of the coffees, his face screwed up in snarl.

"You're welcome," Simon chimed.

"To what do we owe this gift-bearing visit?" I said.

"Finally, a bit of good news," said Simon.

We walked back into the chilly interior of the trailer house, and
Simon caught us up.

"Inge admitted that it was her booze, and she returned the knife. She elected to stay locked up rather than try for bail. Apparently, she has nowhere to go."

"Woman really was homeless then, eh?" I said. Surprisingly, I felt a wave of sadness wash over me for the Crazy Cat Lady, who was actually a Crazy Car-Camping Thieving Cat Lady.

"So she's looking at what? Vehicular homicide?" Kento said.

"It's vehicular manslaughter versus gross vehicular manslaughter," said Simon. "It's one year in jail, versus four. Essentially. But if we can show that Patrick was driving recklessly, or that he also was intoxicated, she might walk. She's got a public defender on it. I hope they don't drop the ball."

I remembered Patrick's aggressive behavior toward me in the parking lot at Grief Group, not to mention the rock and threat situation just prior to the accident.

I said, "Gross manslaughter. Hmm. That sounds like something made up by a teenager."

"But there's some not great news, too," said Simon.

Kento and I traded glances. We were so used to bad being folded into good. Ruining it. Stinking it up.

"Let us have it," Kento said.

"Corinda and Arthur are going to fight you for custody of the baby. Sole custody."

"Fuck!" screamed Kento. "I fucking *knew* it."

Greta barked and raced up to my brother, alert with that dog sense that something had gone horribly wrong.

"But," said Simon, "and this is a big qualifier, the petition was filed the day before the accident. Things may have changed since then."

"Yeah, I think it's premature to freak out," I said, directing my caution at Kento who was, indeed, freaking out. Pacing, swearing, muttering.

Simon, as alarmed as Greta at Kento's unglued behavior, strode up to him, and forcibly placing both hands on his shoulders, said, "We can't have you losing it every time we meet an obstacle. There's already speculation about—"

He trailed off. A knot fisted its way into my gut. "Speculation about?"

Simon still had hold of my brother's shoulders, trying to pry Kento's eyes up to his own. "You know how much fire the LGBTQ community faces in any custody suit, right? The assholes are just waiting for an excuse to point and say, 'told you he's unbalanced.'"

Kento shrugged Simon's paws off him. "I'm aware," he said.

"Good. Calm heads must prevail. We have an excellent case. If this were in Washington instead of Idaho, it'd be a slam-dunk. But things have gotten trickier with the anti-gay legislation around here. The folks trying to legitimize hate as an option. Relitigating legislation. We have got to be above scrutiny, do you understand? And it starts with how we handle ourselves these next few months. Both in the depo, and in court. And, of course, in the media."

"Kento," I said, the knot tightening, "what was that call with Tom about?"

Kento slumped. "I just thought we'd have a better chance if I divorced Tom and agreed to marry Corinda."

My worst fear, recognized, I unleashed. "What? Did you forget she's still married to someone else? No wonder Tom's pissed off."

"It would just be a paper thing. Tom and I would still be together." Kento resumed his pacing. He reminded me of one of the raccoons my father used to catch in his live traps.

Whenever Kento got worked up, the tips of his ears reddened. Right now, they were candy-cane red.

"You cannot afford to piss off your life partner, Kento," I said. "Tom has been your advocate through all of this. Also, it's possible that he's the biological father, isn't it? If it comes down to a paternity test, and Tom has been shoved to the sideline, how would that work?"

Kento simmered in his brooding. His arms tucked in tight, pout on his face. Such a child sometimes.

"If the baby goes full term, it'll be born in three months, right? We have three months to sort this all out," said Simon.

"Meantime," I said, "Merry Christmas?"

# PART THREE

# TWENTY-THREE

LIKE ALL THINGS THAT HERALD A SWERVE in my future, my day began with an unexpected knock at the door. I'd been putting the finishing touches on a forensic sketch of a serial hit-and-run perp, and had my Beats on, so I didn't hear it until the knocking had reached pounding.

"Hey, Benjamin, what's got you all fired up this morning?"

Benjamin Kreutz, purveyor of shitty news, was catching his breath. "Give—me—"

The day was unseasonably warm for mid-March, and Benjamin's pits had bled sweat circles through his T-shirt. I yanked my noise-canceling headphones off and craned my neck for a glimpse behind him. "You ran here?"

"Riot," he said, between puffs. "Them militia folk are on the march."

I had been warned about that possibility since our depositions and court dates had been postponed until next week, when Corinda was expected to be fully recovered from her injuries, the baby due date still two weeks off. Things had been relatively calm with all the legal tussle handled quietly, in the background. Simon, who had kept his distance since Christmas, kept his communication scant. Since the Kwaiken knife had been compromised, it was no longer evidence, and I'd rented a storage unit for the various family heirlooms I hadn't offloaded to my brother. In other matters, I chalked up Simon's low-key contact to a classic No News is Good News paradigm. In spite of that, my bank account had taken a hit, with monthly BB&A statements dinging my inbox with annoying regularity, so I'd taken on twice the usual amount of gigs.

Benjamin was a bit of a drama nut, but the fear on his face, his breathlessness, was over the top, even for him. "On the march? Riot? Where?"

He pointed down my driveway. "They're assembling over to Blair's house. I think they're coming for you."

"For me?"

"In town this morning, at Helen's bakery, I overheard them saying you built the house up here to groom children. That your brother and you are turning kids queer."

If I'd had a beverage in my mouth, I'd have sprayed it all over him with the raspberry guffaw that broke out my lips. "That's absurd, Ben. You know that's just a bunch of crazies spouting weird conspiracies."

"They were serious, Hazel. They're coming up here."

"To do what?" I opened my door wider, as if to prove I wasn't harboring any children.

Benjamin peered over my shoulder, as if needing to see for himself that no Pizzagate level of fantastical malfeasance was taking place.

"Kento isn't here, is he?"

Kento was not here. Not this week. He and Tom had been struggling, and my brother had been commuting to and from Seattle in the face of their difficulties. Corinda, still healing from the accident, had returned to the house she shared with her felonious husband. Neither Kento nor I had heard from her, probably on the advice of the Blairs' high-powered lawyers.

"Do you have a gun?" Benjamin asked.

"Several. Inherited from my father. But they're locked up in a storage unit. Empty of bullets."

"You might think about gettin' a couple loaded up's all's I'm sayin'."

I held my rendering pencil aloft. "What happened to the pen being mightier than the sword?"

The attempt at a joke sailed over Benjamin's head, and he took in a fresh inhale.

"Want to come in for a cuppa?" I said.

"A cuppa whata?"

"Coffee, Benjamin."

"You have decaf? Doc says I have to stick to the decaf."

"I have iced tea. Herbal."

Benjamin stomped in with his mud-clung boots, after half-heartedly kicking clumps off on the mat. My *Please remove your shoes* sign went unread—or, more likely, read and ignored. He trudged in and mounted one of my new bar stools, his gaze shifting like a panoramic camera. I pulled a pitcher of sun tea from the fridge.

Benjamin whistled. "Quite a fancy place ya built yourself."

"Mm. So, what exactly did you hear in town?"

"Oh, it's bad. Like I said, they think you're running some sorta *homo-sex-shul* game up in here. Takin' runaways and foster kids, maybe even some locals, and showin' them vids and what not."

"Oh, brother. Who is behind this fantasy, anyway? Besides Arthur."

"Well, two of 'em, I never seen before, but there was a couple of men been holed up with Arthur ever since his Patrick got killed in that accident. Them's from Utah, I think? Or maybe Arizona. They been flashing your logo around town, too."

Since my brand had been usurped, I had to ditch the Bitterroot Renderings logo, and recreate it from scratch, lest I be mistaken for a White Nationalist, anti-gay, Nazi thug. I hated the fact that I had to change the art *I'd* created because these nefarious assholes stole my identity.

"I'm telling yous; better get prepared. They'll be up here later today, sure as rain."

I filled a couple jelly jars with ice cubes and peach-ginger tea, my head spinning with next steps. "I suppose we could call Detective Coulter, tell him what you overheard?"

Benjamin shook a finger at that idea. "Nah, he won't do nothin'. He's one of them."

I had my suspicions about that as well, but there was no way I was going to call him on what could amount to idle gossip. I slid the icy beverage in front of Benjamin.

"I need to call my lawyer, I think."

"That Simon Aaronson is kinda got a bullseye on his back, too. Folks talking about him like he's got a thing for boys just like your brother. Him with that poodle and all."

"Jesus, are people really that lame? The poodle belonged to his ex. His *wife*. And so what if he is gay? Is that their agenda? To rid Steeplejack of citizens who aren't cisgendered heterosexual cave-dwellers?"

"Huh?" said Benjamin.

While Benjamin slurped his tea, I slipped out to the porch for the phone call I dreaded making. Kento picked up before the first ring.

"You have news?" he said, anxiously.

"Sort of. But not about the baby or the legal stuff."

I gave my brother the short version, ending with a suggestion that we stay in a hotel in Coeur d'Alene for next week's deposition.

"Fuck that. I'm sick of being bullied," Kento said.

"Hate to ask, but what's the latest with you and Tom?"

"Working on it," he said, grumpily.

Benjamin flew out the door, waving his cell phone at me. "They're on their way! Look, I just got this text from Burt Kingset, down on Main."

"Who?" Kento said, overhearing, "the mob? Go get Dad's 45."

I was flanked by hysterical men, one in my ear, one on my porch.

"I'll do no such thing," I said, but my heartbeat was revving. I hung up on Kento and dialed Simon directly. I wasn't about to get tangled in BB&A's automated phone nightmare.

"Hazel?" he said, in the same anxious tone that Kento had greeted me. Was it me? Was I inspiring dread, like a Grim Reaper?

"You hear anything about a militia rally? Apparently, I'm about to be swarmed by White Supremacists. Should we alert those federal agents?"

The feds had shown initial interest due to the uptick in hate crimes throughout the Silver Valley, but someone in seniority had pulled them away since we'd not been killed or maimed in the rock incident. *Stretched thin*, was the official excuse.

"I'll be right over," he said, and abruptly hung up.

I turned to Benjamin who was scrolling on his late model iPhone. For a yokel, he was surprisingly tech savvy.

"I got this covered, Ben. You can be on your way."

He looked up, a pout forming. "Serious? I would think you'd want a witness or at least someone to help you stand yer ground."

It was a sweet gesture. Benjamin Kreutz had been one of my dad's best pals back in his trash hauling days. He'd been one of the last people to visit while Dad was suffering with advanced cirrhosis, he'd given Dad a deathbed promise to "look after yer girl." I felt a well of tears climb up my sinuses.

"Last thing I want, Ben, is to put you in peril. Simon is coming over. He's good at de-escalation."

"The poodle guy? Please."

I patted Benjamin's back in a parting gesture, the way my father used to do when a conversation was over for him, and Benjamin understood. It was, perhaps, one of the unconscious reasons I'd moved back. Familiar body language. Shorthand. The stuff that roots so deep in your fiber, it'd take decades to untangle.

BENJAMIN LEFT AND FIVE MINUTES LATER, Simon roared up the driveway. His bumper still hung lopsided, unfixed since the Inge fender-bender during the ice storm. Greta wasn't with him, and I was surprised that I felt a twinge of disappointment. He wrestled his trunk open to reveal some video equipment, tripods, and a length of electrical cord.

"Is that really necessary?"

He lugged an armful to my porch, dumping the mess on my newly refinished teak. "It is if we want to document these crazies in a way that gets the public's attention. Think George Floyd. Think Charlottesville."

"Can't we handle this diplomatically, though? Last thing I need is reporters driving me crazy while I'm trying to earn a living."

Simon winced. He clearly realized that his legal fees had thrust me into a scramble for gigs. "I hear that," he said, but kept right on setting up his not-so-candid camera on the porch, and followed that with some more stealthily positioned tech in the house.

After everything was installed, we sat on the porch with more iced tea, in wait, the elephant between us, until I just burst out with it. "You've been keeping your distance, I've noticed."

Simon raked his fingers through sweat-tinged hair. He'd grown it long, and it gave him a boyish look. "Yes. Well. Apparently, my billable hours had dropped over the holidays. The partners hauled me in for a talking to."

A slither of guilt squeezed my stomach. "I know our unsanctioned, spontaneous trip to Boise probably didn't go over too well, and I had a feeling you talked the firm out of billing me round the clock hours. So thank you for that."

He waved me off with his iced tea hand.

"You're a kind man, Simon," I said.

"And you're a brave woman," he said, quickly, "after everything you've been through."

I despised being thought of as a victim, and the guilt in my belly morphed into heat. "I'm not a fan of pity," I said, sharply.

He tipped his head, side-eyeing me. "I don't pity you. I'm actually astonished at your coping skills. That balance, centered-ness. It's rare."

"For a woman?" I said, snarkily, filling in the blank.

"For anyone. Listen, this might be unprofessional of me, but I can't help comparing you to my ex. In your position right now, she'd be flipping out."

I laughed. "Who says I'm not? Kento is driving me nuts. And if Corinda crossed my path right now, I'd probably punch her. Not in the belly, obviously."

"I can't say as I'd blame you, but that might complicate things, yeah?"

"Right. Listen, Corinda is like a pesky coyote that keeps sneaking into the hen house and poaching chickens. Been that way since we were kids. She's sneaky, selfish, and, frankly, stupid. Like, dropped on her head as a baby stupid. It's as if she's blind to the right path, and keeps choosing the one that leads to a quicksand bog, thinking that if she tries it just one more time, a diamond mine will replace the sucking mud."

Simon nodded. "Boy, do I know the type."

I fiddled with my wedding ring. "Thing is, after everything, I can't rustle up the gumption to hate her."

"We shouldn't hate," he said, in a half-mocking tone.

We were on refill three of our iced teas when the sound of chanting filled the air.

"Here we go," said Simon, his fingers working on a series of buttons on a remote-control device.

As the mob approached, their sickening chants became clear. Over and over they screamed, "BLOOD AND SOIL, YOUR KIND WILL BOIL! IN HELL! IN HELL!"

The "in hell" sounding like *heil*, and I was sure it wasn't an accident. As they crunched up the driveway the chant morphed into, "GAYS WILL NOT REPLACE US!" before returning to the hybridized Nazi one about blood and soil.

Simon and I stood at the top of the porch steps, our arms crossed, stock still as Buckingham Palace guards. There were a couple dozen of them, led by men I didn't know. Behind the first wave of intruders, some semi-familiar faces, embellished with war paint, seemed the most vocal. They were a rather stocky bunch. Most of them sweating profusely, wiping their foreheads with their branded bandanas—the brand being the one appropriated from me. I glanced down the driveway to discern a whinny that rose from the crowd, and, sure enough, bringing up the rear was Arthur himself, positioned on a swayback horse, brandishing a pole vault pole in the air in front of him.

To be sure, they were a motley crew of amateurs, as if they'd been dressed for a take-your-White-Supremacist-to-work day.

"Oh, brother," I muttered as they marched to the base of my steps.

"Where is he?" growled the fattest of the mob—a man so sweaty and labored of breath, I wondered if I'd be administering CPR before the afternoon was over.

"He?" I said.

"The sodomite! Your kin."

"Sodomite? Really?"

He peeled an index card from his fanny pack and read it in what he likely guessed was a preachery voice: "For there is no authority except from God, and the authorities that exist are appointed by God. Therefore, whoever resists the authority resists the ordinance of God, and those who resist will bring judgment on themselves. Romans, thirteen."

Simon piped up, "That's your justification for trespassing here? You do know you're on private property, right?"

The fanny pack guy continued, "Paul called homosexuals unnatural. *Para physin*. That means against nature, college boy. And therefore, we have a God-given right to cleanse this valley of illegal fornication and buggery."

"Paul, Jesus, you Klansmen types, or whoever you think you're quoting is moot. You are still breaking the law right now."

Arthur trotted his nag forward while Fanny Pack's mouth opened and closed, his rebuttal stuck in his jiggly throat.

Arthur held his pole vault pole aloft and declared, "The evil in your house is responsible for my boy's death, and your Satan-loving brother dared put his seed in my wife. We've come for justice."

"Justice?" I laughed. "You shot my brother. Or did you forget that part. You shot him and then made up a cock-and-bull lie that it was self-defense."

"My only regret is that I didn't kill the bastard," he responded in a harsh tone that I hoped had been picked up by the microphone concealed in the arborvitae that fringed the porch. "He tricked my wife into being a incubator for his perverted scheme. That bugger lookin' to fill the world with his deviant kind."

"Where *is* Corinda, by the way?" I said.

"Never you mind where my wife be holed up. That witch you had lodgin' here nearly kilt her, too."

The chanting started up again, but it wasn't clear that they knew how to channel their hate since Kento wasn't here. Simon had suggested earlier that they picked this particular time to invade because it was the date of the annual St. Patrick's Day motorcycle parade, and local law enforcement was all tied up escorting the procession. Not to mention it being that particular saint's holiday, which, in Arthur's twisted mind, justified direct action in Patrick's name.

Arthur's horse lifted its tail and plopped some turds in my bed of daffodils.

Simon repeated the private property warning and suggested they celebrate hate somewhere else. He had a hard time concealing a smile, and I noticed, for the first time, he had a sizeable dimple in his right cheek when he grinned.

A bald bloke from the center of the mob raised a bullhorn to his lips and yelled, "Fucking foreigners. Faggots. You will not erase us."

That seemed to energize his countrymen and women, and they raised Hitlerian fists in unison. They inched forward, as one blobbish organism.

"Get off my property," I screamed over their chanting. The tenor had changed. They wanted satisfaction, and I realized in that split second that I might actually be in danger.

Arthur dismounted his horse and joined the mass of them as they advanced up the steps. Some of them wielding bats, they began their siege of my porch, kicking, swinging, throwing. The iced tea pitcher was the first casualty, hit with a good-sized river rock. Next, two young women grabbed the cushions off my porch furniture and began tearing the upholstery. Simon stood in front of the door to the house. His face, too, had changed, belying his worry as the frenzied mob turned violent. His gaze shifted to the places he'd set up his surveillance equipment. So far, they hadn't noticed it.

A metal flash of something in the bald guy's hand sent a chill through me. He was armed with what looked like a serrated fishing knife, and he was heading for the door.

"Simon, step aside," I shouted over the chants. "Get out of the way

186 | SUZY VITELLO

of that maniac!"

Simon dodged the knife-wielder and a six-pack of them rushed the door, bursting through it as though running from a fire. I stayed outside, figuring I was safer not following the mob.

"Told you!" I heard one of them scream. "She's a fucking witch!"

The sound of glass breaking confirmed my suspicions that they were addressing—and destroying—my recently hung Kusôzu series. A college portfolio project comprised of nine watercolors that I'd resurrected and put the finishing touches on only a month earlier, hung opposite the Triptych of my mother.

For the series, I'd used the image of a hunted elk, taking it from wounded to total decomposition. My heart tore with every crashing blow.

Simon did go in, though. He had thousands of dollars' worth of equipment inside. Also, I suspected, he wanted double video evidence, and was likely recording the goings on with his phone. My growing terror was mitigated by sheer audacity of this Christo-fascist mob.

Amid the chanting, the crashing, and the threats, another sound broke through. A series of SUVs roared up the driveway, and screeched to a halt inches from the porch. Federal agents disgorged from the vehicles, assault rifles taking aim. Arthur, still on the porch, vaulted the railing and ran toward his horse, who was calmly munching spring grass next to the house. One of the agents yelled for him to stop, but Arthur, still spry enough to leap, scrambled onto the nag, and loped down the hill while the mob, one-by-one, halted, as if engaged in a game of freeze tag.

There was little to no resistance, other than a chorus of whining and pleading, as the feds rounded up the two dozen or so rioters, and hauled them off, and I was left with a giant mess, which Simon documented before I brought out the brooms and shop vac. We'd given an official statement, and we were offered assurance that our recordings could, and would, be used in the legal action to follow.

"So, did someone from your office call them?" I asked Simon after the last of the FBI-emblazoned jackets had left.

"Nope," he said. "No idea who tipped them off."

Benjamin, I thought. Must have been.

Simon's cheeks were rosy, his brow beaded with sweat, and despite my better judgment, a pang of desire prickled.

Simon's expression changed from relief to curiosity as he took in my lascivious stare-down. He removed his glasses, cleaned the lenses with a shirttail, then placed them back on, as if he wanted to confirm the meaning behind my continued eye contact.

I'd never been the initiator with Ethan. Call it a case of gender conformity, or laziness, or, maybe, casual disinterest since we'd been together so long. But my hunger for Simon in that moment felt visceral. Felt biological. I'd always marveled at animals fucking. The way they went at it with unmitigated urgency. In college, I'd sketched a whole series of copulating creatures in my portfolio. Death and sex: the themes that most interested me. Did that make me a sicko? A voyeur?

I'd always thought myself a person of science, recording nature, never the participant. Never the subject. But that afternoon, post-raid, our glee at capturing it all on tape, my hunger for Simon, for climax, penetrated my curiosity. My need for his body was like a wolf tearing up an elk. I couldn't stop it.

I grabbed his hand and dragged him upstairs.

I pushed him down on my bed with one hand and peeled my sweatpants off with the other. I relieved him of his freshly de-smeared glasses.

He responded, fully aroused, but slightly sheepish, bending a leg to hide his excitement.

"Hello, there," I whispered as I pushed his knee down and cupped the clothed tent of him as if I were about to mold clay into a cylinder.

"Are you sure about this," he rasped, one hand on each of my shoulders, pushing me away from his erection.

I swatted his arms, flailing like a caught bird, before zeroing in on his belt, then his zipper. He let out a guttural groan through grit teeth, his intellect fighting his nature. Out of instinct, I longed to draw his face in mid-grimace. The desire. The denial of desire. My mouth found his lips. He tasted lemony from the tea. I nipped, tongued, pulled away.

We were dancing a sort of horizontal tango, and his eyes opened wider, as he whispered, "You're so sexy. So beautiful."

I freed his cock from his trousers but marveled at its form beneath a pair of striped boxers. The hide-and-seek of it, pulsing, throbbing. I slid a hand through the opening and tugged. His groan, less voice, more coital lamentation. My cunt, electric jelly.

"I want you," I keened.

He pulled me against himself, then flipped me beneath him, his hands pinning my wrists. "What do you like?" he whispered.

He released his grip, licked his fingers and slid them down my body to my sex. His fingers played the folds of me until he found my clit. "Do you like this?"

My cunt was wet with want. My toes twitched and curled, and I wrapped my legs around his ass, pushing my pelvis against his fingers.

"I do," I panted. "But I don't have a uh anything—do you have some protection?"

Somehow shirts left our bodies. We were skin against skin, thrusting, wanting, pulsing. His cock twitched against my belly, and he nibbled my earlobe, whispering, "I had a vasectomy, and I haven't been with anyone since—"

He didn't say his ex-wife's name, but the image of Lucinda, her model looks, intruded just the same. For a brief moment the spell broke. Midnight, and my coach was again a pumpkin, my magic steeds once again, rats. But I pushed against the intrusion, my teeth finding Simon's earlobe, his collarbone.

"I want you inside me, now!" I ordered.

He flipped me over again.

"Not yet," he managed. "I want to see you come. I want to make you come. I want to see what your face does when you reach it."

Despite his professorial tone, the way he searched my face had me close. The penetration of his gaze made me shiver. Every nerve, every skin cell, firing. I squeezed his cock between my thighs, staring at him, him staring at me, a game of who'll blink first. Who will come first.

He cupped my ass and maneuvered my sex over the length of him. Another groan, and then his eyes squeezed shut as he plunged himself inside. I steadied myself on my forearms and ground my knees into the mattress, my tits enveloping his face. I yelled his name, pleading for a hard fuck. A fuck that I'd needed for more than a year-and-a-half. The empty, loneliness I'd lived since Ethan died, and even before he died, all that loss, it melted into joy. Into abundance, and he whispered exactly what I was feeling as he fucked me.

"You're so alive in there."

We moved like the tide, stuck together, the two lost souls of us, pining for release while wanting our fusion to continue. A paradox that joined yearning to yielding. Passion to completion.

A mini-wave crested in my belly. A small release, but there was more behind it. His breath became labored and forced as he moaned in the throes of pleasure. Again, we flipped and again I tightened my legs around him. His hands clawed my hair as he pushed into me once more, and that was it. My body, helpless under its molten eruption. His come cry, an animal release.

We stayed locked for a minute. Or an hour. Our heartbeats synching and slowing. Our minds, thankfully, not catching up to our bodies. Looking away, then teasingly, flirtingly, peeking back at one another. It had been so long since I'd been with someone for the first time, and first-time magic was its own universe. Neither of us wanting to break the spell by speaking.

Slowly, though, a gloomy cloud of awkwardness descended. We were in that place between ravished and detumescent. Too cynical for pillow talk. Too caring for dismissal. We'd crossed a line and there was no uncrossing it.

He broke the silence. "Take out?"

"That'd be good," I said.

"Thai or pizza?"

"Anything," I said. "As long as it's solid. After that gallon of iced tea, my eyeballs are floating."

   Awkwardness transcended, we both rose from the sex-smelling bed, and trotted off to separate bathrooms to pee.

# TWENTY-FOUR

I AWOKE TO THE SOUND OF HAIL rat-a-tatting on the solar roof above my head. The weather, overnight, had turned from unseasonably mild to near freezing. Spring in the Silver Valley.

Simon was a back sleeper, and he lay next to me, sprawled. In some ways, he resembled a baby. Rosy, chubby cheeks, long, dark lashes fluttering as he semi-snored. He'd asked me to wake him early, so he could get home to tend to Greta's needs, but early had passed us by hours earlier.

"Hey," I harsh-whispered into his closest ear. "Psst!"

His lips pursed and he burbled, then shook his head, his eyelids resisting the impulse to open. I'd interrupted a dream, and likely a pleasant one, given the status of his boner.

The morning after the first time was always awkward, in my recollection. Especially when the sex was lusty and carnal. After gobbling our delivered pad Thai, we'd returned to bed for an encore. We'd not been tender afterwards. No pillow talk, no intimate nuzzling. He passed out, and I scrolled my phone into the wee hours, trying to figure out who'd called the feds. There'd been no news. No emergency messages. Local media outlets were all covering the St. Patrick's Day parade; nothing about a White Supremacist riot in town.

After almost no sleep, I knew my eyes would be baggy and crinkled, and I felt a stab of vanity and embarrassment pierce my comfort level as Simon, at last, awoke.

"Oh," he said. "Hi there. What time is it?"

His breath was not minty fresh, and I recoiled.

He caught it, too, and raised a hand to cover his mouth as he mumbled, "Sorry. Fuck. I meant to get out of your hair before this."

"You sure know how to sleep," I said, grabbing my discarded shirt from the floor next to the bed.

He leapt up, his morning boner bobbing as he grabbed his clothes. "Mind if I—?"

"Go ahead," I said, pointing to the ridiculously giant en suite bathroom. "I'll use the guest bath."

I watched his toned ass recede from the bed. He was more fit than his modest choice of clothing revealed. Ethan, the last year of his life, had sprouted a mini-gut, and his former quads of iron from his soccer days had softened. But he still dressed as he had in his studly salad days, with shirts a size too small, and form-fitting slacks.

Outside, the wind continued to howl; the hail pounded. I brewed coffee and waited for my overnight guest to join me for a brief redux. I chuckled to myself envisioning line items on my next BB&A invoice:

- Oral sex: $1,000
- Kissing with tongue @ $40.00 per
- Kissing without tongue @ $30.00 per
- Missionary sex: $500.

MY KUSÔZU SERIES LAY IN A HEAP, a smattering of glass fragments in semi-tidy piles littered the living room. I heard myself groan involuntarily, and not in the lusty way. It would take most of the day to reassemble my art and clean up the detritus left by the mob.

As if reading my thoughts, Simon bounded down the stairs, his hands animated in a plea for me to leave the evidence the way it was. "I want our investigators over here to take additional photos. Just in case."

I handed him a steaming mug of coffee, disappointed that now I'd have to sit around in the mess for who knew how long. "The sooner the better."

"Thanks for the coffee," he said, his hand brushing mine as he took the mug.

A few moments of awkward silence hung in the air between us. I spoke first. "We probably shouldn't mention last night to anyone."

"Probably not," he said.

"And, our little activity was a one-time thing, right?" I said, noting an unfortunate squeak in my voice. "Or, uh, a two-time thing?"

He hesitated, nodded and sipped. "I need to get back to Greta. She's probably pissed all over the house. I'll be sending a crew here to gather the footage and clean up."

I aimed my chin at the door in agreement when my phone buzzed, and my screen lit up with Kento's picture. "Hang on a moment. It's my brother."

"Thank God you picked up. Are you okay?"

"Oh, so you heard about—"

"Hazel! She's in labor!"

"She?" It took a minute to wrap my head around the who behind the pronoun.

"They're going to take her into custody as soon as the baby is born," he cried.

"Custody? Kento, what are you talking about?"

Simon's attention piqued, and he signaled for me to press the speaker button.

"So you really don't know? Corinda saved your ass. She informed the FBI."

I was trying to keep up, but I was clearly missing some details. The hail kept pounding.

"Why would she—"

"She had a fight with that asshole husband of hers. I think she called the feds to punish him. After the raid, when he came home from your house, he tried to strangle her, I guess? And she shot him with his own gun. Execution style, I heard. His brains splattered all over the place. Fucker deserved it."

"Whoa, what? Where are you getting all this..."

"It's all over the news. Also, she called me, hysterical, right after she killed him."

*After she killed him.*

The implications of that reality clashed with the last vision I had of her, back in Boise. "Where is she?"

"In Coeur d'Alene. Obstetrics. I'm at SeaTac about to board a plane to Spokane. Can you pick me up?"

Simon was shaking his head.

"Of course," I said, scowling at the lawyer-turned-lover I'd just obliterated boundaries with.

"This situation is getting crazier and crazier," said Simon after I clicked *end call.*

I scrolled my phone, and, sure enough, in the time between my insomniac hunt-and-gather, and this morning's revelation, Steeplejack's latest crime was national news.

*Crime of Passion in the Panhandle*, claimed the AP headline. *White Supremacist Killed by Wife* was another incendiary title. Nothing about the mob visiting my house, but that would surely end up part of the story, and the last thing I relished was the infiltration of journos at my doorstep.

Simon reached a hand toward me in a *We Just Fucked and Now You're Mine* gesture, and I backed away.

"It's his baby," I said. "He has every right to be there for the birth."

"I know," Simon agreed. "However, Kento hasn't proved to be the most stable dude in a crisis. And Corinda is a major chaos engine. Who knows what her state of mind is?"

"The baby is a couple weeks early," I said. "And with all the trauma, Corinda's state of mind, he might need NICU care—likely in Seattle. So there's that."

"Fair point," said Simon, plopping his coffee mug on the counter. "I better go. Greta's probably diarrheaed all over my apartment."

It occurred to me; I had no idea where Simon lived. "Apartment?"

"Haven't had time to buy a house," he said. "There are still some outstanding issues with the divorce."

"What do you mean, outstanding issues? Are you really divorced, or did I just screw a married man?"

Simon didn't answer. He was already out the door.

# TWENTY-FIVE

"CAN YOU DRIVE FASTER, PLEASE?"

Kento hated being a passenger. Especially when I was the driver. He blamed it on his years navigating Seattle's notoriously shitty traffic and nonsensical network of one-ways and can't-get-there-from-here engineering.

"I'm already going ten over the limit," I said, trying hard to eliminate exasperation from my tone.

It didn't help that Spokane's rush hour had become a four-hour ordeal that began at 2 p.m. It was 1:55 when we crossed over the state line, into Idaho. Kento kept refreshing his phone's email and news, as if he expected updates to offer Corinda's maternity status.

"They have cops outside the birthing room," he said. "Can you imagine the extra stress that puts on her? I mean, she's already in pre-term labor."

I forced my lips to shield the words that yearned to blast out my mouth. *Never mind she just murdered someone*, and, *relax, she lives for being the center of attention*. And, *she's only a couple weeks early, so chill*.

Kento's lawyer agreed to a video call once the baby was born. It was important, the lawyer had told him, that he establish custody right away, given the circumstances. I didn't ask about Tom, where he stood on all this and why he, too, wasn't in the car ready to claim his newborn son.

Kento had been a nervous child. In middle school, he'd been a cutter, and went through an anorexic period before his growth spurt stretched out his chubbiness. But once he achieved success on the soccer field, his anxiety melted. And then, in college, he found his people, and lived a mostly closet-free young adulthood. It was only in his dealings with Corinda that he reverted to the anxious mess version of himself.

From the beginning, I'd worried that the life-long entanglement with Corinda as bio mom of his child would be triggering and a tax on his mental health. I was pretty sure Tom felt that way also. And the glimmer of hope I felt that Corinda might do serious time and therefore be out of the equation for years, came with more than a little guilt. Our mother's warning about *that girl* bearing out time and time again.

I let Kento out at the entrance to the hospital, and parked in a far section of the parking lot. The spring storm had abated, but the air was frosty and damp. Spring in the Silver Valley was a volatile thing. A Jekyll and Hyde that even after a lifetime of moody Marches surprised me with its extremes. In the hospital's small children's garden, daffodil blooms struggled to make sense of the forty-five-degree temperature change that had occurred within twenty-four hours.

Before my mother gave up on treatment, I'd bring her to the hospital for her chemo infusions and sit on the bench in the garden, sketching the less-celebrated flowers. Ones in decline from their peak bloom. I marked time sketching the seasonal metamorphosis of the plants. In summer, sunflowers took over with their narcissistic, plate-sized faces until September, when their petals wilted, and they hunched as if infected with osteoporosis. In winter, the curly, skeletal branches of the Japanese maple caught my fancy. In fall, I brought conté sticks to capture the autumnal color. I wished I'd thought to bring some supplies today. I wasn't ready to dive into the high-octane chaos inside. But I'd neglected to wear weather-appropriate clothing for an afternoon in a garden.

A tiny, bald child wrapped in blankets appeared, wheeled out by a dad, whose face forecast bad news. God, how I hate cancer. I smiled at the child, and the child smiled back, weakly. On impulse, I yanked a fistful of half-bloomed daffodils from the soil and offered them. "They'll be happier in a warm room," I said.

The dad slapped them away. "What are you doing?" he shouted.

The child said, "I'm supposed to mask around anything alive."

Shit. I'd forgotten about that whole microbe thing. "I'm so sorry," I said, a flush of embarrassment heat warming my cheeks.

The father was already affixing an N-95 to the child's face, turning now and again to scowl at me. I scurried down the path toward the atrium door, and slipped inside as my phone buzzed with a text from Kento:

> They won't let me in. She's refusing a C-section. I hear her scream-
> ing all the way in the waiting area.

I texted back that I'd meet him up there with coffee.

Since COVID, the rules had changed at the small community hospital. Any visitors on a patient floor were required to mask. As much as I understood the reasoning, I hated how masking hid the full measure of expression. I found my brother perched on the arm of a sofa, his focus on the screen of his phone. Luckily, we were the only folks in the maternity waiting room, because, despite his mask, I saw that Kento was lashing out at whoever was on the screen.

"What do you mean the baby will be turned over to social services? That's insane!"

I placed his coffee on a side table, and mouthed, *easy there, cowboy.*

"Out of my hands," offered the resigned-looking face on the screen. "Idaho is, well, Idaho. We discussed this possibility."

My stomach clenched, and I put my coffee down next to Kento's. I wanted a shot of Redbreast. Why didn't hospitals have bars?

Kento signed off on his contentious video call and glared at the patterned carpet.

I stepped closer, "Bad news, I'm gathering?"

"This fucking state and its anti-gay bullshit," he said.

A scream pierced the room. Definitely Corinda.

"And they won't even let me in there," he said.

"I'm going to investigate," I said. "Stay tuned."

The nurse's station nurse asked if I was family, and I said I was a sister-in-law. "Hmm," she said, her eyes squinted toward her computer screen.

My own eyes darted around the unit until they spied a couple of police officers—both of whom I knew from work.

Another series of screams came from the room where the cops were standing guard. I didn't wait for the nurse to give me the green light, I just casually walked away and sidled up to the nicer of the two policemen.

"Todd, right?" I said, through my mask.

He looked confused, then something in his forehead softened with recognition. "Ms. Mackenzie?"

"That's me! Mind if I check on the perp in there? Need to fill in some blanks."

His eyes squinted in confusion. I wasn't generally called to sketch a suspect who was already in custody. I pulled a lie out of my ass. "Coulter wants to confirm a birthmark on her thigh. I'm pretty sure I'll get a good look at it, given her current activity."

"Oh," he said, glancing at my empty hands.

I patted the pocket of my flannel shirt, "Got everything I need right here."

The other cop, Mitchell or Michael Something-or-other, eyed me suspiciously. I didn't wait for him to put two-and-two together, I just burst in as Corinda let loose a blood-curdling sound.

"Stop!" yelled a nurse attending to Corinda. "Who are you?"

"Oh, thank God!" said Corinda. "Hazel, they want to cut me, and then they'll take my baby and lock me up!"

"What's going on?" I asked the nurse, who was squinting at the monitor.

"Baby's transverse. Her water broke hours ago. Heart rate has gone down a bit in the last few minutes."

Corinda yelled again. One of the screens confirmed that she was having a contraction.

I waited until the pain subsided, then got in her face, "Hey, listen, the baby can't be born vaginally in the position it's in. You have to let them do a C-section."

Her eyes flitted back and forth, before she settled her gaze on me, "They are lying. They just want to take my baby to an orphanage and put me in jail."

"Kento won't let them take the baby anywhere. He's the father, remember? Well, he and Tom are. You just need to authorize him, okay?"

"I'm not going to let groomers raise my baby!" she shrieked.

I wanted to slap her.

"Corinda, if you don't authorize Kento, your baby will end up in foster care. Do you really think that's the way to go?"

Another contraction took over, and a monitor began to beep frantically.

"Okay, we need to get the baby out, now," said the nurse. "Heart rate is dropping fast."

I wrapped my hands around her shoulder blades, "Did you hear that? If you want this baby to live, you need to let them do their job."

She squeezed her eyes shut tight, and nodded as she blubbered.

The nurse told me to get out, and another nurse bustled in. The curtain closed around the bed, rustling sounds joined Corinda's screaming. A doctor ran in, her gloved hands up, and inches from her face. I backed away, but stayed in the room. If they wanted me to leave so badly, they'd need to drag me out.

My phone bleeped with a text from Kento, a row of question marks. I texted:

Stay tuned ...

Behind the curtain, competing sounds of urgency and fear. The doctor barking orders and Corinda, suddenly silent. The nurses throwing numbers out.

I crammed myself into a corner, next to a sink. Kento burst into the room, followed by Todd the good cop. I raised a hand. Whispered, "He's the father, let him stay. Please."

Todd glared at Kento, shook his head, and left the room.

"What's happening?" Kento whispered.

"Cesarean," I whispered back.

Kento's eyes looked panicked. He grabbed my hand and squeezed.

I swallowed a mouthful of anxious spit.

We waited.

The room grew quiet, but for the beeping of machines.

Kento's grip on me was bone-crushing and I nudged him. "Can you relax a little?"

I wanted to tell him everything would turn out fine, but I didn't have it in me to offer such an obvious lie. The last time we clung to each other this way, was at our mother's death bed. Her last ugly throat rattles. Our father sobbing in a corner. I could tell, glancing at Kento's face, that he was reliving that horrible day as well.

I squeezed his hand. "I have an idea."

"Baby's out," came a voice through the fog of quiet. A somber voice, rather than a joyous one.

Corinda's weak, panicked cry came next. "Is it—is he—okay?"

Kento squeezed my hand back. Hard, like that awful Disneyland trip, in line at the Haunted House. Our grandparents shaking their heads when tears leaked down his cheeks.

Our whole lives, I'd bolstered him through the tough times, and it looked like I was going to have to do it again.

"Suction," said the doctor. "C'mon, baby."

Another heart-stopping length of quiet, and then, at last, a yowl.

"Give him to me," cried Corinda. "Is he—healthy?"

"Ten fingers, ten toes," said the doctor. "But we need to get him in a warmer ASAP."

Another doctor bustled in. "Baby in distress in here?"

The new doctor, a pediatrician I assumed, disappeared behind the curtain and contributed to the escalating sounds of business. Kento and I continued to act like wallpaper. So far, it'd worked; nobody seemed to notice we'd remained in the room.

But Kento's impatience was growing. He stretched forward, toward his new son, as if pulling a wagon. My arm was the wagon, and I felt

my shoulder pop. Suddenly, the curtain rattled back on its rod, revealing Corinda pressing an impossibly small human to her breast while
lab-coated and scrub-wearing medical folk hunkered over her. A nurse
said, "We need to take him now. His color isn't good."

Another nurse whispered something about the NICU and beds
and RSV. Kento heard it, and stepped into the inner circle. Through
his double-mask he mumbled, "We should fly him to Seattle, where
he'll get better care."

The nurse who'd been whispering snapped her head around, "Excuse
me? Who are you?"

Corinda yelped, "Get him away from me! Don't let him near the
baby! He's gonna corrupt him!"

"Sir, you need to leave," said the nurse.

"Corinda, what the hell? That's my baby. What are you—"

"Sir, I'm going to call security," said the nurse.

I tugged him back. "It's okay, he's leaving. Kento, let's go. Let's not
get in the way of the baby's care."

Kento allowed me to drag him off, but his focus, his gaze, wouldn't
detach from the tiny thing that lay nearly lifeless on Corinda's chest.

As we left the room, Kento's head still turned toward the closed
curtain, he pleaded, "Corinda, please, you and I just talked on the phone.
Why are you doing this?"

# TWENTY-SIX

DESPITE THE WEIRD, MUDDIED WATERS with my legal representative, I called Simon and asked him to meet us back at my house. His car was in the driveway when we arrived from the hospital, and Simon was sitting on a bench on my front porch.

Kento hadn't said a word on the drive home, but now he announced, "He looks pretty comfy there. You fucking him now?"

The thing about twins is true. We do read each other's thoughts.

"Nah," I lied. "Not that it's any of your beeswax."

The other thing that is true about both Kento and me is, neither of us were good at the casual hook-up. For me, there was always a physical contract between my vagina and heart. I couldn't help it. I was sure Kento suffered from a similar affliction, given his weird, continued attachment to Corinda.

Inside, Simon peppered us with questions. He wanted to know if Corinda had been arrested, and if the baby was okay. Kento answered while I pondered disclosing the idea I had of applying for guardianship of the baby. Was *apply* even the right word though? Weren't guardians appointed? I interrupted the back-and-forth between my brother and Simon.

"What if," I started, "I care for the baby while all this gets sorted? How might that work?"

Both men stopped their chatter and turned to stare at me.

"You?" Kento said. "You've never expressed an interest in being a parent, Hazel. You never even babysat as a teenager."

"It's true, babies have never been on my radar. No biological time clock stuff, but it would be temporary, right? Until the legal system works through the convoluted mess. I mean, wouldn't a judge—even an Idaho judge—place a baby with a relative rather than a stranger?"

Simon piped up, his words carefully spoken and spread out, as though thinking them as they stumbled out his mouth. "But you're not legally a relative according to this state."

Kento waved an imaginary document. "I have a contract."

Simon sighed. "That's only binding in Washington State, Kento. We've been over this."

"There's also," Kento continued, "the matter of a huge hospital bill. If I have no legal rights, this baby's NICU tab will be picked up by the state, correct?"

"Your point?" said Simon.

"Well, if I'm listed as the father on the birth certificate, then I would have rights and responsibilities. Maybe I should appeal to the hospital?"

Simon shook his head. "According to my investigators, Corinda is on welfare. In Idaho, you have no legal ties to her. This was all established during the previous lawsuit."

The other lawsuit. Right. And the bogus self-defense claim. Corinda's flakiness was whiplash inducing. "I still don't know why she alerted the feds, though. I mean, why stick her neck out for us after all the trouble she caused?"

"I have a theory," said Simon. "Arthur must have said or done something to piss her off. Maybe he refused to raise the baby? Maybe her calling the FBI on the mob was in retaliation for that and had nothing to do with protecting you, Hazel. Now that she's facing murder charges, more will be revealed, I'm sure."

Murder charges. How had things gotten so out of hand?

"Look, here's what we can do," said Simon. "I'll file a petition in family court to have Kento declared the baby's father. We'll file a motion for a paternity test."

"Oh," said Kento, glumly.

"Something wrong?" said Simon.

"It's possible that Kento's husband is the bio dad," I said, hoping Simon wouldn't ask for more details.

"I see," he answered, adopting a respectful poker face. "We'll cross that bridge, y'know? First step is to prove paternity. In Idaho, fathers do, actually, have more custody protections than in some other states."

It hit me then. Kento, a father. An actual father. A tear formed, its salt stinging my eye before I had the chance to wipe it off.

Kento had begun to pace. "How soon can this all be accomplished?"

Simon shrugged. "Hopefully this week. In the meantime, stay away from the hospital. I'll have my investigator check on the status of the baby. There's legal workarounds in cases like this, but, Kento, Hazel, it won't be in your best interest to harass Corinda or force your way into the situation until we, you, have legal standing. Capeesh?"

Simon was all business, and my heart ached a little. Did he regret last night?

"Sounds good," I said, matching his emotionless delivery. "Kento and I will just hang out here, awaiting further instructions."

SIMON GAVE ME A SALUTE without making eye contact. He did regret it. The ache in my chest expanded, and I turned away, opening the door for his exit. As he made his way, I whispered, "Was Greta okay last night, on her own?"

"She, um, wasn't on her own," he said, and then strode away.

# TWENTY-SEVEN

IT WAS NEARLY A WEEK BEFORE the judge approved the petition and Kento's spit could be tested to see if he was, indeed, the baby's father. Baby Luce was its name, as Corinda had insisted he not be given Arthur's surname. She'd been in the county jail since the day after the C-Section, awaiting a bail hearing. Even as angry and disappointed as I was with her, I found her postpartum incarceration especially cruel.

"Can she have visitors?" I asked Simon in an email.

"She can, but you're not going to visit her," he responded, tersely, his email signature offering boilerplate warnings against sharing this *confidential matter*, blah, blah, blah.

Ironically, the spit lab was directly one floor below the NICU. Kento hadn't wanted me to accompany him, but I'd tagged along anyway. I'd been hovering, I realized. Maybe it was all the Grief Group warnings about checking in with friends and family members when they seemed depressed. Kento had been even quieter than usual. He'd taken family emergency leave from work, and had been sitting around a lot, sighing, drinking. It was reminiscent of his last year in high school, awaiting acceptance and rejection letters from colleges. Kento had a hard time not being in control—another personality trait we shared.

After his sample was sealed and tagged, he joined me in the waiting room where we debated defying orders.

"They won't know who we are," he said. "We can peer through the windows. They do have windows in the NICU, don't they?"

I knew the layout of the Neonatal Intensive Care Unit from work. A horrible gig where I was hired to sketch a baby on a vent who'd been subjected to an ugly forceps delivery, which had damaged her windpipe. The OB who delivered her was not convicted, but lost his license and fled the area. The baby died a few months later. Despite my obsession with chronicling death through art, I didn't want any part of visually representing the baby's horrific demise.

We approached the unit furtively. Through the glass, we could see several incubators occupied by tiny humans, some so small; they could fit in a jacket pocket. They reminded me of unfeathered baby birds. Nurses and parents all gowned and masked dotted the background. The nurses in the NICU wore pastel-colored scrubs, their hair hidden under pink caps. One mother sat in a rocking chair; the suction cups of a pump affixed to her breasts. Another set of parents hovered over an incubator; their faces lined in worry.

Kento scanned the room, then pointed at an Isolette near the back of the unit. We were too far to read the identifying index card, but it seemed likely it was Baby Luce.

"He's bigger than most of the babies," I said, forcing hope into my voice. He also didn't have gadgets attached to him. He was a tiny bit yellow, sunning under a jaundice light, and Kento worried out loud about the infrared-looking contraption.

"What if they forget to turn it off? He looks like he's roasting."

"It's standard, don't worry," I said with faux authority.

Kento wasn't calmed by my assertion, "But look. Nobody's paying attention to him. All the other babies have people. The first few days are crucial for bonding."

My brother had such a porcelain heart. His anguish worn on the outside, unlike me. I'd always envied his easy way with feelings. Letting them find purchase in a gesture or a declaration. He cried easily. Laughed spontaneously (although lately, that laugh had gone into remission). When Kento was anxious, his skin bloomed with hives. He was already mindlessly scratching the backs of his hands.

I swatted him, just as I always did when we were kids, and he retracted his hand. His head pivoted, his eyes searching mine.

"We can't, Kento. Don't even think about it."

"This is ridiculous, don't you think? I'm here. A father to this baby. And they won't let me comfort him. Sing to him."

"Wait a second," I said. "Maybe you could apply to be a volunteer? I think there's a program—"

He spun around, grabbed my upper arms, his eyes wide with possibility. "Mom did that, didn't she? Remember, once we were old enough for kindergarten? She said she missed our infancy."

A vague memory of our mother picking us up from school, her eyes red, her mascara smeared down her cheeks. She hadn't lasted long. Sad outcomes, all too common in the NICU, spoiled her joy at holding newborns. I kept the memory to myself. It was the last time she'd volunteered. Our father in rage about anything taking her away from her "wifely duties." She hadn't had time to pack him a lunch and he'd had to go without food for a shift. God forbid he'd have to slap ham on a couple slices of bread for his own midday meal.

"I can go by Kento Zapf? Maybe there's still history of when Mom volunteered? They'd recognize the name?"

He was perseverating. We were doomed. I had no doubt that, one way or another, he'd work his way into that NICU.

"We should go," I said, abruptly. I had the feeling that we were being observed.

"I wonder if I can just ask—"

"Kento!"

But my warning fell on deaf ears. He was already knocking at the unit's door.

It opened, and a woman—likely a nurse—inquired if she could help him.

"I'd like to volunteer in here," he said.

"Oh," she said. "Well, there's a process."

She wrote down the name of the contact and handed it to Kento.

212 | SUZY VITELLO

He thanked her and returned to me, only then allowing himself to be led down the hall to the elevators.

I hesitated to rat Kento's plan out to Simon. On the one hand, we were supposedly a team. If Kento intended to get into a lengthy legal battle for custodial rights, we needed to be transparent with Simon, our legal representative. But then there was the issue of Simon's weirdness the day after we slept together, and his warning to stay away from the baby or Corinda, lest we muddy the waters. We'd completely ignored it.

I decided to stick my head in the sand. I was not my brother's keeper. He would do what he would do.

A week after filling out forms and submitting a background check, the hospital called "Mr. Zapf" to let him know they approved his application, and they happened to be short-handed. It was also the day of Corinda's bail hearing. It was unlikely, given the charge of murder, that she'd be granted release. She had a public defender representing her, and two of Arthur's children were apparently in the courtroom, offering their support to the prosecutor.

Meanwhile, I busied myself with work.

The next county over had hired me to sketch the body of a John Doe who'd been scraped off the interstate. I was driving there when Simon called.

"Hey, listen, I need to tell you something," he said, his voice low and tentative out the speaker of my car.

"Okay—"

"I don't regret that night. Not at all. But it shouldn't have happened. Probably."

A wave of embarrassment hit me. I swallowed, but said nothing.

"Hazel, the thing is—"

The pause lingered like a sticky fog.

"She's back, isn't she? Your ex?"

"Lucinda is in rough shape," he said. "That woman she took off with, she turned out to be pretty awful. Identity theft, tax fraud. Anyway, she's traumatized, and I've agreed to let her stay with me for a bit."

"Yeah, fine. Thanks for the update. Bye."

After I pressed the red icon on my Apple Play console, sadness swelled beneath my seat belt. A rush of anguish bursting upward from my gut, into my nose, my sinuses. Years of tamping down feelings had taught my body containment. A refusal to weep. But I was alone, and on the very highway where Ethan, holding onto a deceit he'd never shared with me, breathed his last breath. Outside my car, a beautiful spring day. Inside, an atmospheric river of regret and hurt. A lifetime of suppressed feelings. The dam burst. And it burst with such force, I had to pull over.

The intensity with which I pined for Simon shocked me. I hadn't consciously processed my growing fondness for him. As tractor-trailers zoomed by, shaking my car as they passed, my own inner self vibrated to its sorrow. Sobs roiled through me, and I couldn't even take a complete breath before another spew of grief erupted. Was it all about Simon, or had I finally reached critical mass?

It felt ugly to admit that betrayal was the common factor here. Not illness, not accidents, not death. Ethan's fling with the QAnon chick, Corinda's big lie, Kento having the rug pulled out from under him so cruelly, and now a man I'd opened up to taking himself out of the equation and falling under the spell of a prettier, more complicated woman than I could ever be. I deserved this one-woman pity party on the side of the interstate, no doubt, but why hadn't I cried this way when my mother died? When my husband succumbed to an early death? Or was grief a trickster, taking form in adjacent sorrows, sneakily invading my heart while my mind pretended all was well?

My dashboard alerted me to another call coming in. This time, Kento. It took everything in me to decide to ignore the call. My knee-jerk maternal instincts to protect my brother be damned. Let him negotiate his own way out of his dilemma, I had work to do. Work, the balm for me, always. I drove on.

The sketch took more than two hours. Why they didn't simply take a photo of the John Doe was evident in the degree to which the man resembled road kill. With renderings sensitive to potential loved ones, my pencil could de-emphasize gore, while highlighting features that might be recognizable to family members. My training in facial anatomy filled in the blanks, and the poor chap, whose entire right side was caved in, his cheekbone pulverized, was rendered whole again, under my hand.

By the time I returned to my car, and turned my phone back on, there were seven missed calls and two voicemails from Kento. Three from Simon. Two from unknown callers.

I turned my phone off for the drive home.

# TWENTY-EIGHT

I OPENED THE FRONT DOOR to see an entire nursery set up in my living room. A car seat, a portable crib, mountains of toys and diapers and doll-sized clothes, and Kento in the kitchen, sterilizing bottles.

"No, you did not kidnap a baby from the NICU," I bellowed.

Kento spun around from the sink. "*Kidnap* isn't exactly the right term for a parent's rightful custody of his child."

"Kento, please. Please, please, please tell me I'm not harboring a stolen baby in my house."

"You didn't respond to my messages," he said, holding a bottle scrub brush aloft like a fairy godmother wand.

My stomach flipped as if Kento had just crammed the brush down my throat and was massaging my intestines with it. "I was working, Kento."

"Relax, Sis. The baby is still in his Isolette in the hospital."

He tossed the brush behind him and it thunked against the enamel farmhouse sink. "The paternity test results are in, and I am too nervous to open the email. What if, what if—"

I pushed my hand, palm out, toward him, "Why did you buy all this stuff?"

"Didn't you talk to Simon?"

"I did but—"

"Well, it's part of showing I have all the equipment to be ready for the little guy. He's been cleared to leave the unit. Oh, Hazel, I got to hold him today. He's perfect."

"And the baby's *mother*? Did she get released on bail?"

Kento shrugged.

"Don't you think Corinda's legal status needs clarification before you feather the nest?"

Kento turned and pointed at his iPad, the silver rectangle of it isolated on the kitchen counter as if quarantining with a lethal virus. "The email from the lab, Hazel. Can you open it? And let me know the verdict?"

"Okay," I said. "Here goes."

We made it through the various safeguards and passwords, and arrived at the confidential lab results page. Kento's eyes were squeezed shut. I clicked on an image, and a graph greeted me, showing the paternity index chart. One column was headed with an all-caps CHILD and the other column's heading read ALLEGED FATHER. There were all sorts of numbers that meant nothing to the layman, but scrolling down, at the bottom of the chart was the answer.

Kento's eyes were open now, trying to read my expression.

I turned the screen his way. "I hope you can patch things up with Tom," I said, quietly.

"Fuck," he said, striding into the living room.

"You should call him."

"Fuck, fuck, fuck."

It was the same response he'd given when the rejections to his reach schools trickled in.

"Look, you guys are still legally partnered, right? Don't you think Tom's tune might change once he knows the results?"

"We both said a lot of things. Hard to unsay things, you know?"

"Welcome to your typical hetero-norm marriage, dude. You think Ethan and I didn't have our rough times? Remember that Christmas at your in-laws'?"

My stomach turned evoking Ethan's name. I hadn't told my brother about his affair. About his dabbling in anti-gay, Christo-fascist, hate-fueled activities.

Kento kicked the car seat lightly, sending it against the sofa where, not too long ago, he'd been shot. "Maybe you should dial up your boyfriend," he said.

"Huh?"

"Your solicitor," he said. "The guy you give money to and also shag?"

"Simon is not my boyfriend."

"Pants on fire," he sneered.

It was a phrase from our *I don't* days. Whenever we reached an impasse, having had our fill of constructing horrendous suitors for each other, we'd settle on whatever kid was cooties material that particular week. As in, "Admit it, you want to kiss Robert Potersack." Back and forth we'd chant the denials, and then the counter denials. Childish. And now Kento was regressing into the least palatable version of our twinship. I picked up his phone. Holding it with an outstretched hand I said, "Call him."

He snatched his device and pressed a button. Good, at least Tom was still in his *favorites*.

He marched out of the room for privacy, while I made a call of my own.

"Hey, Simon, listen," I started, wanting to clear the air before getting back to the legalities at hand.

But he interrupted me. "They denied bail. Which makes our next step an interesting one."

*Our* next step. Just hearing those words laid out in a line like that pierced me in my raw heart. I knew we were back to a business only relationship, but my train was still, a little bit, on that other track.

"Did Kento get his—?"

"Yes. Paternity is unlikely. As in less than 5 percent chance. He's clearly not the bio dad; his estranged husband is."

"Hmm. Okay. So that makes the petition for you as guardian somewhat a stretch. What's the latest status with Tom? Is he agreeable to a court battle for custody?"

The whole thing was getting messier and messier. "I don't know. My brother is talking to him now."

I wanted to tell him about Kento's volunteer gig but wasn't ready for him shitting all over it. I'd had enough contentiousness this week,

218 | SUZY VITELLO

and there was no talking Kento out of it. It was clearly best that Simon didn't know anything about Kento's baby stalking.

From the den, Kento's voice escalated. He sounded just like our father. Same inflections. Same emphasis. The way the last word in a sentence squeaked out, angrily.

"I have to go," I said, abruptly. "I'll get back to you."

I hung up while Simon was still talking, which gave me a teensy bit of satisfaction.

As if we'd planned it, Kento hung up at the same time, his phone skittering out of the den, whizzing by my feet.

"Well that didn't sound very promising," I said, as his late model device smacked against the leg of the coffee table.

"He's being completely unreasonable," he said.

"How about we make a pot of tea and calm down," I said.

Kento shook his head, defeated. He sat on a chair, opposite the infamous sofa, and stared straight ahead.

I heated some water and brewed some sencha leaves the real way, in our mother's raku teapot. The aroma made me heady and nostalgic. Tea was the antidote to our father's temper tantrums. Our mother would put a kettle on in the wake of Dad's storming out of the house. The way some folks sage smudge to rid their house of bad juju, she believed in the power of the leaves of Camellia sinensis.

"They grow only in the places where sun warms the land," she'd say. "Sun warms your heart, that way, too. Get rid of all bad things."

Kento was no fool. He knew what I was trying to do, and he wasn't going to be cajoled out of his foul mood.

I waited until the refill to press for details.

"It's his parents. As usual. Their shame and guilt all projected on me."

"You did tell him the baby has his genetic imprint, though, right?"

"He's not so sure. Says that with Corinda's flaky history, she may have gotten knocked up prior to our contract."

The baby had black hair, almond eyes. Unless Corinda had been screwing another Asian guy, Tom's accusation was unlikely. But I held my tongue.

"Is he willing to take the test?"

"He doesn't want to, but I told him he has to."

"Oh?"

"It's the least he can fucking do, right?"

I stroked Kento's arm, long soothing pets, another of our mother's calming strategies.

"He refuses to come here though. He's getting swabbed in Seattle."

"That's a good compromise," I said.

Kento shrugged. "Even if it's conclusive, he told me he's not contributing to some lengthy lawsuit that we'll probably lose anyway."

I wanted to agree with my brother, but Tom was probably right. Idaho had all but banned same-sex couples from engaging a surrogate or even adopting a child. If only the baby had been born in Washington. It seemed so arbitrary that a child's future, and the rights of a parent, would be decided by the fact of twenty miles. Had the baby been born a stone's throw to the west of Coeur d'Alene, Kento and Tom would be filling out his birth certificate right now.

"I'm sorry, Kento. Sorry that this has become so complicated. Maybe it wasn't meant to be?"

Kento glowered. "You know, I've heard that my whole fucking life. That because I am what I am, I don't get to partake in stuff you all take for granted. Everything has to be a fight. Whether it's marriage, making a family, even holding hands in public. You wonder why I kept everything under wraps in the hometown for so long? This is why. This is *exactly* why."

We finished our tea, and I slapped together some ramen. Kento cooled down, but I worried that he would do something crazy.

I wasn't wrong.

# TWENTY-NINE

I WAS PUTTING THE FINISHING TOUCHES on the gruesome sketch of the highway accident victim. Shading the missing cheekbone, getting it ready to scan, when the cops showed. Two of the newer detectives from town—ones I'd yet to cross paths with. My first thought was, *They really want to ID this guy in a hurry.* It took only a minute to realize they were not here for my rendering. This had nothing to do with my latest gig.

"Where is he?" said the lead detective, flashing his badge.

"Beg pardon," I said, still not understanding.

"Your brother. He hiding in here? Can we enter?"

Out of habit I asked for a warrant.

"Oh, it's going to be like that, is it?" said the sidekick.

The first detective leaned in, his eyes grazing the swath of interior available to him from the porch. Legally, he could keep his feet outside and stretch his torso inside, and not violate the "illegal search and seizure rule."

Kento and all the baby equipment had disappeared sometime in the night. He'd left no note and had his phone turned off. I'd told myself to give it half a day before my next level of anxiety-fueled reconnaissance kicked in.

Calmly, but sternly, I asked, "Why are you looking for him?"

The first cop squinted at me. A sneer, really. Playing the intimidation game.

"We're done here," I said, giving the door a little shove toward closed.

A mud-splattered shoe stopped it from shutting all the way. An ominous, "We'll be back," followed by retreat. Stomping. Engine revving. Gravel spraying.

My gut sounded an alarm. The last time Kento pulled a disappearing act, he ended up married. My brother was in the "It's easier to ask for forgiveness than permission" camp. It was unlikely that he'd contacted Tom, but he was my first call.

"He what?" Tom said in a harsh, whispery tone. He was probably at work, so I got right to the point. "Police are hunting him, and I'm pretty sure it has to do with that baby."

"Christ."

"Tom, did he say anything to you yesterday? Anything you can remember that might help track him down?"

Tom groaned. Then, "I'll call you in a few minutes. Hang tight."

Before Tom could call back though, Simon rang in.

"He really screwed the pooch," he said, by way of greeting.

I took in a labored breath. My heartbeat ramped to elevation-gain levels.

He said, "We could have sorted this out, eventually, but he did the worst thing a person can do when filing for custody."

"He didn't take the—"

"He did."

Silence.

My phone alerted me that Tom was calling back. "Simon, I need to take this. Hang on."

"He's probably crossed the border," Tom said, no longer whispering.

"The border? Canada?"

"He was making noises about it. Said he had money—which I suspect came from the sale of your parents' house? Said he had been researching underground channels, ways to apply for emergency asylum."

Time passed. I didn't know what to say.

"Hazel? You still there?"

My head filled with pinpricks, and I realized I'd been holding my breath too long.

"Which province?"

"I don't know, but I can get into his VPN via his backup laptop. Maybe there're some email exchanges?"

His voice was tinged with the same desperation I felt roiling in my stomach. Did my brother really flee the country with a stolen baby?

"Okay, but maybe don't call my cell? I'm on my way to you, and we can meet at—the place where this baby was, um, made? And if he did leave the laptop at your condo, maybe bring it with?" I was treading in the dangerous waters of aiding and abetting just with that suggestion. But I had hoped we could track Kento down before the feds did. Maybe he hadn't attempted to cross the border yet.

I met Tom in the lobby of the Four Seasons—site of the now-infamous turkey-basting. Sweat beads gathered at his hairline. You could smell the stress leaking from his pores. But he did, thankfully, have the laptop in his hands. I followed him to a bank of cushioned benches hidden behind a jungle of rent-a-plants.

I nodded toward the machine. "Did you get in?"

"Hazel, before I show you what I found, you have to swear to me that you won't take this nonsense any further."

"Nonsense?"

He leaned in. "Regardless of my biological connection, I don't want to pursue custody."

"You've made that clear."

"Also," he said, leaning close enough that I could smell a tinge of garlic on his breath, "I love Kento, you know I do, but our marriage, our relationship, has become untenable."

*Untenable.* That was a word Kento and I had once confessed to hating, along with *passive-aggressive*, *regardless*, and *henceforth*. Terms in the legal-meets-pop-psychology sphere, terms meant to intimidate and/or gaslight.

"Oh," I said, simmering. "I'm sorry to hear that."

I wasn't going to acquiesce and there-there him. Yes, Kento could be unpredictable. He could be hardheaded and impulsive. But he'd always been that way. That was the Kento he married. What had changed?

"Regardless," I said, unironically, "we need to find him before this gets worse."

Tom nodded in agreement, but something in the way he set his jaw told me he'd like nothing better than to wash his hands of the whole deal.

"Open it up. Let's take a look," I said.

Tom set to work hacking into Kento's laptop and turned it around to reveal an exchange between my brother and someone named Alberta Wolf. The text was cryptic, full of secret codes and misdirection, which alarmed me in its programmed stealth. Clearly, Kento had been in communication with this Wolf person for quite some time. "I can't decipher any of this," I said.

Tom turned the screen his way, clicked on something, then turned the screen back my way. A Word document with a translation key faced me.

It took a while, but from the last exchange, it appeared that Kento would be breaching the BC border within the hour. This Alberta Wolf person had a "guy" there. This was a twenty-thousand-dollar transaction. The money sewn into a blanket. This had been in the works for a bit. At least a week. I was shocked.

"See what I mean?"

"Untenable," I agreed, shitty words be damned.

"Even if we drove to the border now, it'd take a couple hours. He'd be deep in the Western Canadian hills by then."

"But he has a newborn," I said. "Which I would imagine will slow him down."

"You bring your passport?" Tom said, in a tone that gave away his hope that I had not.

I patted my backpack. "One thing I can say about Ethan? He was a proponent of the Go Bag. Survivalist instincts passed down from his paranoid family."

Tom shook his head in resignation. "You driving, or should I?"

# THIRTY

TOM KEPT THE SPEED TO NINE over the limit to avoid a ticket. The border was a mess. Western Washington sophomores lined up for a weekend of under-twenty-one drinking in Vancouver. We weren't sure what to do once we crossed into Canada, but Tom had a thought. On their one-year anniversary, they'd stayed at a vine-covered, iconic hotel at the edge of Stanley Park.

I wasn't so sure, but asked, "You really think he'd go there?"

"He was fixated on a family with triplet infants when we were there. Almost stalking them. It was the first time he brought up hiring a surrogate."

When it was our turn to offer our passports and answer questions: What is your purpose in Canada? How long are you staying? What is your relationship to each other? My stomach flipped at the thought of my brother trying to sneak a baby out of the United States. Clearly, they wouldn't let a single man with a newborn in without reams of documentation. Had this Alberta Wolf person procured a passport for a six-pound, newly hatched human?

We were waved through, and joined the traffic jam of eager nineteen-year-olds into the city.

Tom's stomach growled. He was a slightly built guy. A marathon runner who needed, according to Kento, to eat every three hours lest he fall into a low blood sugar crisis. I consulted my phone, and suggested a fish and chips place with good Yelp reviews.

"You should put that away," he said. "If the feds track you up here, they'll figure something's up. Also, international roaming charges."

"Fuck," I said, powering down.

The fish was greasy and the chips, chewy. Served us right for eating in a place five minutes before closing. Over conciliatory ice cream cones in a hip, trendy Denman Street dessert place, we worked on a narrative. In reception, I would claim I was desperately searching for my brother, who had likely checked in that afternoon. That's when Tom, playing the part of my boyfriend, would walk up in a faux rage, and we'd pretend to quarrel before he stormed away.

We huddled at the back of the parlor, whispering our parts of the scheme over honey fried chicken ice cream (me), and vodka-gooseberry sorbet (Tom).

The idea was to convince the hotel receptionist that I needed space from my abusive boyfriend. I would say that my brother often traveled under an assumed name because he was famous, and wanted privacy to bond with his newborn son. The idea was a ridiculous long shot, hinging on, one, Kento actually staying at the hotel; two, a gullible receptionist; and three, plausible acting by me—a woman who couldn't lie her way out of a speeding ticket. I felt somewhat guilty pretending to be a DV victim, but karmically, maybe it was owed me.

It was nearly 10 p.m. by the time we felt confident in our fakery. The kids behind the ice cream counter were already lifting chairs on top of tables, pulling out the oversized mop and rolling bucket. Closing rap streamed out the speakers, replacing the low-key folk music meant for paying customers.

As we trudged out of the parlor, my limbs felt heavy, as though sunk in sand. Where was Kento? Why had he become so obsessive? The hotel's ivy-shrouded façade loomed, shadowy under an almost full moon. I had the feeling I was in the middle of one of my childhood *I don't* sessions. One that had gone on too long and lapped into the territory of dark fantasy, and our faux intendeds sprouted extra body parts. Why was I even here, in this foreign country? Was this simply a wild goose chase?

(Vodka-gooseberry chase?) With our parents long-dead, I'd taken on the role of the sensible sibling. Me, a person who drew carnage for a living.

As we inched toward the hotel, a wave of failure roiled in me. I'd fallen for Simon, and now his beautiful ex-wife had reclaimed him. The mensch. The patsy. How was it that both Simon and I kept allowing our lives to upend out of duty?

My mother called it *giri*. The obligation one has toward others. It was why, when we were given gifts, we had to reciprocate with even larger gifts. This confused all the white people with whom we exchanged. When Mother was dying, the neighbors organized a meal train. Glass pans full of gelatinous concoctions we would never consume, could only be returned filled with our dashi-based dishes. Instead of simply toasting bread and scooping applesauce into a dish (all Mother could eat), we were tasked with disposing of the nausea-inducing casseroles, then preparing a "better" quality of meal and penning a thank you note before hunting down the giver.

*Giri.* My legacy.

The reception desk was empty when we entered the lobby. "Let's walk around a bit before we do the deed," Tom suggested.

I felt like a robber about to demand money from a bank teller. My feet were getting colder by the minute. Tom led us to a bank of elevators, and we followed a guest inside one. "Floor?" he inquired as he pasted his room key to the interior sensor. "Uh—" I began.

"Four," said Tom, definitively.

We exited, and Tom strode down the hall like a boss.

"Are we headed toward your anniversary room?" I said, meekly.

He didn't answer, but his increased pace served as confirmation.

At the hall's end, he made a right-angle turn, and came to a stop at the third door of an exterior-facing room. He pressed an ear to the panel and waved me back, lest I disturb his surveillance.

But even without proximity, I could hear a faint, high-pitched cry. It sounded like a Siamese kitten. A stunted yowl, followed by shushing.

Tom straightened, and faced me. I nodded. He knocked.

There was a Do Not Disturb hangtag suspended from the brass door handle, so it was no surprise when the knock resulted in no response.

Tom knocked louder, and harsh-whispered, "Kento? Open up. It's me."

My stomach cramped. I should not have eaten ice cream. Soon, I would require a toilet.

"Let us in," he repeated.

"Us?" said the voice of my confused brother. "Do not tell me you brought law enforcement with you."

"Kento," I said. "This is madness."

When the door yawned open, offering the vision of Kento's rocking body, the baby enveloped in the folds of one of those carrier wraps, for a moment I had a déjà vu of our mother in the NICU, her volunteering cut short without explanation. We'd later found out that a racist nurse who didn't like the way she "smelled" had talked her into quitting the gig.

"Shh," Kento whispered. "He's almost asleep."

For the first time, Tom let down his guard. His face relaxed and he peered over Kento's shoulder to view the child.

It was a moment.

All the adversity, the drama, the trauma, evaporated for one perfect second. A triad of love unfolded before my eyes. The top of the baby's head was covered in hair. Black licorice-colored hair. His crying, now gentle mewling.

Beyond them, piled on the bed, lay the accouterments of infancy. Diapers, a bucket-shaped car seat, pacifiers, and bottles. And something else. Something that didn't belong.

"Kento," I said in a quiet, baby-soothing voice, "tell me you didn't raid my storage unit.

Tom followed my gaze. "Is that a gun, Kento? And the Kwaiken knife?"

Kento continued to jiggle his armful of baby. The only answer from him was the shushing sound of comfort.

"So in addition to international kidnapping, you've crossed the border with weapons? What the fuck, Kento? And who the hell is Alberta Wolf?"

I didn't have to wait too long for an answer, because at that moment the door burst open and in strode a face I recognized from photos. Those cheekbones set in that hauntingly gorgeous face. She momentarily froze, then carefully placed a filled ice bucket on the dresser. Her gaze swept the room, coming to land on me. She pointed, "You're the twin sister, yes? The one Simey's been sleeping with?"

*Simey?*

I couldn't begin to organize all the questions floating around my brain.

Something about Lucinda's high-pitched voice startled the infant, and he cried out.

"What the fuck is going on here?" I managed.

"I'm his solution," said Lucinda, aka Alberta Wolf. "But now, now that you've foolishly complicated the plan, we'll have to Plan B this whole thing."

Tom plunked down on one of the antique full-sized beds and covered his face with his hands. He let out a muffled sigh. The baby quieted again and Kento glared at me, then at Tom.

"You shouldn't have come here," he said.

I directed my next question at Lucinda. "Simon—?" I said. "Does he know—"

Lucinda shook her head. "That man. Poor Dear. I've put him through so much. But it's his own fault, really. Everything so by-the-book. Except fucking you. That was a departure from his usual Boy Scout compliance. You must give a really good blowjob."

I ignored the insult, went for the jugular. "You know you're facing major charges, right? What do they call this? Human trafficking? You used to be an attorney, didn't you? Sworn to uphold the law and all that? You'll be disbarred at the very least."

I was aware that my accusation was undermined by the *extra* in my posture: wagging finger, stomping foot. But it matched the over-the-top swagger of Simon's troubled ex.

"There is no law," she said. "The right-wing Christo-fascists have taken the rule of law hostage, so, *viva la revolución*, baby!"

In her fiery eyes I saw heart-stopping mania. Her small fist shot up toward the ceiling, as though posing for a magazine shoot focused on rebellion. She had out-extra-ed me with her affect.

"I'm tired of playing defense, Hazel," said my brother, as he bounced his armful of fussy baby. "I'm through with basing my decisions on the whims of a population who'll never accept me."

A fury rose in me. "So now you're in some sort of Canadian witness protection, or are you just going to be on the lam until they catch you and throw your ass in prison?"

He struggled to counter, and in the silence, Lucinda said, "We're on the right side of history, Hazel. Think Harriet Tubman and her underground railroad. Rosa Parks and her refusal to be told where to sit. In their time, they were outlaws. Now? They name high schools and streets and parks after those brave souls. Well, at least in states that haven't banned truth."

It seemed a stretch for this diminutive white lady to compare herself to racial justice heroes, but there was a seed of truth to her statement. I pointed to the newborn in my brother's arms.

"Fine, but what about this poor child? Kento will be locked away once he's caught. And he *will* be caught. Simon, uh, Mr. Aaronson, had a workable plan, and now that's moot."

The baby unleashed his lung capacity, and I took that to be a sign of agreement.

"Shh, shh," Kento whispered, turning his light bouncing into frantic swinging.

The baby quieted, and began a sucking sound.

Tom rose from the bed, and faced Lucinda. "Now what?"

"Well, you've probably been tracked here, so now you need to lead whoever's following you away," she said, whinily. "We will need to vacate ASAP, which is problematic, because our first contact house is a half-day's journey, and they won't be ready for us until tomorrow evening."

Tom peered over Kento's shoulder again and swallowed hard enough for me to hear it. His expression softened, and he said, "Is he okay? Healthy, I mean?"

Kento finagled a pacifier into the baby's suckling mouth. "He's fine," he mumbled.

Lucinda opened the mini-fridge from which she plucked several baggies of whitish-blue liquid before cramming them into the ice bucket. "He'll need to eat before we take off," she said, dispassionately. The robotic way she handled the breast milk, the way she ticked off the agenda, got my wheels spinning. Her actions and demeanor were so cold. So task-oriented. Was she the force behind Simon's vasectomy?

"Wait," Tom said. "What if I came with? I am the biological father, after all."

Lucinda spritzed water into a hotel cup and shoved it in the microwave, pressing the 30 second button. She spun around on her tiny heel.

"Kento said you weren't interested. I don't think you understand the risks here. The ones we've already undertaken. Also, with every variable I add, the chances of success diminish."

"I'm not a variable," Tom said. "I'm a—person."

"Why the sudden change of heart?" Kento asked, softly.

Tom's forehead wrinkled in thought. "I'm here, aren't I?"

A buzzing from a phone caught us all off guard. Who had left their device on?

Lucinda sighed, and reached into her pocket. "It's my burner," she said. "Only Simey has the number."

Again with the 'Simey'? My stomach clenched. She didn't answer it.

"He's probably tracked us down," she said. "And I owe it to him to not make him an accessory, so, here, take it, and leave. Hit the road and don't answer it or call on it until you're back in the States." She tossed the burner to me, and it buzzed in my palms.

234 | SUZY VITELLO

I don't know what made me defy her. Whether it was a spontaneous impulse, or resentment that she'd coerced my brother into committing a felony, or just a case of banal, lowbrow jealousy, but I answered the phone, and I answered it with the query, "Is this Simey?"

# THIRTY-ONE

"WHAT THE—? HAZEL?"

"You have some 'splaining to do, Lucy," I said into the staticky void.

Lucinda moved toward me, her hand outstretched and ready to snatch the phone back, but I shifted quickly, sending her crashing into an antique rolltop desk.

"Tell me you didn't know what she was up to?" I said.

"Where are you?"

"Alberta Wolf, Simon? You must have known her alias."

Lucinda scrambled to her feet, made a guillotine slashing sign across her neck.

I waved her off.

"If you're in Canada, you just complicated our case times a million," said my alleged lawyer.

*Our* case? "Last I checked, Kento had his own lawyer for the custody case."

"I fired him," Kento called from across the room. He'd been bouncing the baby, unsuccessfully attempting to quell his hunger with the pacifier. Tom had taken over warming a baggie of milk in the zapped cup of water.

"You haven't answered my question," I said.

"Let me talk to her," he said.

"Too bad these cheap burners don't have a speaker function. She'll only destroy the phone if I hand it to her."

"It doesn't matter now. You've compromised the whole deal," Lucinda said with a defeated tone. I'd be lying if I didn't admit to a bit of schadenfreude at the sight of her newly slumped posture.

I turned away from the others, and strode to the bathroom, where I closed and locked the door, lowering my voice to a whisper. "Where are you, anyway?"

"Seattle. Where I suspected you'd gone to find Kento."

"Is that where law enforcement is, too?"

"I didn't know, Hazel. You have to believe me. I thought she had that phone to avoid being tracked down by that woman she left me for."

The co-dependence in his voice, his words, angered me. But, then again, here I was, committing my own felony in the name of enabling. Projection is indeed a bitch.

"Okay, what should I do now? What do you suggest?"

"You need to bring that baby back across the border. Like, now. And Kento, too. He needs to face the music."

Lucinda pounded on the door. I turned on the faucet. Whispered, "You're forgetting one little detail. Your crazy ex."

"Let me speak with her. I have an idea."

The next several minutes unfurled in a flurry of confusion. Lucinda weeping into the phone, Kento and Tom huddled on the floor together, feeding the infant who was gulping his bottle amid a staccato of sobs.

Lucinda had agreed to refund part of Kento's cash—a sum that was not disclosed to me—and she disappeared into the night. I gathered the weaponry on the bed and stuffed it back into the same Rubbermaid bin I'd packed them in when relegating it to the storage unit. The guns, the ammunition, the Kwaiken knife. But I paused upon the discovery of an envelope marked with calligraphic kanji. I was ignorant of their meaning, but I knew Tom had studied in Tokyo as an exchange student. "What is this?" I said, waving the envelope.

"Family history," Kento said. "Your late husband had these bound for the dumpster. In the aftermath of his accident I rescued them."

Tom approached the envelope and studied the Japanese characters. "Yes. Family history," he repeated, tracing his finger on the kanji.

I hadn't remembered running across such an envelope when I cleaned out our parents' house. "What do you mean, Ethan had these bound for the dumpster?"

"In a pile, along with Mom's artifacts. The knife, a ceremonial tea service. He'd tossed them in a Hefty bag."

I peeked inside the envelope and found a bundle of mail. Letters, it looked like, yellowed with age. Some of them enclosed in antiquated onionskin airmail envelopes. The missives themselves were addressed in English, and as I thumbed through them, I was surprised to find a few sent to the Tule Lake Relocation Center in Northern California, postmarked in the mid-forties.

"Have you read these?" I asked my brother.

He nodded.

"Have you?" I asked Tom.

He indicated that, yes, he had.

I felt deceived. Left out. "Would have been nice to be looped in. I mean, these people were my family, too."

I knew that our grandfather, the one Kento was named for, had been a baby when his father served as a Nisei interpreter during the Second World War. That he'd spent the first few years of his life in an internment camp. In my hands I was holding the stories of my family. Their endurance. Their grace.

Tom reminded me that we needed to hit the road. The baby, finally satisfied and changed, was now asleep on Tom's shoulder.

"Okay," I said, hoping that an all-points, international Amber Alert search for the child was still pending.

# THIRTY-TWO

STRANGELY, THE TREK BACK TO WASHINGTON STATE went smoothly. Kento had been briefed on the best time to cross. Midnight was shift change. 11:45 p.m. was optimum for that reason. At least that's what Lucinda the Wolf had counseled.

I sat up front, trying to look all mommy-like, the baby's fake passport in my hand. Despite the munitions and Amber Alert passenger in Tom's car, we were waved through. For once, bureaucratic ineptitude was on our side.

Once in Washington State, however, we had a target on our backs. Or, more accurately, on our car, since Simon had confirmed Tom's license plate was on the "persons of interest" list. Alberta Wolf, a.k.a. Simon's ex, helped us out with that as well.

We pulled off the I-5 in Bellingham, and drove a few miles to a wooded dead-end road to switch plates for ones from Alabama.

The phrase "accessory to a crime" kept wiggling itself into my sleepy brain like an annoying alarm clock's snooze button. I'd tamp it down with all manner of justification. This baby was the son of my brother and his husband. They were his parents. He wouldn't exist if it weren't for Tom's contribution to his DNA. We were saving this child, this itty-bitty infant, from the tangled web of the foster care system. We were in the right. Even Lucinda and her questionable tactics, appeared to be fighting for justice—though admitting such was a hard pill to swallow.

The letters from our family's archival history lay rubber-banded together in the bottom of my bag. Our mother hadn't said much about her father's internment, but she'd obviously known about it, given the correspondence she'd kept hidden. A feeling of triumph mixed with terror coursed through me as we continued south. The baby fussed in his infant carrier, and Kento worked the pacifier in his mouth like a gag.

"It's okay if he cries, Kento. Let him cry it out," Tom pleaded.

But I knew why Kento was consumed with quieting the baby. Our mother's constant appeals for peace in the family home. Our father was the only member of the household allowed to vocalize frustration or anger. Any temper-tantrums or fussiness emitted from our mouths was met with the back of his hand. The smell of alcohol on his breath, his clumsy footfalls after a night at the bar, elicited a Pavlovian rush of adrenaline that reverberated through our child bodies. Our bedroom, sliced down the middle by two opposite-facing dressers, rattled in the wake of his thunderous explosions.

As small children, we huddled together in my bed, me, soothing Kento with back pats as he muffle-cried into my pillow. When we reached middle-school age, during his tirades, we'd escape out our bedroom window, into the night. Sometimes climbing into the family station wagon until dawn, curled in the back-back, under the Pendleton wool blanket our mother kept back there to hide "valuables" when she went shopping in the "big city" of Spokane.

Our clandestine trip down the interstate felt similar. The need to stay quiet. The terror-induced paralysis felt in our limbs. Tom, who, by all accounts, had a calm upbringing, raised as he was by doting, albeit cold, parents, drove silently forward. Finally, as we exited the freeway at the rendezvous spot Simon had dictated, Tom uttered an audible breath.

"Kento, I was wrong to get cold feet on this. I'm in. One hundred percent."

Kento's hand reached his husband's shoulder from the back seat. Sobs choked out of him. But they were happy tears. The first happy weeping I'd heard from my brother since their wedding.

Simon met us at a 24-hr truck stop diner south of Tacoma. The burnt-coffee and rancid bacon grease of the place did nothing to quell my appetite. Apparently, being a fugitive was hard work, and I was famished. We settled into a booth where Simon had evidently been parked for a few hours. A stack of documents sat piled in front of him next to an untouched trucker's all-night special of pancakes and congealed sunny side up eggs.

Kento hefted the infant carrier between him and Tom. The baby's eyes were slitted in sleep, a miniature Carhartts hat puffed up like a mushroom from his tiny head.

"He really is adorable," Simon muttered, then turned his face to me. I'd been careful not to cozy up to him there in the booth, having placed my large handbag between us.

"Thanks for getting us out of hot water," Tom said.

"Oh, you're still in plenty of it," Simon responded.

My stomach growled and I waved the server over. He was a ginger-haired, acne-ridden kid, barely out of high school, was my guess. He dealt a handful of sticky, laminated menus before asking if Simon was done with his platter of cold breakfast food.

Simon nodded and thanked him, but asked for a fresh refill on the coffee. We all asked for coffee.

"Your lawyer was kind enough to send me a copy of your surrogate contract," said Simon, thumbing through his papers. "He's a good dude. Obviously pissed off at how this thing has blown up, trampling your rights."

Tom and Kento leaned forward.

"Unfortunately," Simon continued, "you're in violation of several laws. And the fact that Corinda is claiming she was coerced into the surrogacy is paramount among the complaints. Seconded only to the fact that she resides, and gave birth, in a state that no longer recognizes same-sex marriage."

"Seems to me, she resides in prison now," Tom said. "Federal prison, yeah? So, Idaho law doesn't—"

Simon cut him off. Gave him a *Bingo!* salute. "That's the hope, eventually. But for now, she's awaiting trial, and is still in the state's custody. They moved her out of town though, to Orofino, to avoid a local uprising."

Kento's earlier happy tears were a distant memory.

The pimply server returned with three chunky diner mugs and a carafe. "Decisions?" he said, flatly.

"Basted eggs, dry toast, butter on the side," said Tom, waving his unread menu in the air.

"Basted? What's basted?" said the server.

"Poached will do," Tom said.

I detected an eyeroll.

"I'm fine with just coffee," Kento said, in a more polite tone.

My brother tended toward anorexia when upset.

"I'll have—" I said, scanning the numbered items accompanied by bleached-out photos, "number four. With the hash browns *and* the fruit."

"That's extra," said the server.

"And a slice of pie," I added. "Cherry."

"Oh, that's seasonal."

"What do you have for pie?"

"All the cream varieties. And lemon meringue."

"Lemon meringue it is," I said. I was the stress eater of our twinship. Ethan used to say that the yin-yang of Kento and me was nature's need for balance. Ethan. I realized that I hadn't thought about him a while.

Simon's head snapped up. He went pale. We all followed his gaze.

Law enforcement.

"Fuck," I said, and, as if in scold for my swearing, the baby began to howl.

The next several minutes were a blur. Four uniformed officers descended upon us. The other diners aimed their phones our way to capture whatever this was, and I knew, I just knew, this fiasco was a viral arrest in the making. They all converged on Kento, whose likeness was, apparently, plastered all over social media.

That's when Tom took over.

"It was me, not him," he lied, jutting his arms out for cuffing. "I am the biological father of this baby, and I have rights."

Kento made a move to stop him, and Tom pushed him away. I realized then that the gesture was performative. The words, though true, were spoken clearly, in hopes that all the vids-in-progress would emphasize "rights" and "biological."

The cops looked dumbfounded, searching one another's faces for protocol.

Simon stepped into the fray, glancing from face to face. "I'm their lawyer, and they will not say another word."

A female cop reached into the booth and yanked up the carrier by its handle, tipping it inadvertently and spilling the infant out onto the booth. I scooted under the table and caught the baby before he hit the greasy floor. When I emerged with the bawling infant, cheers rang out. Now it was my turn for performance.

With all the sanctimony and drama I could muster, I bellowed, "Are you crazy? You almost killed this child!"

The cop stepped back, her face frozen in horror for just one second. And that second was enough. "I'm, uh, I'm—" she sputtered.

THAT, IT TURNED OUT, WAS THE MONEY SHOT. By the time folks were rolling out of bed a few hours later, X, IG, TikTok and the like were awash with the images of police overreach and incompetence. Protests and marches and a media blitz were already in the works. My phone blew up with requests for interviews.

The baby's custody, however, was in limbo, until Simon stepped in, granting me temporary guardianship. Hashtag #StolenBaby—which had originally served as an Amber Alert, describing my brother as the perpetrator—now couched the "system" as culprit. The incompetent police officer, caught on tape botching the seizure, was put on administrative leave immediately. Due to the dustup and subsequent media blitz, when Idaho attempted to carry out extradition, Washington State refused, and granted bail to Tom and Kento in addition to providing stealth accommodations thanks to the recent Safe Harbor Law, originally created to protect abortion seekers from one of the red states—mainly Idaho.

Meanwhile, Simon, the baby, and I holed up in a Seattle-area Airbnb owned by an anonymous sympathizer of the suddenly trending #StolenBaby mob.

# THIRTY-THREE

"I CAN'T BELIEVE PEOPLE CHOOSE to do this," I said, patting the gassy newborn's back as he screamed.

The temporary guardianship role was a stopgap while the various jurisdictions battled for the right to decide the baby's fate. As well as Kento's and Tom's. An "underground railroad-esque" effort for our collective food and shelter needs was underway, and we'd been awaiting word from our latest benefactor on when Kento and Tom would find their way to us.

We were down to two pouches of donated breast milk (carried around in a cooler like a liver awaiting transplant), but more was on the way, apparently.

Simon, who'd had the foresight to achieve Washington State licensure in the month prior, was deep in LGBTQ custody case law, his laptop and documents splayed out on the wobbly kitchen table. He had parted ways with Beacon and Bright—the polite way of saying they bought him out and showed him the door—and Kento was his sole client at the moment. How we were going to compensate him was still a mystery, as my bank account was empty, and Kento had only the reimbursement from Lucinda. The whole money thing was weighing on me, and I had to admit a growing resentment at being stripped of my gigs.

The wailing infant didn't seem to bother Simon. And then I noticed the earbuds. I tapped his shoulder.

"No fair."

"Let me spell you," he said, rising from his studies and reaching out for the still-unnamed stolen baby.

"His lungs sure work fine," I said. "Can I borrow your buds?"

Simon and I exchanged the requested items. "I think he just shat, by the way," I said, wrinkling my nose.

"Of course he did," said Simon, as he lowered the child to a toweled spot on the kitchen counter.

I flopped down on the worn sofa, stared at the ceiling, and tried to declutter my anxiety-filled brain, but the sadness and injustice embedded in the Nisei letters kept intruding.

I'd spent the past couple of days reading through the bundle of missives Kento had rescued from the trash heap. Still, after all this time, I wanted to believe Ethan hadn't tossed them on purpose, but the growing evidence of my late husband's distain for my family could not be ignored.

The letters were startling. My mother had never spoken of her father's early life in a concentration camp while his own father served in the military, but as I read one after another revelatory missive, I realized she had carried the ugliness to her grave. Written in perfect English, a gruesome timeline revealed itself. Apparently, my maternal great-grandfather, George Utaka, had been recruited to active duty in the Pacific during World War II, while the rest of his family, including the grandfather for whom Kento was named, were rounded up from their small farm in Western Washington, and sent to a camp in Arizona, and then moved to a notorious Northern California segregation center, Tule Lake, where they spent more than three years behind barbed wire. They were sent to the worst of the camps after submitting a poorly written loyalty questionnaire, wherein my Japanese-born great-grandmother misunderstood a question, and marked "no" when she meant "yes" due to the word "emperor" appearing in the context of loyalty. She thought she was rebuking the Japanese Emperor, when the "no" answer meant the opposite.

Nisei were first-generation Japanese Americans, exploited by the U.S. military for their Japanese language skills and familiarity with the norms and customs of their ancestral culture. Great-Grandfather George wrote of the segregation he endured in his division, how he was called "Jap" by his fellow soldiers. Whenever a commanding officer required his assistance, whether day or middle of the night, he, and a couple others from his unit who had proven useful, were pulled into service. In one letter, one that haunted me, Great-Grandfather George wrote about the first nights after landing in the Solomon Islands, bushwhacking through bamboo and waist-deep mud on the Munda Trail. He wrote about being ordered to decipher the contents of blood-soaked diaries peeled from the pockets of dead Japanese soldiers, his visit to a POW camp, and his role as a translator. His bout with malaria. His bout with dysentery. And finally, in late August of 1943, his surprise meeting with First Lady Eleanor Roosevelt while healing from a bullet wound in his thigh. Friendly fire, that bullet wound. At least that's what I figured out, reading between the lines.

I stood and stretched, yanked Simon's buds out of my ears. The baby, now freshly diapered, had quieted. Simon was still rocking him, but the infant's eyes were closed, occasional sleep burbles emerging from his pale, thread-thin lips. Simon's nurturing posture clanged a bell in my head. I'd forgotten all about Greta.

"Where is your dog?"

"Your Crazy Cat Lady friend has her. She's housesitting for me."

"The felon?"

He shrugged. "Greta loves her. That's all that matters."

Was it though?

The vehicular manslaughter case had been dropped, thanks to some fancy footwork Simon performed before his ousting at the law firm. Apparently, tire patterns at the scene proved inconclusive in determining which car slammed into which. The icy conditions had complicated the reconstruction, and it seemed just as likely that Patrick had slammed into Inge, rather than the other way around.

Talk of the dog Simon shared with his ex was my opening.

"So how'd you leave it with Lucinda? Did you really not know about her side job in international trafficking?"

I could read his jaw-setting reaction from across the room. Enabling and defending his way-too-pretty ex-wife, even now.

I pressed. "Did you know about her alias? I mean, if my brother was able to find her—"

I stopped mid-sentence, hating the sound of my whiny, jealous voice as it echoed off the sterile walls of the room.

"I can't talk about it," was all he said.

"What do you mean, you *can't talk about it*," my whiny tone now replaced with fury.

Simon put a finger to his lips and tilted his head toward the sleeping baby.

I bit my lip and folded my arms, fully aware that I was acting like a child, but feeling justified all the same. I longed for a field trip. A walk to a café would do. Or even just a brisk constitutional through the nearby park. Spring, and all its colorful glory, had blanketed Seattle, and here I was, stuck in this cheap tract house, under what amounted to house arrest.

While Washington and Idaho squabbled over Tom's and Kento's fates, the partisan #StolenBaby factions dueling on social media as well as daily protests in front of the states' respective capitols, we needed to stay hidden. Even though an anonymous benefactor allegedly donated this "safe harbor," it was starting to smell like Alberta Wolf—a.k.a., bipolar, kind-hearted Lucinda—was involved in this as well.

"He really is cute," Simon said, glancing down at the doll-sized bundle in his arms in an obvious move to change the subject.

The baby had an effect on all of these guys: Kento, Tom, now Simon—who'd had his sperm channel pinched off to avoid fatherhood. All of them turned to jelly over this mini human.

"Babies," I mumbled.

"Didn't you and Ethan want children?"

"He did," I said. "I wasn't ready."

"You sound like Lucinda," he said.

"She's the reason you got snipped, then?"

Simon's head nodded less in confirmation than thought. He peeled his glasses off, set them on the counter, all without jostling the sleeping infant on his shoulder. He turned to face me.

"I notice you still wear your wedding ring."

I glanced down at my fingers. The ring had become part of my body. Less a symbol of marital commitment than an object of rebellion against the in-laws. In that moment, looking at its waning sparkle, I realized I no longer had a need for the Mackenzie heirloom. If Mac and Skipper wanted to die holding onto this bit of their family history, who was I to stand in their way? But I wasn't going to lose this argument.

"I'm a widow. Not a supposedly divorced spouse still pining for the ex."

"I'm not *pining*," he said, in a mocking voice.

"Well, you are still under her spell. That much is clear."

Simon opened his mouth to say the next thing, but at that moment, a rap on the door announced we had company. Instinctively, I ducked, eyeing the Rubbermaid tub across the room where the Zapf family cache of weaponry sat packed amid diapers and burp cloths. I motioned for Simon to stand by while I made my way over to the bin. There had been too many violent visitors over the last year; I wasn't going to take any chances.

But then my brother's voice broke through the fog of tension. "Open up, guys, it's us."

# THIRTY-FOUR

KENTO IMMEDIATELY SCOOPED THE BABY off Simon's shoulder.

"How'd you—" said Simon, clearly as befuddled as I was with this odd turn of events.

"The wolves," Tom said. "Lucinda's gang of underground social justice folks."

"Not sure that's the best idea," Simon said, looking longingly at the baby that was just snatched from the comforts of his body. "I was hoping you'd lay low until my court filing on Monday."

"This house is pretty secure," Tom said. "At least that's what the driver who brought us here told us."

"The whole state is on our side," Kento said, his tone notched up toward joy—a quality that had been dormant for some time. "Have you seen the buzz on the socials?"

"To be clear, not the *whole* state," Tom added.

"Well, west of the Cascades, anyway," Kento said. "At least according to my three million followers."

"We have our devices turned off," said Simon.

"That explains your surprise at our arrival," Tom said. "We messaged you."

Tom went on to fill in the missing pieces. Lucinda's underground network spanned the West Coast from San Diego to Alaska. A woman Tom referred to as Seattle Wolf had been shuttling him and Kento from house to house all week. This was to be a brief stopover. A delivery of breast milk and some of what the #StolenBaby movement (it was a movement now?) referred to as "parental bonding time."

Kento and Tom were betas. The network was building a guerrilla infrastructure set on countering the flurry of anti-gay laws and legislation. The west and northeast coasts were gearing up. It turns out that, thanks to the viral episode in the truck stop diner, Tom and Kento's plight birthed a revolution. In the week that followed, many safe harbor volunteers raised their hands, willing to risk consequences by opening their homes to disenfranchised same-sex couples whose marriages and adoptions were hanging in the balance.

Idaho, however—the Panhandle in particular—was a different story.

"It's about winning the war through winning a series of battles," Tom said. "Hazel, we need you. We need your help."

"*My* help?"

"You're the legal guardian for the moment, and apparently untouchable as long as you and the baby go back to Idaho."

My mind was playing catch up with an agenda that had been decided already. "*Me* and the baby?"

As if in protest, the infant farted, and then spit up.

Simon turned on his device, and scrolled through emails and messages, while I paced, trying to figure out how not to sound like a total dick when I refused this mission.

Simon murmured some legal mumbo jumbo. Words like *Ad Litem*, *informal discovery*, and *representation*.

"English, please," I said.

Tom translated. "Since Simon is licensed in both Idaho and Washington, he's been appointed to oversee the custody dispute, which means, he can no longer represent us. What it boils down to is filling out a bunch of forms."

"A bit more than that," Simon said. "And this whole thing reeks of sabotage. I can smell a 'conflict of interest' suit a mile away. I can't accept the position, clearly. And Hazel can't continue as the temporary custodian."

The infant screamed. Kento patted his back. "Fuck," he said.

"The Guardian Ad Litem needs to be a neutral party. An attorney or a social worker who acts in the interest of the baby and has no ties to Corinda or the two of you—"

"What about Patriot Root," Kento interrupted. "How can we be certain that some homophobic, anti-Asian attorney won't end up deciding the fate of our kid?"

"The system—" Simon began, but facing a roomful of people for whom the system has never worked, he clearly understood the fallacy, and his mouth stopped mid-thought.

The infant escalated his wrath. "It's called purple crying," Kento said. "You know, colic. At the hospital they showed me this technique."

My brother began swinging the child in his arms, supporting his neck and head while rocking side-to-side like a metronome on steroids.

It was reminiscent of something. Something dark and far in the past. My heart ticked wildly in alarm, "Stop! Kento, stop!" I yelled.

All eyes turned to me.

"You'll drop him. You'll hurt him," I gasped.

Simon stepped closer to me. His two hands on my two shoulders. But whatever compelled me to scream in fear, the un-worded terror within me, now caused convulsive sobbing. Rage and sorrow pushing out of me. Even the infant couldn't compete with the sounds that poured, like a waterfall, from my body.

And finally, words joined my sobs. "Make him. Make him stop."

# THIRTY-FIVE

I SLEPT HARD. When Kento brought me a mug of tea and pulled back the drapes, the sun had been up for some time. My head throbbed. The deep skull-pounding pain of a crying hangover.

He sat on the edge of the bed, his hand squeezing each of my toes through the cheap IKEA comforter.

I sipped the tea.

It was another act reminiscent of our childhood. Our mother bringing us tea in bed the morning after one of our father's tantrums.

"I don't have to ask what that was about," Kento said.

"Next topic," I said.

Kento stood, turned his back to me. Something was coming.

"What?"

He pivoted again, but his eyes didn't meet mine. "Don't think I'm not scared, Hazel. The way Dad was—I'm on guard all the time."

"The swinging. It seemed excessive."

"I protected his neck and head. I wasn't Dad."

"Was he really the monster we thought? Did he even have a gentle side?"

Kento shook his head. Methodically. A finger in the air, but without revelation.

"How do you know we aren't similarly cruel, Kento? How can we be sure that his rage, his evilness, didn't take root?"

He paused. Then, "I need to tell you something."

I waited.

"You always questioned the Corinda thing. Why I don't hate her. Why I'm always sucked back in."

I took another sip of the now lukewarm tea.

"Do you remember prom night?"

"Vaguely. As you recall, I didn't go." Ethan and I had our first breakup a few days before prom. We got back together the week after, just to break up again before heading to our respective colleges.

"Right. The fucker. Anyway, after prom, Corinda and I were out back on Dad's riding mower, smoking weed. I was trying to work up the nerve to tell her. To come out to her."

I searched my brain to recall that night, but I was pretty sad. I was probably streaming Amazon romcoms and tearjerkers in the house.

"I made the mistake of leading with 'I love you,' and before I could muster the courage to say, 'but I'm gay,' Dad's friend's pickup pulled up the drive."

"Benjamin Kreutz?"

"Yeah. Dad's main enabler. Always the designated driver when Dad went out on one of his binges."

"I think he was secretly in love with the old man," I said.

"Quite possibly. Anyway, that night, he must have smelled the weed, because he stomped right up to us, all drunk and pissy."

"Yeah, well, he did his own share of blazing, so, I don't know why he'd care."

"It was all show. He rambled on about my worthlessness, the usual. But it escalated. It's as if a switch got turned on. Corinda in her slinky prom dress still, half covered with shawl. He ripped the shawl off. Said something about her breasts. About his son not being man enough to take what he wanted, blah, blah, blah. And then he basically assaulted her. Right in front of me. Grabbed her arm, pulled her off the mower, and started pulling her straps down, touching her, and I just fucking froze."

My stomach turned. I put the mug down on the nightstand. "He what?"

"But that's not the worst of it. Do you remember Corinda's reaction to the Kwaiken knife during the gender reveal fiasco?"

"Yes, but..."

"Mom. She threatened her with it."

"Wait, what?"

"She stormed out of the house with that thing, and you would have thought Corinda was assaulting Dad rather than the other way around."

I stared at Kento. "That's nuts."

"She called Corinda a whore. Told her to get off the property, and stay away from our family. Waving that god damn knife around like a sword. You know, she always had it in for Corinda. And what did I do? Nothing. Not a fucking thing. So you want to know why I keep cutting her slack? To make up for our parents. To make up for my pussy-hearted passivity."

My brother's face all screwed up with the pain of it. I reached an arm out to him, but he scooted back. "Kento—I had no clue about any of that. I'm so sorry."

But there was more. My brother's expression turned sour, the way he'd get when his feelings were challenged.

"Talk to me."

His gaze, up, down. "You are a straight, white-passing woman, Hazel. We're twins, but we don't even look like siblings."

"You don't think I know? Every time I look in the mirror, I see our father. Big treat for me."

He turned from me, his focus landing on the pile of stationery, now loosely scattered on the bed. "Did you read them? The letters?"

I nodded.

"Our legacy. Well, mine, at least."

"You're right, Kento, I don't experience the level of racism and oppression that you do, but that doesn't mean I'm any less impacted by it. I was raised by the same people you were. The same intergenerational trauma leaked its sewer water into my blood. When I saw you rock that baby? I swear, I had some kind of pre-verbal PTSD."

"Yeah. Well. It's likely that you were spared Dad's physical abuse, but you witnessed some shit."

My obsession with drawing decomposing bodies. The darkness that kept me in shadows and denial. How did I not know that Ethan lived a double life?

"You've always been better able to see and express truth, Kento. I envy you that."

Kento picked up a random envelope from the pile of fragile stationery on the nightstand. He fanned it in front of my face.

"I'm the namesake, okay? Every time our mother looked at me, she saw the evidence of what this country did to our family. Her great-grandmother died of cancer in that internment camp. Her dad, brought up by a battle-scarred father, carried those scars."

"She never shared any of that with me," I said, not even disguising my bitterness.

"Well, consider yourself lucky. She bent my ear plenty. About her upbringing. The way our father used her—claimed her, basically imprisoned her."

"What are you talking about?"

"So many things you don't know."

It's true, our parents' marriage was a complex puzzle. How they met, why they married. They never discussed it. At least, they never talked about it in front of me. And, until this moment, I'd assumed Kento was likewise in the dark.

"Our childhood game," Kento said. "*I don't*, remember?"

"What does—"

"I invented that game as a way to deal with the stuff Mom told me. I was her diary, okay? The keeper of secrets I wasn't allowed to tell."

"Your grooms were always handsome, impeccable."

"And my brides were warty and hideous, remember?"

I did.

"Mom was supposed to marry a Japanese man. It was arranged. Some guy named Akio from Seattle, supposedly descending from the Imperial Fujiwara family—remember her fixation on that?"

"Yeah. It was a weird obsession she had." I always equated it with the way conservative white people brag about their *Mayflower* ancestry.

But it hurt that Kento knew of this arranged marriage, and I had been in the dark. "So, what happened?"

"She worked as a cleaner up on Whidbey, for some admiral's family. She and her mother. One night, they had to work late. Something about the admiral's wife throwing an officers' party. Mom stayed later, and her mother had a migraine, so left earlier. It was nearly midnight when she walked home, and that's when Dad and some other drunken navy halfwits saw her walking alongside the road and basically kidnapped her."

I had no idea about any of that.

Kento's face took on a strange shape, as if he was trying to fold an uncomfortable truth back inside.

"What do you mean by kidnap?" I said.

"The way Mom told it, the guys were tossing her around in the back-seat like she was a ragdoll. Dad, who was driving, was the most sober of the bunch, if you can believe that. And he made them get out of the car. Mom, at this point, was hysterical. He calmed her down, brought her home, but not before asking her out. Apparently, he was quite the doting boyfriend. And then, he knocked her up with twins, and that was that."

I'd known that our seven-months-after-the-wedding birth was suspicious, but twins often come early. At least that was the official Zapf company line.

"No wonder our grandparents were so shitty to us," I said.

"Yep. We're bastards. Big surprise."

"But Mom enabled Dad's behavior. That victim-blaming thing with Corinda? What the fuck?"

"Exactly. Loyalty's a weird deal. If you read the letters, you might think Mom's whole legacy was based on an intergenerational Stockholm syndrome sort of thing. The twisted idea that marrying a white guy would elevate her."

The tea was too cold to enjoy. I set the mug down.

Kento continued. "She kept one foot firmly in her ancestral pride, though. The Kwaiken knife, the claim to Japan's imperial past. While secretly resenting her parents and aligning with our drunken shithead of a father. She lived and died a conflicted woman. So un-self-aware. And I see the same thing in Corinda."

My brother looked on the verge of tears. I reached a hand toward him, making the slightest of contact. "And you thought you'd save her from that. Kento, you have such an enormous heart."

"What is that gaslighting phrase? 'Mistakes were made?'"

My gentle twin brother. My heart. "Tell me how I can help."

# THIRTY-SIX

WE HAD A PLAN. QUESTION WAS, would I be able to pull it off? My first stop—Mac and Skipper. When I pulled up in front of their house, I was blindsided by the degree of neglect. Sections of their once-white picket fence had blown down, and random pieces of dry-rotted wood lay about the yard. Early spring weeds claimed cracks in their walkway, bolting through shattered flagstones. A total tripping hazard for elderly people.

Skipper's past pride in her flower beds—the perennial parade of blooms planted to provide a continual sequence of color—had been replaced with a series of lawn signs. Some espousing rightwing grievances, some scolding potential solicitors. Despite my issues with the Mackenzies, evidence of their sad bitterness pained me. Outliving their only child, suffering financial ruin due to a blind, ignorant belief system. If only they'd opened their minds. Their hearts. Now, it was too late. I knocked on a door badly in need of paint.

Shuffling from inside. A scratchy voice punctuated with coughing. The words were indistinguishable, but the tone was clear: who would dare defy their signage and trespass on their sacred path?

It was Mac who opened the door a crack, his expression, a spectrum of surprise, disdain, hope. "Hazel," he grunted.

"Mac," I responded, matching his growl.

"What do you want?"

"May I come in?"

The door hinges creaked as he stepped back with his walker.

"Skipper isn't doing well. She's been in bed a week," he said.

"A week? What's going on?"

He sniffed, dragged a filthy handkerchief from his pants' pocket and honked into it.

"Mac, I've come here to give you back your family ring," I tugged the heirloom over my knuckle and held it out. "I realized that I was holding onto it for selfish reasons."

Mac blew another wad of crap into his hankie. Then, "Could have done this a year ago."

"Take it," I said, the thing still resting in my palm.

He reached a yellow-nailed hand toward my outstretched one, and snatched it up, then folded it into the gross handkerchief before cramming it in his pocket. He was skeletal, and his trousers hung on his frame like a scarecrow that had lost its straw.

The house smelled of grease, urine, and Simple Green. "Do you have any help around here?"

His raised his head, his rheumy eyes into mine. "My son is dead."

"I want to help," I said. "I don't have any extra money right now, but I'm going to sell my place. Downsize."

"Spent your windfall, did you?"

He was struggling. Wanting to appear tough, but the façade wasn't holding. This man wouldn't last a year without significant intervention. His wife was likely in worse condition. I took a deep breath. It was worth a shot. "I'd like to say hello to Skipper."

"She's rough."

"Still."

He tweaked his head in the direction of a nearby bedroom, from which low, muffled moans were emanating.

What greeted me in that room was a stench so bad, I had to stifle a gag. My mother-in-law lay in a squalid bed, likely in a pile of her own shit. Her hair, a gray nest corona-ed around a pale, sunken face. She wasn't yet seventy, but looked twenty years older. When her eyes met mine, she yelled, "No!" A frightened animal in a rusty trap.

I had no idea how to handle it, so I stood, frozen in the doorway. Mac clunked up behind me. "She's demented," he said.

I turned to him. "She needs care."

"I promised her I wouldn't stick her in one of those places," he said, his voice wavering.

"So you just let her lie there? In her filth?"

"I clean her up, usually, but today I had the flutters." He clutched his chest.

"I'm going to make some calls, Mac. This is no way to live."

"Don't you dare," he seethed.

"Where are all your supposed friends? Your community? All those organizations that happily took money from you?"

He waved the back of his hand toward my chin. "They got bigger fish to fry. Country's going to hell."

"Well, on that we can agree. But, Mac, Ethan must be rolling in his—"

Mac swatted at me. "You had him burned. There is no grave."

I backed away from his flinging claw. "So, you just want to die like this? Without dignity? What if you keel over with a heart attack, and she starves to death?"

"The Lord will take care of us."

"Oh, brother."

I'd had enough. I wasn't going to debate a losing argument. I scooted by him, turned around for a final shot. "I will be making those calls, Mac. This is elder abuse."

"You should have died, not him," he launched. His need for the last word. Just like my father.

BACK ON THE ROAD, I thought about calling Simon, but we'd left things so weird. Besides, if I was going to make visiting hours at the prison in Orofino, two-and-a-half hours away, I had to break speed limits, and focus on driving.

Simon had the foresight to have me apply for visitor status before the whole debacle with the baby, and I knew Corinda would want an update. She'd even reached out, leaving a message on my cell phone. I fishtailed a bit over the pass, my mind wandering through my agenda. This was my only shot. Our only shot. But I was exhausted. By the time I turned into the prisoner's "guest" parking lot, I was a quaking mess, and I had less than a half an hour before visiting time expired.

I don't know what I expected, really. I'd been inside plenty of prisons—mostly of the county jail variety. Had seen my share of bedraggled, angry inmates. Incarceration does nothing for skin, hair, disposition. But on Corinda, the orange jumpsuit and fluorescent lighting was a step up from her usual somber black outfits. She'd possibly hit the weight room; there was new definition in her arms.

I took a seat across from her—since she was still awaiting trial, she was allowed visitations in an open room, though I was cautioned there could be no skin contact, nothing shared.

I had hardly sat down when she began drilling me. Had I seen the baby? Was he with Kento? Had Tom also taken a paternity test?

"Slow down, we still have fifteen minutes," I said.

"You look like shit," she offered, head cocked, nose wrinkled.

"It's been a long day. Long week, actually."

Her foot tapped nervously, as if she'd been given a stimulant. I confessed that Kento had screwed up, taking the baby, but he'd done it out of love. "They were going to stick him in the foster system," I said.

Her foot froze midway through a tap. Her eyes widened and focused on a space behind me. "I'm going to plea," she muttered. "Five years."

I nodded. Simon had indicated this as a possibility.

"You don't want your child—Kento's child—with strangers until you get out, right?"

"I don't want the kid to turn queer though. Life ain't easy for kids these days. Worse if you're living an alternate lifestyle."

"Corinda. Stop. You know that's a load of crap, right? A baby needs love. That's all. And there's no such thing as *turning* queer. Arthur is—was—a violent, angry man. A fear-driven, homophobic bully who abused you, and gaslighted you."

"Well, you're not wrong about that," she said, quietly.

"I have an idea," I said, sensing a small opening. "One I think you'll see is the best solution for all of us. Especially the baby."

A guard began to move toward us, offering the wrap-it-up motion with his hands. I spilled the plan. My role, Kento and Tom's role. A promise that she'd continue to be part of the baby's life once she got out. All she had to do was tell the truth about Arthur's invasion the day of the aborted gender reveal party. Agree to honor the contract, and allow Kento and Tom to raise the baby in Washington State. "You might consider moving there yourself once you're out," I said.

"What about you? You planning on moving to Sin-attle?"

"No. But I am going to sell my house. I want to downsize, and Leona and Marcia are putting their place on the market, so—"

"That house you just built? You crazy?"

"It was a dream I had a lifetime ago. With someone I didn't really know. Besides, Leona and Marcia's house is super cute, and it comes with a killer hot tub in a private back yard."

Corinda twisted her mouth, narrowed her eyes. A snarky comeback on her tongue, but to her credit, she held it.

But I had something to say. It was now or never. "My brother told me something I didn't know. Something that happened prom night."

In her face, a streak of pain flashed, but she sniffed it away. "Ancient history."

"Not really. Corinda, you were assaulted, and nobody came to your rescue. I am so sorry."

"You know what they say about what doesn't kill you and all, right?"

"That's a load of crap. My parents were sick, but that's no excuse. I want to make you a promise. Nothing like that will ever happen to your baby."

"It isn't my baby," she shot back. "If it was Tom who made him, not Kento, I don't want him."

Her words struck me like a bullet to my heart. But at least the truth was out now.

"That's fair, and that's honest. But you still need to sign over custody. Admit you weren't coerced into surrogacy."

The guard loomed, pointed to the overly huge clock on the wall.

"Yeah, I'll do that," she said. "But Hazel? For the record, I never hated you. I ruined my life for you. Called the feds against Arthur and that group of shitheads. No way can I ever live in Steeplejack again."

"And I'm grateful, Corinda. Truly. But maybe you'll feel differently when you get out. Maybe we can start over?"

"Time's up," said the gruff voice of the prison guard.

Corinda stood, biceps flexing under her rolled-up sleeves. She turned to leave, the guard herding her toward the inmate door, but then, she pivoted to face me. "Take care of yourself," she said.

# THIRTY-SEVEN

## NINE MONTHS LATER

HE STOOD THERE, ARMS FULL OF GREENERY. An oversized elf hat slipped over one bespectacled eye. "Are you some sort of would-be Grinch?" I said, guarding the entrance to Marcia and Leona's former cottage.

"Ho ho ho," he said, releasing the evergreen swag festooned with flocked ribbons and plastic doodads to my frosty stoop. "Never too early to introduce Akio to the holiday traditions, right?"

"But do they have to be so banal? I was thinking more of a solstice celebration. You know, paper lanterns and whatnot. Christmas isn't a huge Japanese holiday. At least not in our family."

His mud-splattered Patagonia jacket hung on his slender frame, a size or two too large. "Admit it, you simply don't care for my Christmas kitsch." He whistled for Greta, who was on a sniff-ari in the bushes. She bounded up and raced past us, into the house.

"I hope she didn't find any cat turds left over from Marcia's menagerie."

"It's been four months; I would think they're part of the soil?"

"Yeah, well, she fed all the strays, and they keep coming back, hoping."

Simon grinned. "You're such a hard ass."

"My ass is getting harder, actually, now that we've joined the Steeplejack hiking club." I stretched over the pile of holiday cheer, and pecked him on the cheek.

"So, Kento and company haven't bailed yet, I hope," he said, air-smooching me in a return gesture.

"I texted him this morning. They did the Saito Yuletide family gathering last night. Tom's family is coming around. Apparently, they're doting grandparents, and it was quite the haul, gift-wise. But Tom's folks are super uptight. I think they're ready for a less formal gathering. I was thinking Hot Pockets?"

"And maybe tater tots for a side dish?"

"Brilliant minds," I said. "I'll warm up the toaster oven."

Simon hopped over the embellished greenery and plucked the elf hat from his head before hurling it into the room, stripper style.

"Damn, boy," I said.

"How much time do we have?"

WE'D TAKEN WHATEVER THE THING we had to the next level. Or maybe half a step to the next level. A friends-with-benefits meets Fitbit-rivals sort of arrangement, neither of us keen on defining it. Given our last run at marriage and our spouses' secret lives, it was fair to say we both had trust issues. I hadn't anticipated my horny reaction today, however. With my brother and his adorable family due within the hour, this would have to be the quickest of quickies.

I stripped as I walked through the house, tossing clothing like confetti onto the floor, the sofa, the kitchen counter. I grabbed some towels from the laundry basket near the back door, and headed out the slider to the deck. Simon, already at the lip of the covered tub, free of clothing, his cock a half-hard beacon as if deciding whether or not to point my way.

"Never a good idea to get busy in a Jacuzzi," I said.

He took me in. An up and down glance that answered his questionable arousal. "We can figure it out."

"Ah," I said, returning his appraising gaze, "I see where this is going."

I pried the lid to the Jacuzzi open and folded it back, beckoning him into steamy waters as I stepped in.

He moved next to me, cupped my chin in his hand. His kiss, wet and long. Upon release of his lips he said, "Hazel, I want to clear the air about something. I never explained or apologized for the whole Lucinda deal."

"You know what?" I said, "I don't want to discuss it. You are a total mensch, and you did what any mensch would do when faced with a manipulative she-devil. You caved. Let's move on."

He pulled back, his eyes now skimming the bubbling water. "There's so much I want to say. To do. To make up for—"

"Damn it, Aaronson," I said, "I've never seen such an apologetic lawyer. You compartmentalize like it's your main job. You're here now. She's gone for good. And she did try to help my brother, even if her tactics were a little shady."

I drew a question mark on his torso. A gust of icy wind blew across the deck, and we sunk deeper into the mother-warmth of the tub, where we slowly merged.

# THIRTY-EIGHT

"I LOVE WHAT YOU'VE DONE TO THE PLACE," said Tom, sarcastically.

I followed his gaze to the wall where all my decomposing bodies hung, newly framed.

"Akio doesn't mind," I argued. The baby was babbling, clapping his chubby hands, focusing on his grandmother's freshly dead countenance. "I think he's conversing with her."

Kento laughed. "He is named for the man she was supposed to marry, after all."

"And you call me creepy?" I said.

We were gathered around a picnic table in the alcove between the kitchen and living room. Having sold my house furnished, I hadn't had time or inclination to replace major pieces, so I'd dragged the half-rotted table from the yard. In deference to my trendy brother and brother-in-law, I'd at least covered the monstrosity with an Italian washed linen tablecloth.

"Speaking of *may*-widge," Tom said, pointing to Simon and me in turn. "Any plans?"

"Way to be awkward," I said, hoping my FFG glow face wasn't too obvious.

"We enjoy sinning," Simon said, winking at me.

"Also," I added, "we enjoy giving the good folks of Steeplejack something to talk about."

"You're really determined to stick it out here, then?" Tom said.

"There are more allies than you'd guess around here," I said. "We just need to be a little more vocal. Besides, now that Simon opened his own practice specializing in advocacy for marginalized people, we're committed."

"*We're*," Tom said. "As in plural?"

"Hazel volunteers at the women's prison, leading art classes once a week," said Simon.

"It was Corinda's idea, actually. She's sort of a ringleader in Orofino," I said. "Found her calling, channeling her bossy tendencies for good."

The baby slapped his hand into the pile of Cheerios on his high-chair tray, sending the oaty bits flying.

"Chip off the block, huh?" I said. "You have your hands full with that one."

Outside, the late-December sky darkened as we nibbled on heated Saito Christmas leftovers, and sipped Tom's version of his mother's glögg.

In an impulsive yet glorious move, Kento led a hand-grasping blessing, the circle of us, all connected. "For all the ancestors, everyone who made us, nurtured us, or failed to nurture us, we give thanks. May we bloom where we're planted."

I glanced at the dead people on the wall surrounding us, daily reminders of humanity's perseverance and resilience. When I returned my gaze to my family, a gust of wind rattled a loose pane behind Kento, but my brother didn't seem to notice. Tonight was impervious to disruption. We, at least, had that.

# About the author

**SUZY VITELLO** writes and lives in Portland, Oregon with her husband and a mischievous Rottweiler who is sometimes known as Bad Dog Carl. She holds an MFA from Antioch, Los Angeles, and has been a recipient of an Oregon Literary Arts grant. Through her editing/coaching business she's a proud midwife to dozens of book-babies and their creators. In addition to *Bitterroot*, her own novels include *Faultland*, *The Moment Before* and *The Empress Chronicles* series. Check out suzyvitello.com for info on books, events and upcoming workshops.

**Enjoy more about**
*Bitterroot: A Novel*

Meet the Author
Check out author appearances
Explore special features

# Acknowledgements

So much gratitude to the team at Sibylline Press. Particularly Vicki DeArmon and Julia Park Tracey for the courage and conviction to build a press that elevates the work of women-identifying authors over fifty. The passion, energy and heart that you bring to your books and our growing community is unique and has filled me with hope for the future of publishing.

I want to thank Natalie Hirt, my road-trip ride or die, for introducing me to Susan Penfield's ranch and patiently waiting for me to catch up on our various mountain hikes.

Thanks, as always, to my husband, Kirk, who has ferried countless mugs of tea and fruit slices to my desk during various NaNoWriMo-type obsessive writing sessions.

To my brave and wonderful daughter Maggie, and her wife Ayla, and the family they've built.

# Book Club Questions

*Bitterroot: A Novel* by Suzy Vitello

1. At the story's end, how is Hazel's sense of community different than at the beginning?

2. Hazel and Kento are twins, but in some ways, they had polar opposite experiences growing up. What are some contributing factors to those differences?

3. Corinda switches allegiance a few times. What psychological elements might contribute to these shifts? Do you have friends, family or acquaintances who have changed affiliations in the last few years?

4. Steeplejack is a fictional town based on a conglomerate of several actual small towns in the Idaho Panhandle region. The area has a reputation for attracting radicalized individuals, as well as adventurers. What features do you think contribute to extremism in small, rural areas?

5. How are extreme governmental measures that limit access to women's healthcare related to laws that infringe on the rights of the LGBTQ+ community?

6. How are Tom and Kento's marital struggles the same or different than those of a hetero-marriage?

7. Hazel and Kento were partly shaped by injustices suffered by their parents, having to do with class and race. Can you think of key events in your own life that were informed by ancestral baggage?

8. Which of the characters did you relate to the most and why?

9. On paper, Simon and Hazel seem an odd couple. Why do you think they're drawn to each other?

**Sibylline Press** is proud to publish the brilliant work of women authors over 50. We are a woman-owned publishing company and, like our authors, represent women of a certain age.

### *Rottenkid: A Succulent Story of Survival*
### BY BRIGIT BINNS

Pub Date: 3/5/24
ISBN: 9781960573995
Memoir, Trade paper, $19, 320 pages

Prolific cookbook author Brigit Binns' coming-of-age memoir—co-starring her alcoholic actor father Edward Binns and glamorous but viciously smart narcissistic mother—reveals how simultaneous privilege and profound neglect led Brigit to seek comfort in the kitchen, eventually allowing her to find some sense of self-worth. A memoir sauteed in Hollywood stories, world travel, and always, the need to belong.

### *1666: A Novel*
### BY LORA CHILTON

Pub Date: 4/2/24
ISBN: 9781960573957
Fiction, Trade paper, $17, 224 pages

The survival story of the Patawomeck Tribe of Virginia has been remembered within the tribe for generations, but the massacre of Patawomeck men and the enslavement of women and children by land hungry colonists in 1666 has been mostly unknown outside of the tribe until now. Author Lora Chilton, a member of the tribe through the lineage of her father, has created this powerful fictional retelling of the survival of the tribe through the lives of three women.

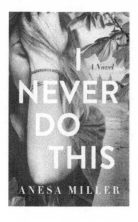

### I Never Do This: A Novel
#### BY ANESA MILLER

Pub Date: 4/16/24
ISBN: 9781960573988
Fiction, Trade paper, $17, 216 pages

This gothic novel presents the unforgettable voice of a young woman, LaDene Faye Howell, who finds herself in police custody recounting her story after her paroled cousin Bobbie Frank appears and engages her in a crime spree in the small town of Devola, Ohio.

### The Goldie Standard: A Novel
#### BY SIMI MONHEIT

Pub Date: 5/7/24
ISBN: 9781960573971
Fiction, Trade paper, $19, 328 pages

Hilarious and surprising, this unapologetically Jewish story delivers a present-day take on a highly creative grandmother in an old folks' home trying to find her Ph.D granddaughter a husband who is a doctor—with a yarmulke, of course.

### Bitterroot: A Novel
#### BY SUZY VITELLO

Pub Date: 5/21/24
ISBN: 9781960573964
Fiction, Trade paper, 18, 296 pages

A forensic artist already reeling from the surprise death of her husband must confront the MAGA politics, racism and violence raging in her small town in the Bitterroot Mountains of Idaho when her gay brother is shot and she becomes a target herself.

For more books from **Sibylline Press**, please visit our
website at **sibyllinepress.com**

Printed in the USA
CPSIA information can be obtained
at www.ICGtesting.com
JSHW020040300524
64007JS00005B/455